THE IMPROBABLE THREE

Mel Frances

This is a work of fiction. The characterisation and narrative are entirely fictitious and purely a product of the authors imagination. Any similarity to actual persons, living or dead, or actual events, is purely coincidental.

It is not legal to reproduce, duplicate, or transmit any part of this document in either electronic means or printed format. Recording of this publication is strictly prohibited.

ISBN: 9781836542162 (paperback)
ISBN: 9781836542179 (ebook)

For Eileen, Cate and Helen

"There can be no keener revelation of a society's soul than the way in which it treats its children."
Nelson Mandela

1

Newcastle, March 2015

FOUR CRUMPLED BLOUSES lay on the wardrobe floor. Maia stared at them. They'd slid off their hangers again. The fabric folds looked like smirks, mocking her like mischievous children. They did it deliberately she was sure. Her wardrobe was packed and as she attempted to separate the snarled up hangers clinging together like a monkey-puzzle, she became more annoyed, 'slippery little sods.' Maia picked up the offending garments, one-by-one, with pure resentment and re-hung them, buttoning them up at the collar, satisfied they couldn't pull that trick on her again. She smirked back at them, smoothing the fabric between the palms of her hands, hoping she wouldn't have to iron them.

Two thoughts entered her brain, I need to get some non-slip hangers, and some of that crease-release spray her mam was always banging on about. She knew every labour-saving hack known to humankind. Firmly sliding the mirrored wardrobe door closed, Maia glanced at her reflection, then grabbed her phone from her bedside, reacting to the

Pavlovian stimulus of her ringtone. The early morning call interrupted daily scrutiny of the merest hint of a wrinkle on her face. She'd be thirty this year, another thought, she must start using a daily face cream with sun protection factors, or she'd be an old crone by forty.

The familiar deep tones of her older brother, Andy asked, 'you at home? Okay if I pop over?'

'Of course.'

'See you soon.'

'What's the rush—' Maia looked at her phone, Andy had abruptly ended the call. She was going to ask if he'd gleaned any details to divulge about her thirtieth-birthday party plans later that year. She was keen to be involved in the celebratory organisation palaver, but had been firmly advised by her younger sister, Nik, *"it was all being taken care of."*

There was something different in Andy's voice, something ... desolate, even urgent. Twenty minutes later, the intercom buzzed. Taking in the minimal style of her new rental on Newcastle's Quayside, she walked to the door and pressed the access button. There was no usual quip from her brother, asking whether he had the correct address for; the local brothel, Alcoholics Anonymous, or his favourite, *"is this the correct address for the IPNS?"* The acronym for, The Institute for the Preservation of Northern Spinsters. Oh, how he laughs ... every time.

Maia opened the apartment door, about to offer one of her usual retorts; *wife kicked you out again?* when her greeting was immediately neutralised as Andy barged into the room. There was no smile, none of his usual easy warmth, as he firmly encased his sister in his arms and whispered, 'Tom's dead.'

Maia froze, hardly breathing, she looked into her brother's watering hazel eyes. Her body trembled. Andy gently lowered her onto the sofa, his arm around her shaking shoulders.

With shallow breaths, she said, 'oh god no, no ... how?' She slumped into a tiny self-protective foetal ball, hands pressed firmly over her face, fingers raking through her hair with an irrepressible urge to yank it out.

Andy held her forearms gently but firmly to prevent any self-harm. He rasped, 'they found his car, crashed into a wall.'

The siblings remained entwined, sobbing, nothing could be said. Maia heaved frantic breaths to draw in oxygen. Andy gently lifted her up to cradle her. 'How could we have let this happen to him?' Andy held his head in his hands as he released her, unable to say anything more as he wept.

Maia took sleep-walk steps to get some tissues from the bedroom. She glimpsed the transformation in the mirror from the relaxed image an hour ago, to the crinkled over-ripe peach, gazing back at her with empty eyes.

Numbing days followed, interspersed with many calls about the devastating news. Andy, Maia and their younger sister, Nik, gathered at their parents' home for solace. They talked together, cried together and shared memories. Maia could see Tom's smiling face in her mind's eye, and echoes of his full-bodied, joyous laugh resonated in her ears. She managed to smile and talk about his terrible attempts to play guitar. 'His version of, 'Message in a Bottle' was a complete disaster.' Forcing a smile, 'remember that?'.

Andy smiled broadly, 'but he was a great front man,' reminiscing about their teenage band playing days.

'The best. A true extrovert,' Nik sighed sorrowfully.

Tom's funeral eight days after the devastating news was unbearable. How fitting it was on this Friday morning, 20 March 2015 at 9.30 am, the sun was eclipsed as the moon drifted across its surface until it was gone entirely at 10.40 am, creating an eerie atmosphere as mourners gathered for the service.

You couldn't get a better metaphor if you had tried Tom, thought Maia, why did it have to be today when I say goodbye to you. The date you knew nothing about, but I should have told you. She pulled her heavy shawl tightly around her shoulders, encasing her body to keep it from falling apart in the swirling, icy cruel wind. She watched the zombie-like congregation dragging their feet into the cavernous church as palpable grief echoed around the walls. Maia clasped the small jade heart in her pocket from the necklace Tom gave her for her sixteenth birthday. The grating tension in her throat was agonising as she gulped for air and moisture, she was drowning in sorrow. She desperately tried to suppress the brimming, volcanic eruption of crying out, he isn't dead, he can't be! She inhaled deeply to calm the visceral sorrow draining her core.

Maia looked at the coffin. Tom was in there. Her brain was shrieking inside her head, no! he isn't in there, he can't be dead, this can't be happening. She thought any moment now he's going to stroll down the aisle and say it's all a big joke, but the most terrible joke of all. The photograph on top of the coffin showed his beautiful face, his tousled hair falling around his neck. Those green eyes glowing, and his wonderful smile, it caught the moment before Tom would burst into laughter. Maia noticed a glimpse of the rune pendant she gave him for his eighteenth, he always wore it. She was struggling to comprehend she'd never see Tom's face again, or hear his voice. Her parents, and her siblings stood at either side insulating Maia's emptiness, but the inner welling damn had to break. She joined many others who were openly weeping.

Following the emotional non-religious service, Maia held Tom's mother, Pauline close. Her expression concerned Maia.

'Tom seemed content lately,' said Pauline, 'I can't believe he would take his life? But when the police officer brought his belongings, she told me there seemed to be no reason for suspicion. His mobile was missing, but he never went anywhere without it. Something isn't quite right Maia.' Pauline was pensive, 'and I found this notebook with rows of numbers, and—' Pauline was interrupted and distracted by a passing mourner offering condolences.

'I'll call in to see you and Mike soon,' said Maia as the women embraced. Maia joined her parents, and her brother and sister, they left the church, with arms around each other, tears welling and spilling on this bleak, soul-splintering day.

2

Durham 1995

MAIA'S PARENTS KATRIN and Phil bought a new-build family home on the Woodside Estate, to house their three growing children, Andy was twelve years old, Maia was nine and Nik was six. The estate was located on the outskirts of Deyton Village, north of Durham city. Neighbours, Pauline and Mike Cassidy who offered foster care for the local authority, lived opposite with their four children.

Phil was staring out of the kitchen window. 'Hey, looks like they've got another one, 'she's got a heart like a lion that woman.'

'Who's got another what?' Katrin puzzled, with her back to her husband whilst putting the shopping away in various kitchen cupboards.

'Another little feller. Another waif and stray, looks about our Andy's age. I dread to think what the poor little soul has been through.'

'Oh, that'll be Tom.' Katrin twigged who Phil was referring to. Pauline always introduced her fostered children to her neighbours, at least those she knew would be accepting of, and kind to them.

'Apparently he ran away from a care home to find them. He's nearly eleven I think, in between Andri and Maija's age.' Katrin always pronounced her children's given names with Icelandic inflection, not the shortened version of Andy and Maia they preferred to use. 'She has a heart that seems to expand with every child they care for, and Mike does too.'

'Must be a real handful, looking after teenagers.' Phil slightly shook his head. 'Still, the Cassidys had four of their own, so probably been through a lot. I recall their eldest was a bit of a tearaway when he was younger.'

'I often wondered where they put them all when their children were still at home.'

'Mike built an extra bedroom in the loft, which must've helped.'

'But the expense. I mean, I know there's a fostering allowance, but at times, they must have had five or six hungry mouths to feed.' Katrin craned to see Tom out of the window, a skinny tousled-hair youth was walking into Pauline's house. 'He's going to be a heartbreaker that one, lovely looking lad.'

Over the next few months and years their son Andy and Tom became close friends. They would have sleepovers; the two families went on camping holidays together and the children spent a lot of time in each other's company. In later years Andy discovered, and encouraged the showman in Tom. They'd sit in the bedroom, Andy playing guitar and Tom attempting to play, but he had a great voice, and would belt out pitch-perfect songs with abandon. Eventually the teenage boys got a band together and played gigs at local youth clubs, school events; they played at a few pubs and minor summer festivals as they grew older too. Tom was a brilliant lead singer.

In 2001, at age fifteen Maia was not too enamoured with a seventeen year old Tom. They'd always got along as younger children, however when she attended band rehearsals at the local community centre, she deemed him, *"a massive big-headed show off."* However secretly, she and her teenage-ignited hormones, found him devastatingly attractive. Not long after her last attendance at a rehearsal, Maia was doing her chores at home one day when the door-bell rang. She took off her rubber gloves, and plonked them in the sink, pleased to be distracted from washing the dishes. Tom stood there in jeans and a faded red T-shirt, he really suited red she thought. He held a folder with the lyrics for the new songs he and Andy were learning with the band. His green eyes shone, his bright but slightly imperfect smile and natural playfulness lit up the room as he entered the house.

'Andy about?'

'Not back in from sixth form yet.'

'Your boring brother spends hours studying, he really needs to get a life.'

Maia retorted, 'he wants to get a place in a good university, so he's got to get the grades.'

'I know that, chill-out Maia I'm only kidding. He'll go far your brother.'

Maia's face flushed at her over-reaction. Tom could easily wind her up.

'I haven't got the concentration to study,' he continued, 'nor the brains.'

Maia said with a cheeky grin, 'well ... I'm glad *you* said that, saved me saying so.' Touché, she thought.

Tom took it in good spirits and laughed. 'Mike's trying to get me into a trade, wants me to be a mechanic or a joiner, summat like that.' He shrugged. 'I've joined the countryside ranger volunteer service, which is great. Love being in the outdoors, out in the open spaces.' Tom was quiet, even wistful. 'No-one bothers you there.'

Maia noticed these moments of disconnect with Tom. Most of the time he was bolshy and brash, always joking, never still, leaping around, but at times, the complete opposite, introverted and vulnerable. She didn't know anything about his past, but the fact he'd been in care meant there was an experience there. Tom never mentioned anything prior to living at Pauline's.

Maia was aware there were loads of girls wanting to go out with him, they had asked her to arrange dates, but she never did. One of her friends told her when she, the friend, had been alone with Tom at a party, he was really shy, and didn't seem keen on kissing her or anything. The friend concluded he must be gay to deny her advances. Maia thought not, he probably didn't fancy her. Maia knew he had a girlfriend for a few months, but that seemed to have fizzled out, which pleased her. She noticed a reticence for intimacy whenever they were alone, however they could always talk and laugh about their shared family experiences, and chat about music, tv shows or movies. They often had movie nights with her siblings and Tom's foster family at each other's houses.

'Drink? There's cola, lemonade or orange.' Maia went to the fridge. 'Here you go, you like Fanta don't you?' She handed him a freezing cold can, took one herself and they opened them simultaneously with a sharp sounding, pssch. The two sat for some time chatting, and glugging their drinks. Maia enjoyed these intimate chats with Tom and wondered if he deliberately called, knowing Andy and her parents weren't in. She did hope so.

Tom asked, 'there's a new film out called, *A.I. Artificial Intelligence*, have you heard about it? No surprises it's about a robot that wants to be human.' Then in a rush he said, 'fancy it?'

Maia was nodding at his first question, then surprised by his second, stuttered a little and replied, 'er, um ... yea, why not, I like a bit of sci-fi.'

'Great, none of the lads are interested,' Tom faked nonchalance. 'It'll save me going on my own.'

Maia studied Tom as he feigned distraction looking through the song sheets in his folder. Was his face slightly flushed, it certainly seemed so. She knew Andy would definitely have gone to the movies if Tom had asked. Tom looked up, they smiled at each other, it was a little embarrassing but exciting, both recognised they were going on a date.

The date was arranged and the two headed into town to the multiplex cinema, Tom bought some goodies for them to share. During one of the darker scenes, Tom slipped his arm around the back of Maia's seat, so his hand rested on her shoulder. She moved in toward him, at one point he turned his face toward her and gently kissed her neck below her jaw. Tremors of the most wonderful feelings hit her and rippled throughout her body. She wanted to kiss him, and kiss him passionately. Maia wasn't sure she could wait the few months until her sixteenth birthday before they had sex legally. Maia and Tom became a couple, and it would be many weeks before they got an opportunity to explore each other intimately.

Tom and Maia had been dating for a year in 2002, and were celebrating their anniversary at the cinema in recognition of their first outing as a couple. They returned to an empty house as Pauline and Mike were over at the Hewsons, a pre-arranged event to allow the young lovers some space. Tom stared at his hands, then turned to Maia and asked, 'have I ever explained how I came to be living here?' He looked around the cosy front room, anywhere to avoid eye contact.

Maia shrugged. 'Not really, I mean we know you're fostered and everything.' She then said hurriedly, 'not that it matters one bit, not to me anyway.'

'No worries, I'm glad to be here,' repeating Maia's words, 'fostered and everything,' Tom gave a wry smile. 'Pauline and Mike have legal guardianship. I am now Thomas Cassidy, their son.' It was a firm statement. His smile turned to a sigh. He straightened and looked away. He couldn't look directly at Maia as he recounted events from his past. Maia realised, he needed to tell her, she was a *safe* person. She promised to never tell a soul, not even Andy, and she never did.

Tom sat upright and began to recount his early memories, trying to piece together what had happened, anything at all he could recall from his early life; being removed from his family after his baby sister Abigail was born, he believed because of his behaviour and his mother's depression. Maia listened intently to every word.

Tom's eyes brightened when he reached the part where he was first placed with Pauline and Mike. 'I came here a few times on respite, it was always great fun and I really wanted to live here with Pauline and Mike, but there wasn't enough room to stay permanently. They had their own kids and fostered other kids too.'

Tom hesitated when he spoke of being placed in a children's care home aged ten, meeting other children who had their own story to tell. Tom was shaking as he spoke of the excruciating pain and humiliation of sexual abuse he suffered at the hands of a perpetrator at the home. Tom still couldn't bear to speak his name. 'People wonder why you didn't say something at the time, they ask, why didn't you tell anyone? But you can't, no-one understands unless it's happened to you.'

He leaned forward, elbows resting on his knees and his head in his hands as his body shook with desolate sobs. Maia did not ask questions or comment, she understood his need for silence. After some moments she said, 'oh Tom,' in the softest tone. Maia's hands gently pulled at his shoulders as she encouraged him to lay back and rest beside her.

It was the first time Tom said anything about his past to anyone other than Pauline. He rested his head on Maia's shoulder as the two teenagers lay on the sofa. His tousled hair fell around his face. He inhaled deeply and closed his bright green eyes. He was still, and hushed as he wilted into her warm body. Maia wrapped herself around him, her shoulder was damp from Tom's tears as she gently stroked his soft, sun-streaked hair. There they remained, warm ... safe ... silent ... simply breathing.

Tom and Maia dated for many months, taking train rides from Durham into Newcastle city to, Bell's Burger Bar and the, Hustler games club, where lots of young folk met up, for games of pool and darts, then would partake in a wander around the shops, and a mooch around the music stores. Maia went to all of their gigs, knowing there were lots of green-with-envy girls looking at them when he came off stage to embrace her. It was a thrilling time in her life. She went on holiday to her mother's homeland, Iceland, and brought Tom a bronze rune pendant back for his eighteenth birthday. He never took it off, he loved it. He bought her a small jade heart on a delicate gold chain for her sixteenth birthday, and they wore their love tokens everyday they were together.

When Maia was studying for the exams that would give her access to a good university, Tom seemed to become distracted. In the past he would happily lay on her bed as she completed homework, he'd listen to music, or read magazines, but he wasn't great at sitting doing nothing. Andy by this time had left for university, so Tom became bored having no-one to engage with. Their dates became less frequent as their prospective future lives grew apart. Maia was destined for a professional career, whilst Tom had got into motocross with a bunch of lads, who weren't the most reliable, and there were rumours of drugs amongst the wider network.

Their love affair gradually came to an end when Tom stopped calling around as often or he'd make excuses saying he was meeting his mates. Maia gave him an ultimatum one night, to which he seemed relieved that the relationship, with all the commitment it brings, was over. Maia had hoped Tom would buck his ideas up, but it wasn't to be. He was soon seeing an array of other girls without, it seemed, much attention or loyalty.

Maia was studying hard for exams, she had ambitions to go to university to qualify in journalism, and had a sense she would eventually leave Tom behind in many ways. They rarely bumped into each other, but when they did, it was nice to catch up. She would always have a soft spot in her heart for the wild, but at times vulnerable, young man who took her virginity and showed her the thrilling rush of first love.

3

Newcastle, April 2015

AS SHE ENTERED her apartment from a long riverside run along the Quayside on this cool April day, Maia's phone rang as she was taking off her hoody. It became bundled up as she fumbled to release it from the pocket. Noticing the caller display, 'here we go again.' She sighed, tapping the green answer symbol, preparing her voice to be gracious for inevitable rejection. 'Hello, Maia Hewson.'

'Hello Maija.'

Hearing her name spoken with the subtle inflection of Icelandic pronunciation was pleasing, though Maia expected nothing less from Harriet Cooper, creator of the environmental magazine, Earth Chart. Typical of Harriet's attention to detail which she picked up from Maia's recent interview.

Once greetings were completed, Harriet said, 'we were impressed with your article of the environment climate change resilience report, particularly your scrutiny of bio-energy, carbon capture and storage. I'm happy to say Maija, it will be published in the next edition of Earth Chart.'

'That's wonderful,' Maia was inwardly suppressing the shrieking excitement bubbling up within.

'We'll get you back into the office next week to discuss your fees and signing up for a retainer. Good to have you on board, there is solid competition for these articles, well done.'

Remaining calm, Maia thanked Harriett for the feedback. She'd spent over a year trying to secure a retainer agreement with the company, with submission after submission of the most current issues, and finally it happened! This could lead to investigative work on environmental matters around the world, as Earth Chart's online and printed publications were globally recognised as a leading voice in highlighting climate change issues. She threw her phone on the sofa and couldn't help but fling herself around in a joyful jig, punching her fist in the air with every, 'yes, yes, yes!' On her final twirl she knocked the resilient Peace Lily plant off the side table, spilling the contents all over, which abruptly halted her twirling celebrations.

'Oh bugger it!' She scooped as much of the massacred moist compost back into the pot hoping the plant would survive, then thought, she can't even look after a plant, never mind a pet, or even a baby.

'Baby' … Maia realised had said that aloud, and froze where she crouched. Sneaking tendril thoughts crept into her mind; she shot upright to whiplash them away. Quickly she grabbed the vacuum and cleaned up the mess, then rang her mother, Katrin.

'Hey Maija, any news?' Maia sensed the trepidation in her mother's voice, preparing to be invited over for a comforting, traditional Icelandic stew and kind words at yet another disappointment.

Maia sighed, 'Hey Mamma,' paused, then said brightly, 'you are now speaking to a newly appointed associate writer for Earth Chart!' She could hear Katrin's shouts to Maia's dad, Phil.

Maia knew she wouldn't have to call anyone else as her mother's phone would be red-hot from all the calls and messages to their friends and family. Predictably Maia's phone began ringing after speaking with her parents. She plopped it onto the sofa and let it ping away, she would savour this moment for herself. She grabbed a bottle of Einstök lager from the fridge, a little early in the day perhaps she wondered ... hell no, she deserved this. She flipped the top off and the, hoppy citrusy, aroma caught her nostrils, preparing her throat for the ice-cool, sharp nectar. Maia always raised the bottle, 'Skál' as a respectful nod to her maternal heritage.

Sitting on the cushioned chrome balcony chair, overlooking the iconic view of Newcastle's seven bridges over the River Tyne; she enjoyed this moment, gulping down the quenching liquid, it was bliss. Still sweaty from her run, she became acutely aware of change, as her warm running gear turned cool and clammy. The late afternoon breeze brushed her bare skin, raising fine hairs on her arms. A veil of fatigue suddenly lowered over her mind and body as she longed for warmth to relax her aching muscles. Soon she was enjoying a luxurious bath, she'd catch up with all of those messages later.

Wrapped in a fresh towel, she slid open her wardrobe

doors and perused the smart-casual capsule within. Maia reflected on her employment experience, joining a local newspaper after Uni, then a spell in broadcasting on local radio. Her current work as a beauty editor for a mediocre magazine was well-paid, but the novelty was wearing thin. She tapped her phone checking her social media platforms, not quite the major influencer, but gathering more followers daily. It was all so ... superficial. She was never comfortable encouraging young women to spend a fortune on designer clothes, and extortionate beauty products.

'All absolute bollocks,' a broad grin spread across her face as she considered the inflated fees Harriet Cooper had proposed in the interview. Maia planned to buy new clothes, in fact, new everything, maybe a new car. Inner shrieking excitement bubbled up again.

The Hewson family were corralled for celebrations at the parents recently purchased downsized new home in South Tyneside. Katrin and Phil made the decision to move to be nearer to Andy once their first grandchild made an appearance. Katrin called her youngest daughter always by her full name, Monika, known as Nik to everyone else. Andri was Andy, whilst Maija dropped the rogue 'j' in her birth name to prevent pronunciation and constant spelling corrections. She would forgive the occasional use of the spelling, *Maya*, however on official documents or in formal situations, she pronounced and spelled her birth name correctly with pride. Family gatherings at the Hewson's consisted of blended bi-lingual conversations in Icelandic and English. It was somewhat muted on this occasion, as they were collectively still grieving, stunned at Tom's death not a month ago, and spoke warmly about their memories.

Andy, his wife Jen, and their two young children were already there when Maia arrived. A few conversations would be ping-ponging around the huge wooden table, interspersed with cries from new baby Nathan, and noisy singing from their three-year-old daughter Kate. The family would all be able to understand each other simultaneously, despite the distractions.

'First here again Jen?' enquired Maia, 'any excuse to have your dinner made for you eh?'

'Too right,' Jen bounced baby Nathan in her arms. Jen took no prisoners when it came to speaking truthfully and could often be guilty of a lack of tact. Her experiences working as a medic in areas of conflict had finely-tuned this personality quirk. Her athletic broad frame matched her robust personality, her fair hair scraped back in a no-nonsense pony tail, befitting her character.

'When are you due back to the surgery?' asked Katrin, 'I'm happy to offer extra child-care for my beautiful grandchildren.'

'Another five weeks, and thanks for the offer Katrin, we'll need it if I end up working late.' Jen looked dolefully at her husband, 'Andy is still suffering from his birthday celebrations at the weekend. He's driving tonight, so I will raise a glass or three for your achievements Maia, for a change.'

'What was the final score of the Architects versus Doctors volley ball game in the end?' asked Maia recalling the late-night antics from Andy's birthday garden party.

Andy shook his head with the memory of the alcohol-induced shenanigans. 'Can't remember but we've offered to pay to re-turf the damage to next door's lawn,' he said sheepishly, rubbing the dark stubble around his thick set jaw.

'*You've* offered!' retorted Jen, 'seems it wasn't such a great idea to use the dividing hedge as a net.'

Andy picked up Kate and at first bounced her on his knee, then quelled the motion so they could tuck into various delights from the sumptuous buffet food on the vast kitchen table. Maia noticed his sandy hair and clothing wasn't as neat as usual. His hair was receding, and his waistline was expanding, she wondered whether he was still able to get out cycling. Her thirty-four year old brother was going to end up the same shape as their dad in a few years. She giggled inwardly at the thought.

Andy asked, 'still not retiring Dad. How long have you been Head of Physics now?'

'Seven years, and I still enjoy sharing my knowledge with the students, I'll know when to stop,' said Phil rocking back and forth on his toes, glass of beer in hand.

Maia's mother, Katrin, had retired early from her work at the local council's environmental protection department, to work as a custodian for the protection of the North east coastline. Maia can't remember how many times Katrin had the children litter-picking at the coast. She often reminisced to Maia, how she was attracted to Phil's free-thinking, inquisitive mind and his commitment to climate activism when they met on her gap year working in the UK. Phil had qualified as a teacher and was forever grateful he popped into the bar where she was working.

Maia observed her parents fussing around the kitchen area of their new open plan Scandi-style home. She was a younger version of Katrin; petite frame, dark brown eyes, button nose and thick brunette hair resting heavily on her shoulders. A former colleague once remarked Maia looked, *"cute"* referring to her having, *"a soft puppy face."* Maia wanted to respond with; at least I won't end up looking like a wrinkled old bat like you in my fifties. She was grateful for her youthful Nordic, genetic inheritance. Maia's dogged curiosity, however, was certainly a paternal influence.

Maia observed the genial family scene and raised her voice above the cacophony. 'Okay!' she lifted her glass, 'let's not forget why we're here. It's all about me … me … me!' The family joined in the congratulatory toast for the exciting new opportunity in Maia's career.

Turning to her younger sister, 'Nik, have you brought any goodies for the occasion?'

'Nah, didn't have time to bake.'

'Not so impressive from someone who runs one of the premier artisan bistros in Durham City.'

Nik shrugged, she always shrugged. She was quite the, plain-Jane with a natural beauty, no frills; a jeans and T-shirt kind of girl, with long mousey hair, which was never groomed. However, there was still a familial look between the sisters.

'I've often wondered whether you're a freak of nature with your unnaturally slow heart rate. You never seem to get rattled about anything,' suggested Maia.

Nik said, 'it's one of the reasons why me and Sophia

are so well matched, similar personalities,' turning to her partner with a wry smile on her face.

The room erupted into laughter. Nik's partner Sophia stood, and the bold, block colours of her outfit, which draped her plus-size beautifully, almost dazzled them. Her abundant dark auburn hair flecked with golden highlights cascaded over her shoulders like molten lava. With a fake-shocked expression on her flawless face, she countered, 'what are you all trying to say?' She held out her arms, flashing fluorescent tangerine, perfectly manicured nails, and soaked up the attention, 'I am rather understated and modest as you all know.'

Even Nik laughed aloud at this. 'Oh yeah, really understated. Especially when you're tirelessly trawling the entire internet for a pair of luminous violet, patent brogues you saw in a magazine in the dentist waiting room, like your life depended on it!'

Sophia threw back her head and her coral-tinted, highly-defined mouth broke into a deep throaty chuckle. Their personal and business partnership worked fantastically well. Living in the apartment above their bistro, Nik and Sophia enjoyed the social contact and the demands of running the business. A combination of Nik's diligent business skills and Sophia's entrepreneurial marketing genius, had rocketed Café Dalvik to the most successful hospitality venue in the area. Katrin was proud they named the café after her home town in Iceland, Dalvik, and never missed an opportunity to tell everyone.

On returning home, and still fatigued, Maia decided to write down everything Tom had told her about his past experience, for some reason she felt compelled to record his own words as he'd never be able to tell anyone now. She placed a brand new notebook and her favourite pen on the balcony table. She loved new notebooks and had a compulsion to buy brightly coloured journals, with crisp lined, unmolested pages, already having three she'd begun writing in. This one was special, it was from Iceland and depicted a beautiful snowy scene with sweeping Aurora Borealis above, it even had a slight glittering sheen which appealed to her eight-year-old self. She'd been waiting for a significant moment to open it, and begin writing. She headed the page, *Tom Cassidy, in his words. Friday 13th September 2002*, recognising the irony of an unlucky superstitious date, when Tom revealed his past to her.

Maia played Avril Lavigne's song 'Complicated' from that year on her phone, it had been a favourite of hers and Tom's at the time. She began singing, *'chill out what you yelling for, lay back it's all been done before, and if you could only let it be, you would see, I like you the way you are …'* she knew every single word, even though it was well over a decade since she heard it. Maia began writing and before she knew it four pages were filled with her memories, as accurately as she could recall.

Tom Cassidy, in his words 13.09.2002

I was about four or five when I was taken to somewhere like a clinic, and they were examining me, like, intimately. The place smelled of disinfectant, like a hospital and it sounded echoey. I was alone and scared, and it was freezing cold. I don't remember much, but I felt sick. I was undressed, laid on my back, and a doctor, a nurse and someone else was in the room. The nurse was trying to amuse me with a toy, a red wooden double decker bus, I'll never forget it. The doctor pressed my stomach, then examined between my legs and backside. I was taken to a dormitory or a ward of some kind. Had no idea why I was there, or for how long. I missed home, I didn't understand why mam or dad didn't come for me. When I did return home, it was never the same. They didn't seem to want to play with me or hug me anymore, so I guess I tried to constantly get attention in other ways. I asked my parents about that memory when I was older, but they said I must have imagined it or dreamt it, but I definitely had not, it was real. I know there was a child abuse scandal in Teesside in the late 1980s, when loads of children were removed from their families, so it may have been connected to that. I was told I could get my records to find out, but what's the point, it's in the past, it's gone.

The next thing I remember, I was maybe ten or eleven when this old woman from social services turned up at our house, so it was probably 1995. She'd been a few times before, can't remember her name. That's when I had to stay at Pauline's, so mam could have a break from my behaviour. The woman explained I had to go and stay elsewhere for a few days because mam couldn't cope again. She asked me why I wasn't happy at home, so I said 'cos my parents are dicks and they treat me like crap. All they did was shout at me, and dad would shove me out of the way. I knew they weren't interested in anything I did. I was really good at footy but he never came to watch me play.

So, off I went again, I knew I'd be back in a few days, I got used to moving around. I stayed here at Pauline's on an emergency foster placement a couple of times when mam was freaking out. On this occasion I asked to come here to Pauline's, but couldn't, maybe no space. The old woman said to get some things. I took my Game Boy, pjs, other clothes and my football. I didn't bother saying goodbye, it was one of the last times I saw my family.

I remember being in the back of a car, looking through the windscreen, could hardly see anything in the dark. The wipers couldn't keep up with the rain. The old woman, pulled up at Linden House. I followed her into the building with my belongings in two carrier bags flapping about. It was a wild night, the rain stung my face and you could hear the storm swirling around the trees. We went inside, the place stank like dirty carpets, vegetable soup and cigarette smoke. You could smoke indoors in those days. Didn't notice the smell after a while, you got used to it. It was the first time I had to go into a home, not with foster carers.

A younger woman, Cath, spoke with the old woman, then took me to a small bedroom down the hall. It was basic but clean. I put my stuff in the drawers and she gave me a toothbrush and paste as I had none. Down one hallway there were about eight bedrooms, and down the other; a games room with a pool table, a bookcase and a HiFi stack. There was a communal sitting room with saggy sofas and stained chairs with a few older kids lounging around watching Byker Grove. A girl shouted, "hey look a new kid, ah bless him, isn't he canny!" That was Aimee.

Next to the sitting room was a basic canteen with a few big grey Formica tables, and orange plastic moulded chairs. I remember some of the chairs had cigarette burns around the edge, which looked sort of like a pie crust. We weren't allowed in the kitchen opposite. I was starving, so Cath brought me some left-over pizza. We had to follow strict rules, but it was alright really. I met Jordan on the first day. His bedroom was next to mine, he was about a year older than me maybe, all the others were older. I can remember every single thing about that first day at Linden House.

4

MAIA ARRIVED AT Pauline's home, she clicked the key fob and the satisfying quiet clunk of the car lock resonated. She walked to the back door and let herself into the kitchen. It was all so familiar; she'd been visiting this house since she and Tom were teenage sweethearts. Pauline wore a cornflower blue top, draping her ample chest, and flowing over light linen trousers. Maia noticed the crisp, fresh scent of fabric conditioner around Pauline. They greeted each other with a gentle kiss. The soft skin of Pauline's cheek brushed Maia's, and she imagined the comfort Pauline gave to fretful children, holding them close if they were willing, to soothe and reassure.

Pauline congratulated Maia on her new job, but her blue-grey eyes didn't sparkle so much today, and Maia noticed more soft lines on her face. The half-inch of harsh grey around her hairline was in stark contrast to the line of deep-chestnut hair colouring, Pauline was usually meticulous about covering her grey. All testament to age, also the burden and joy of raising four children, caring for numerous grandchildren, and the foster children she and Mike had opened their hearts, and their modest home to over the years.

Mike was sitting at the kitchen table; the comforting aroma of a traditional Sunday roast being cooked filled the space. His copious silver hair caught the sunlight streaming through the window, and his tall thin frame was encased in navy overalls. Hugs all around, then they sat with a coffee having a catch up. Mike found it difficult to talk about Tom as the emotion hit him like sledgehammer blows. It was Mike who encouraged Tom to volunteer with the Countryside Rangers, which eventually led to employment. They had a deep fulfilling relationship and shared interests. As a younger boy, Tom would tinker around in the garden and the workshop, and help fix things with Mike. He was Mike's shadow, his little buddy.

Pauline repeatedly glanced at Tom's picture, pride of place on the windowsill, 'I still talk to him you know. Everyone is so devastated, I still can't believe he's gone.'

Maia stared at the photograph. 'Me too.' She loved the imperfection of his two ever-so-slightly crooked teeth on the right side as he smiled, even his flaws were perfect to her. Mike left to go and tamper with his latest project; an assemblage of car parts on the driveway.

'Off to play with his big-boys Meccano again,' Pauline said with a gentle wry smile, loud enough so Mike could hear. Then quietly, 'the distraction helps, but he's struggling, Maia, really missing Tom.'

They were a loving couple who provided Tom with happiness for most of his life after the terrible abuse he suffered. Maia put her arm around Pauline and reminded her of the happiness and security they offered him. For an hour they laughed and cried reminiscing about Tom, and occasionally clasped hands over the table to feel a human touch, and tangible connection to him. It was only a month since Pauline lost her beloved son, and life would never be the same.

'Tom lived life to the full, and he was truly loved,' said Maia, but it didn't really soften the blows of grief that often punched her in her gut.

Pauline stood and checked to ensure Mike was busy outside. She leaned towards Maia and spoke softly, 'Mike thinks I'm mad, and he doesn't want me to fret ... but Maia, those strange numbers in Tom's notebook, and his personal phone is missing, they found his work one in the van. It's really odd,' she puzzled, glancing at Tom's photograph. Maia knew the mystery was eating her up.

'Would you like me to take the book and have a look to see if I can figure anything out from the numbers?' Maia confided, 'and, Mike doesn't need to know, I get it, unless anything comes to light perhaps?'

Pauline offered a knowing nod. They hugged. Pauline reached into the back of a drawer and handed Maia the notebook. With another item clasped in her hand, she said, 'I want you to have this.' She held out Tom's pendant, the one from Iceland Maia gave him for his eighteenth birthday.

A huge rush of emotion at the visual memory of Tom, collided into Maia. She put it on, swearing to never take it off as she hugged Pauline. As she left, Maia shouted, 'see you Mike,' and waved from the driveway. She got into her car, held up the small bronze, elongated rune pendant, she caressed the indented silver etchings, and recalled looking at lots of pendants on a trip to Iceland. This one fit Tom best, though she'd forgotten the exact meaning, it was along the lines of; protection, love and family, she kissed it and felt the cool disc rest on her neck.

Maia returned home in the evening after shopping, with mixed emotions. Sometimes her grief was unrelenting, yet she had the excitement and challenge of a new career in environmental journalism with Earth Chart, and would soon finish with fashion for good.

Maia couldn't shake off her uneasy feelings about Tom's notebook, and whether it would reveal secrets best left uncovered. It did seem odd, and she trusted Pauline's curious instincts. As she slouched on her sofa with a glass of red wine, Maia recalled opening a bottle of red at 10.30 am three days following the news of Tom's death, when grief overwhelmed her. She relived the shame of her compulsion to gorge the huge chocolate easter egg she'd bought for her niece, Kate. On one desperate occasion, she had trawled the cupboards and found a pack of gigantic cookies and stuffed half the packet down, but it didn't satiate the gaping hole inside her, only served to make her stomach feel sicker.

On those lost days of disbelief, Maia recalled the familiar weight of her special wine glass in her hand, comforting her like a trusted friend. She would take a large swig, then become anxious that the comforting elixir would run out too soon as the bottle emptied. She stopped when nausea arose half way through the second bottle, but it hadn't stopped her slaving to the same ritual for days.

Maia recalled throwing-up on a few mornings, then the bleary-eyed humiliation as she disposed of the evidence in the communal refuse bin below the apartment block. The wine bottles clashed on top of an empty half vodka bottle she'd purchased from the local, late-night express store. She had forgotten she'd even drank it. Maia always took the empties to the bins late at night, as the bottles taunted her in the kitchen bin the next morning, and she would despise herself even more.

Many times she was tempted to visit the shop again, as she did now; she wanted anything to dull the ache in her stomach and eliminate the self-destructive process of cruel relentless grief. The guilt of not saving Tom would crush her some days, she should have been able to prevent his death. Today was one of those days. She held his pendant, cried, and wanted to scream her bloody head off! No-one understood, and they were all going about their daily lives as if nothing had happened. Tom had moved in with Pauline and Mike when he was ten years old, twenty one years ago, but the beautiful soul aged thirty-one, was gone. Maia still spoke to him, she still loved him, even though they hadn't been together since they were teenagers. She took out her journal and wrote down more memories. When she finished, she needed solace and light relief, and that could always be found with her best friend since primary school, Rosa. She tapped out a message inviting herself over to Rosa's for a catch-up.

Tom Cassidy, in his words 13.09.2002

I ran away from Linden House after school one day. I'd saved my allowance and took a bus into Durham city, then another to the village where Pauline and Mike lived, as I thought I'd recognise their street. I got off the bus where it looked familiar, and the bus driver must've noticed I looked lost and asked what was wrong. I lied and told him I'd got on the wrong bus to visit my gran. He was really kind, and told me the number of the bus I needed for Deyton Village. I was lucky, as I would've been dragged back to Linden House once they knew I'd ran away.

It was getting really dark, but I somehow found Pauline and Mike's house. Should've seen her face when I arrived on the doorstep, she was in her dressing gown. Soon as I stepped inside and got a hug off her, I felt safe and it felt like home, been here ever since. They went to court for legal guardianship and that's how I came to live here permanently. They are my real mam and dad and I love them to bits.

I've got a sister by the way. By the time angelic Abigail came along when I was five or six, my parents completely ignored me. They fed me, but I was left to my own devices. I used to try and "play nicely" with Abigail but she was a toddler, a real spoiled brat, and I would get in trouble if she started whining. They treated her like porcelain, but she was a boring little whinge to me, I had no interest in her, still don't care where she is.

I hated school and had no friends at first. I couldn't concentrate and messed about all the time. I did get along with a few mates who were just like me, always in bother, we were often sent to the Head. They could cane you in those days, it stopped hurting after you'd been hit a few times. I wonder what those lads are up to now?

5

ROSA'S ELEVEN-MONTH-OLD BABY, Anthony was in bed when Maia arrived at Rosa's home, emotionally drained from visiting Pauline recently. Rosa suggested she called in after bedtime, so they could enjoy some quality time and chat about Maia's exciting career opportunity. After joyous congratulatory new-job hugs, they had a sneak peek into the baby's room to whisper beautiful things about the alabaster cherub curled up in his cot.

Rosa whispered, 'he's over three Curly Wurlys long now.'

Maia, puzzled at first said, 'oh yeh, forgot you measure everything in confectionary.'

'Well, I can't do numbers as you well know. You're hardly eleven Wispas tall, you short-arse, and I'm almost six Toblerone's tall.' Rosa preened, grinning.

'Rosa,' Maia paused, 'seriously, wouldn't it be easier to simply learn measurements?'

'Maia!' Rosa indignant, 'it's a visual thing. I can imagine the length of a Curly Wurly or a Toblerone far easier than someone saying two feet six inches or, god forbid anything in metres and centimetres, and weights are a pure mystery, it's all unnecessary by the way, and makes my teeth itch.'

'Bet you're a joy for Anthony's health visitor.' Maia gazed at the beautiful child. 'Ah, poor baby. Your mam is wonderful ... but bloody bonkers.'

Rosa had been a constant companion to comfort Maia after Tom died. She could always cheer Maia up, recounting the madness of their girls nights out and holidays before Rosa had a family, and they would laugh 'til they ached. The friends often spoke of successful and failed relationships over the years, and more recently joked about Maia's current lack of love interest, largely due to her ex-partner, Ryan's behaviour. Ryan would try to assuage his jealous guilt with gifts of jewellery and flowers after he'd upset Maia with his possessiveness. He demanded to know everyone present on her work nights out, making her life miserable with accusations of affairs. When Maia began lying and omitting details of her work life, and refusing invitations to social events, it was time to leave him. His sneering, miserable face was the first thing she saw as she walked through the door every evening. Nothing was ever good enough. Ryan demanded his clothes were immaculately laundered, and vanity motivated him to have his hair and designer stubble trimmed perfectly every day. He'd spend hours at the bathroom mirror, whilst Maia ended up with approximately seven and a half minutes to get ready to go out, then Ryan would be sulking accusing her of taking ages.

'Ever see bloody Action Man Head then?' asked Rosa.

'No, thankfully.'

'Remember the breakfast?' Rosa clamped her long slim fingers over her toothy grin. This one always made her guffaw.

'Apparently I couldn't cook a fried egg like his precious mam, too sloppy apparently.' Maia joined in the involuntary laughter.

'So, did you cook him another one after he complained, like the good little girlfriend you were?'

'Nope, the full English; sausage, bacon, beans, mushrooms, tinned tomatoes, fried bread, the lot was slid into the kitchen bin with the sloppy fried eggs last. He should've made his own breakfast shouldn't he?'

'I so wish I'd seen his face. A jaw dropper eh?'

'Was tempted to put my finger under his chin and closed his stupid mouth, but it wasn't worth the bother I'd get afterwards.'

'Did he ever mention it?'

'Never, I just went to work, and saw him putting some bread in the toaster. Wasn't long after that I went home, had enough of his demands and jealousy.'

'Dodged a bullet as they say,' said Rosa, by the way are we still on for tomorrow? Girl's sesh at the amazing Cafe Dalvik with the amazing Nik and Sophia?'

'Absolutely, be lovely to catch up with Daphne too, haven't seen her for ages.'

Maia left, after hugs with Rosa and another peep at the beautiful baby boy, still sleeping soundly. On the drive home she recalled the compressed feeling, like a vacuum storage bag having all the air sucked out, until she was flat and lifeless, sitting crying in her car, unable to face walking into their flat. She sensed the momentum of Ryan's aggression increasing daily, with hostile accusations of her having affairs. No matter how many times she insisted her male colleagues' proximity was unavoidable, as they sat at the same work station, it was useless; Ryan had deemed the affairs were true, with no evidence whatsoever.

Maia recalled with fondness, the morning she woke in her childhood bedroom at home after she left Ryan. It was scrumptious! She snuggled down under the familiar, fresh scented duvet and burrowed her head into marshmallow pillows. In the still calmness, she watched the fractured sunlight streaming through the blinds and felt her body soften into the bed. A gentle knock on the bedroom door, which opened slowly. A mug appeared, carefully held by her mam, tip-toeing into the room trying not to spill the brimming offering of strong, sweet tea.

Maia could hear her mother's words now. *"We're so glad you left him,"* she'd said as she sat on the bed stroking her daughter's hair.

Her dad peeped around the door and added, *"don't worry, we'll deal with him if he calls."*

Maia felt that familiar flat vacuum-bag feeling now, for a different reason, as the reality of Tom's death slammed into her so hard some days. She knew Pauline was concerned over the circumstances of his death, however Maia had some misgivings; she had witnessed Tom's periodic moments of recklessness and utter despair because of the abuse … but suicide …?

Early the following morning after a fitful night, Maia made a strong coffee and took the bowl-size mug out onto the misty balcony, shrouding herself in her favourite cosy blue shawl, a welcome Icelandic Christmas gift from Katrin.

Maia thought affectionately about her first sexual experience with Tom one afternoon in her bedroom, when everyone was out. She smiled, recalling the quiet awkwardness, and whilst the first time wasn't so fulfilling for her, with a bit of practice it became thrilling and natural to explore each other's bodies. She was physically responding to those bittersweet precious memories now as her breath accelerated. It felt cosy as she huddled, dream-thinking about Tom's touch, and the innocence, passion and warmth of first love. She was startled by the intercom buzzer! Pressing the button on the phone by the door, a monochrome image of her dad appeared on the tiny screen. She smiled at his familiar rotund shape and thinning hair.

Phil responded to the click, 'keep forgetting the blummin code.'

In a few minutes he puffed through her door. 'Walked up the stairs'... catching his breath ... 'your mother keeps saying I should do more steps.' He blew his cheeks out as he glanced at his fitness tracker. 'Look what she's bought me, it's a bitfit thingy, I've no idea how it works,' he said shrugging with a pink, bemused face.

'Think your losing your marbles Dad. How come you know loads of complex scientific formulae in your lectures, but you can't remember my entry code, or how to use your new watch?' She glanced at the tracker on his wrist and switched the kettle on smiling, at her beloved brilliant, but scatter-brained dad.

Phil handed over a pack of giant chocolate chip cookies.

'Thought you might like these.' Maia was grateful for the comforting gift. So that's where those others came from, she smiled wryly to herself. They settled on the sofa with a hot drink and the pack of cookies.

'Been thinking of Tom, he was a good lad.' Phil laughed. 'But he could be trouble eh? Bet he wasn't an easy kid for Pauline and Mike at times, often in and out of disputes at school. He always got along with Andy though ... and with you of course.' Maia noticed her father's lingering glances, trying to judge how his bereaved daughter was coping.

'He did have a devil-may-care attitude, though nothing was ever malicious or vindictive. He was easily led and would do anything for a dare, or a laugh. Remember when he climbed up and over the motorway signage?' recounted Maia. 'He couldn't be bothered to cross at the walkway further along so decided to use the workmen's route over the gantry.'

Phil nodded, 'I do remember it was one of his particularly death-defying antics, and the police had to intervene stopping the motorway traffic below. He did really calm down not long after that caper. You were good for him Maia, he settled down when you started going out together. If not for you, our Andy, Pauline and Mike, Tom may not have been around as long as he was. There were the drug years afterwards, but he came back around from that too, thankfully.'

Maia nodded. They chatted for some time. She knew her dad was itching to have another cookie and he recognised she had sussed him out, glancing sideways. 'Better not, or your mother will have my guts for garters,' he said, looking longingly at them, then rolling his eyes at his tracker.

'True,' she laughed. 'Hey, what's the time? I'm meeting Rosa and Daphne at three o'clock.'

'Okay sweetheart, I'll be on my way.' A warm hug and a peck on the cheek and off he went.

'Love to mam. Do you remember where you parked the car Dad?' Maia's words followed him on his way out of the door, she heard his muffled retort and grinned.

Maia recalled with clarity the self-destruct darkness within Tom. The small boy inside, who struggled to trust, who feared intimacy and had moments of silently crying inside. They dated for a year and a half from when she was almost sixteen. She knew Tom needed to be out in the wider world and have many girlfriends; he would never have been content with plodding village life. They parted amicably, but she was deeply heartbroken.

Maia met Rosa and Daphne at Café Dalvik for, Fizz-Friday lunch, and were welcomed with sumptuous greetings from Sophia in a harlequin-coloured tunic top; her red lava hair piled up on her head straining to be contained with a huge blingy slide, verging on the tiara! The bistro had an outside area of a few seats and tables for passers-by to grab a coffee which overlooked Durham market square. Maia recalled a lovely evening with Rosa and Daphne last autumn as cocktails flowed. Sophia had produced thick warm blankets to drape around them, so they could enjoy the rest of the evening outdoors.

Café Dalvik was etched in huge letters on the frosted panelled windows. They entered into the bar area where Nik offered a quick, 'hi.' She had popped out from the busy kitchen to hug them. There were four tall tables with high stools opposite the bar, and the room opened up into a bright area of a dozen tables with Scandi style pale wood furniture. The chairs were adorned with bright geometric upholstery, definitely a Sophia touch Maia thought. One wall was decorated with a wall-covering depicting Icelandic newspapers and magazines from the year the bistro was first opened in 2013. There was a hum of customer conversations enjoying a light liquid lunch of sherry and tapas.

The three friends walked through the bright area towards an archway leading to a more subdued area, containing four booths which seated up to six people. The colour choices were muted and Maia recalled Nik had challenged Sophia for the design choices. The subtle lighting was reflected back into the room from a bronze mirrored wall above the booths. The table settings were classy. It was a sumptuous, elegant area to relax. The height of the booths gave privacy from other diners. The three women were seated with a cold bottle of fizz and mini savoury treats for starters.

'Those two certainly know how to make a place feel welcoming.' Rosa sighed.

The women began to catch up, 'I was thinking of Tom last night, I'm sure I dreamt about him,' Maia began.

'Hmm nice!' said Daphne, with a knowing smile on her face.

'Unfortunately no passion. Think I was ugly-crying in my sleep by the state of me when I woke and looked in the mirror.' Maia contorted her face.

Rosa raised a hand and asked impatiently why it was, the heroines depicted on screen always cried so beautifully?

'There's no snot and saliva. No puffy, piggy-eyes from stinging mascara or black tracks down their cheeks, and no swollen bulbous red nose either.'

'True Rosa. I've seen you cry.' Daphne flashed a smile

'Thanks Daph, charming! The single tear rolling down a perfectly blushed cheek is utter tosh,' added Rosa.

Maia delighted in the nonsensical chatter, the catching up on the latest gossip, and numerous happy memories which inevitably arose when they met. This, was interspersed with Sophia faffing efficiently around the tables, checking on everyone, throwing a metaphoric warm blanket over all of her customers.

Maia had worked with Daphne at the newspaper and enjoyed their personal and professional discussions. She was pragmatic, yet compassionate. Her low-key manner was in contrast to her choice of quirky footwear, colourful vintage clothing and bright jewellery, which further enhanced her Nigerian beauty. Always wonderful to catch up and indulge in the gorgeous food on offer, enjoy freshly made cocktails, and finish off with another bottle of fizz. A belly-aching, perfectly joyful and emotionally restorative afternoon was had by all three friends.

Following flamboyant goodbyes at Café Dalvik, Steve, Rosa's incredibly patient husband agreed to do the taxi run and get the three squiffy women safely home. Maia got out of the car and embarked upon her tipsy walk, stumbling at one point severely enough to nudge her bag right off her shoulder. It swung away in front of her, as she frantically grabbed at the air before it finally dropped onto the ground. She turned to look for any witnesses, then peered behind at the ground for the imaginary culprit that had caused her inertia. Bag back on her shoulder, she regained composure and walked in a deliberate straight line, avoiding the large concrete planters along the Quayside, as she made her way home.

Maia scrambled for her keys, spied Tom's notebook, and took it from her bag. She held it in her hand and stroked the cover. Briefly flicking open the book she saw Tom's handwriting, quickly closed it, returning it to the depths of her bag. She wasn't sure she could deal with this, but she had made a promise to Pauline.

Maia sat on her balcony with a large glass of iced water, hoping to dilute the alcohol levels, dreading tomorrow's headache, gazing at the condensed spacing of Newcastle's seven bridges over the River Tyne. The nearest to her apartment was the white contemporary, Gateshead Millennium Bridge, for pedestrians and cyclists, which mechanically tilted open like an eyelid when boats need passage beneath. Then towered the majestic, Tyne Bridge in industrial green, echoed by its younger, and bigger relative, the Sydney Harbour Bridge in Australia.

The low-level red and white Swing Bridge was next, a remarkable feat of engineering, with its capability to swivel on a central pivot for passing nautical traffic. Maia's favourite was the next bridge, the unique stone-built, High Level Bridge with an upper deck where the railway line ran above the road.

There followed the bright blue, Queen Elizabeth Metro Bridge, conveying it's daily commuters; then the no-nonsense battle-ship grey of the, King Edward Bridge for mainline rail routes in and out of Newcastle City's Central Station.

Finally and only just visible around the sweep of the river, was the imposing, sand-coloured concrete, Redheugh Bridge, so exposed to the elements it is definitely to be avoided on blustery days.

Twinkling sunlight dazzled and danced upon the river surface capturing Maia's trance. Often the river was in sync with her mood, sometimes reflecting dark-blue foreboding depth, or choppy with anxiety; but today, life sparkled and she was full of contentment in this moment, however there was something missing in her life. She thought about her friends and family; Daphne and her partner Zain, Rosa and Steve with their son, also her siblings' content relationships. Maia was happy for them, but wondered if she would meet someone, maybe she was now ready for a relationship after Ryan.

First, she had to return to the task in hand, Maia took Tom's small weather-beaten notebook out of her bag. The cover was a pliable black, non-descript fake grain leather. Nothing on the first page, then rows of numbers scribbled out, and four sets of random numbers a few pages in, but nothing else. She scanned the detail to ascertain if a pattern or sequence emerged. The combination of numbers didn't look like phone numbers, maybe they were serial numbers for something? It was exactly as Pauline had described ... really odd.

Maia wondered if Tom had been a closet train spotter. He'd be devastated if such information was revealed posthumously. It would definitely ruin his street-cred, and she gave a little laugh, tracing her finger over his writing. The numbers may represent something scientific, which her dad may recognise. Could they relate to astral activity; he liked a bit of stargazing, maybe the next equinox or eclipse. Again the painful reminder of Tom's funeral drifted into her brain. She mentally pushed it aside, considering memories of his fascination with the universe, as he could name many planets, and constellations, but who knows what it all meant? However, it must have meant something of interest to Tom. It was late she needed sleep and tried her best with nagging doubts in the back of her mind.

6

MAIA RECEIVED A text message from Nik on their joint chat with Andy the following lunchtime. *Still ok for tonight?* Maia was lost in research for her commissioned Earth Chart article. It was now Saturday 18 April, and she had five weeks to hit the deadline to submit a draft proposal of her report to Harriet Cooper. She'd completely forgotten in her musings the previous evening she'd messaged Andy and Nik to invite them over for a, Saturday sibling supper, to discuss Tom's notebook. She'd exhausted her own hypotheses and with no point trying to fathom it alone, she enlisted her brother and sister's analytical skills for the task. Her thinking was, Andy's technical skills were precise and meticulous, with good attention to detail. Nik had been a brilliant mathematician at school, accountancy was an obvious career choice for her, yet she loved cooking and baking, hence buying the cafe. Their logical brains and aptitude for numbers may help decipher the codes.

Maia hurriedly responded to Nik with emojis for pizza, and two beer glasses, representing what was on offer for supper.

Andy replied with a thumb's up emoji.

Nik replied. *Great!*

After warm greetings, the three sat catching up over supper. Maia showed them Tom's notebook. Andy and Nik agreed Pauline may be searching for a non-existent reason to explain the tragedy, however both were intrigued by the entries. After much discussion, Andy suggested the sets of numbers may indicate map coordinates, he recognised the presentation of the numbers from an orienteering and survival course he'd completed years ago. He entered the first set of two long digits in Maia's iPad which pin-pointed an area in Northumberland National Park.

'Oh, wow!' said Maia, she felt excited. There were four of these references.

'Well … he was a Countryside Ranger for years,' commented Nik, 'so the areas may simply represent places he loved, could be SSSI's.'

Her siblings puzzled faces warranted further explanation.

Nik continued, 'a Site of Special Scientific Interest, where there may be rare species of plants, habitats or important geological features.'

Andy and Maia shared a know-it-all expression toward Nik, then Andy said, 'not just a pretty face.'

Nik shrugged, she always shrugged, she spent her life shrugging, nothing phased her, no matter how huge the issue.

'I guess it could be that, but I doubt very much Tom would need map references to visit them,' said Maia.

Andy agreed commenting, 'Tom would've kept the locations in his head.'

The three siblings had at least made inroads into the mystery. When Andy slumped into the sofa with a jaw-breaking yawn, it was time to go.

'Little one keeping you up?' asked Maia.

Andy nodded and yawned again, shuddering with a nod as he expelled the remnants of exhalation.

'Sophia has offered us a lift home, I'll ring her,' suggested Nik.

'Ah Sophia, she's great, she really is my favourite sister now.' Andy said raising his arms as cushions flew in his direction.

Once they left, Maia entered the map references into her iPad and kept a record of the locations, which were to the north of Northumberland County, although the first was strangely, a coastal town car park. Maia was highly motivated to find out if anything had been going on for Tom, as she understood his vulnerabilities. It may offer some explanation for Pauline, although the myriad of outcomes, and potentially nefarious dodgy dealings she conjured up, did concern her.

Stretching and yawning the following morning, Maia padded from the bedroom and saw her list of locations on the coffee table. She knew about Tom's drug-taking for a little while after they separated, though she was certain he had grown out of that stage; he had held his job and been with his partner Fiona for many years afterwards too.

Pondering on what to do, lounging on the balcony, Maia watched a group of rowers on the river. Ripples streamed from several sculls breaking the calm river surface during a training session. She almost spat out the coffee in her mouth as she exclaimed the name, 'Craig!' Her thoughts were directed to her good friend from university who, as an excellent athlete, had captained the university rowing team. Following some years as a journalist, for which they'd both qualified, she recalled he had joined the police service in recent years and trained to be a detective. It was ages since they had spoken, only Christmas and birthday messages these days. She knew Craig wouldn't mind considering a few questions about what Tom may have been up to perhaps, and it would be great to catch up with him. The mobile number she had for him was no longer active, so after a bit of research she contacted the main police switchboard, and was given the number for Yorkshire North CID, with confirmation a DS Craig Pedrick was stationed there. Maia left a message. It was Sunday, she didn't expect a reply, but a few hours later her mobile rang, an unknown number appeared and, an oh-so-familiar voice greeted her, 'DC Pedrick here returning your call.'

She replied, 'it's Maia Hewson here. Is that *Craig* Pedrick? What on earth are you doing working on a Sunday?'

'Hi Maia Hewson, thought it must be my old mate from Uni. What a lovely surprise, and yes, working on a Sunday in this job. How the hell are you?' Craig seemed genuinely delighted. It took them both directly back to the student flats they shared, the inebriation, and the laughter, well into the early hours.

'I'm good Craig. How are things for you?'

'I tried journalism as you know, but the frustration of

only going so far with investigations through subterfuge and getting nowhere drove me crazy. So, years ago I opted for a route with the law on my side, which at least gave me the option to investigate crimes legally. It's going well, interesting work.'

'Good move.'

They enjoyed catching up on the present, with much enthusiasm about Maia's new work prospects and joyfully reminiscing about the past. During a natural pause in the conversation Maia said, 'Craig, there's something on my mind I'd like to run by you, it's not in the public domain, or official work research or anything, it's more personal.'

'Okay, if there's anything I can do, I will. There may be some obvious confidentialities I can't disclose and I couldn't investigate anything unofficially. Are you okay Maia?'

'Yes I'm fine, it's nothing drastic I don't think, just something nagging away and I know I can trust you one hundred percent.'

There was a silence between them, both knowing why their deep mutual trust of ten years was inextricable.

Craig suggested, 'let's meet for a coffee, be great to see you.'

'Or a night on the black velvets?' Maia's comment eased the slight apprehension between them.

Craig laughed at the memory of drinking many a Guinness with a shot of Tia Maria and added, 'who on earth came up with that concoction? We had some great times didn't we?'

'Certainly did, look I can travel down to you anytime, let me know where and when.'

'I've got four days off shift coming up, let's not waste time. How about Thomson's Bar for old time's sake next weekend, Friday at two any good for you?'

'Yea, great. Friday the twenty fourth, it's in the diary, looking forward to it.' Maia took Craig's personal number.

DS Craig Pedrick looked at his cluttered desk, smiled and thought, four rest days coming up and a chance to see the lovely Maia again. He was glad life seemed to be working out well for her after those traumatic months ten years ago. He and Maia had some fabulous times at university, however as the years rolled away, inevitably their social contact faded as the responsibility of adult life took precedence.

7

MAIA RETURNED FROM a run the following morning after the uplifting call with Craig. She took a long shower, and pulled on her new style workwear, enjoying the soft fabric of casual leisure clothing. So much more comfortable than the restrictive tailored suits and heels she had to wear for appearance sake, when attending meetings with the team at the fashion magazine HQ. Now she didn't have to worry about blouses committing hari-kari by slipping off their hangers. With a mug of minty hot chocolate she focussed on the new article she was writing for Earth Chart, *Leading the Urban Environment*. She was planning interviews with key people in northern business, whose pay-off would be positive exposure in Earth Chart, also to create competition to reach their national top ten list.

Earth Chart had its core scientific wing; however, her role was to interpret and critique, everyday life in running large corporations. Maia was on a basic financial retainer and expenses, however there was deadline pressure to produce coherent, evaluative reports frequently and precisely. If and when she was published, especially cover stories, it was rather lucrative. She felt blessed to have this opportunity and congratulated herself for being where she was, and couldn't wait to see her name in print, *Maia Hewson, Environmental Journalist*.

After a few hours work, she sat back, feeling positive about the future. The aroma of another sweet-smelling spring storm wafted through the open balcony doors, and pattered constantly outside. It may thankfully clear the muggy air, she thought, as she laid out her yoga mat. She enjoyed her practice with the sound of real relentless rainfall, instead of a recording from her yoga playlist. Some distant church bells were ringing in the city which distracted her; churches reminded her of Tom's funeral these days, they were not happy comforting sounds.

After the yoga session, she felt motivated not to dwell on the enduring sorrow she felt and decided to remember the positives. She retrieved a large floral storage box from under her bed which contained old photos and mementos that had survived from childhood. Maia played her, mixtape, playlist songs from teenage years which reminded her of her siblings, and Tom messing about together at home, and on holidays and trips.

She came across the jade heart Tom gave her, she caressed the smooth surface between forefinger and thumb recalling how thrilled she was to receive the love token, proof of his love for her. She inwardly smiled at the innocence of their youth and her naive romantic dreams of a life to come with her beloved. She promised herself to get a new chain for it, and took off Tom's pendant gently placing it alongside her jade heart. The past rushed towards her with every mental image, particularly the mobile phone photo she had printed of Tom in his navy Countryside Ranger gear, standing proudly outside his cosy ramshackle, tiny Northumberland cottage.

It reminded her of a time, over ten years ago in the summer of 2004 when Tom had been employed as an apprentice Countryside Ranger in rural Northumberland, thanks to Mike's encouragement. Tom's years of volunteering had paid off, and he was accepted with a requirement to attend college courses to obtain relevant certificates to fully qualify. Pauline helping him find accommodation near to his work base in Northumberland National Park. She was convinced it was beneficial for his mental wellbeing to be away from any hustle, bustle and bad influences, so they offered him financial support until he was on his feet. He was living with his partner Fiona in the tiny cheap rental, Edera Cottage, with only basic facilities. After his turbulent later teenage years, Tom reached his twenties unscathed and the young couple seemed very content together in their gentle rustic surroundings. Maia had met Fiona when they visited Pauline and Mike to celebrate a wedding anniversary. She was a happy-hippy, in Maia's opinion, a sweet gentle woman. Fiona worked at the local farm shop, she made a respectable living by selling her hand-made jewellery and dreamcatchers to tourists during the summer months. She was four years older than Tom, a settling influence.

Maia had arranged to meet them for a drink in the bar nearest the cottage, which was a three mile walk away, as she would be leaving for York University, and was doing her farewell rounds. Maia drove there to meet them, and Tom was waiting outside the bar. She noticed he still wore the rune pendant. Fiona, was apparently, staying with friends on the south coast at a music festival, and as Maia had too much to drink to drive home after getting caught up in the wonderful evening, Tom invited her to stay. Maia trusted Tom implicitly, with her life in fact, so she was fine with the arrangement. Typical of Tom, he lit a flickering fire that crackled away at the back of the cottage overlooking the huge expanse of dusky, rolling fields. They drank more beer and listened to some new music Tom was keen to share. The evening cooled, so Tom brought out a huge heavy blanket. They watched the fire and reminisced about the mutual people and events in their lives. Maia recalled turning her face towards Tom to ask him a question, and they both became lost in a still moment.

Maia looked at Tom's photo now, in 2015 in her new surroundings, 2004 felt like a million light years lost in the past. Taking a sip of the cool gin and tonic she'd made, she closed her eyes, and could almost smell the burning wood, and could distinctly visualise the memory of Tom's face highlighted by the glowing fire.

Their eyes had met that night, then their mouths met. It felt so familiar to her, the feel of his breath, his body scent, her fingers running through the back of his hair, the way he held her around her waist, it was like it had always been. Maia recalled every single detail. Tom pulled her around to sit in front of him, with her back to him, and he engulfed her in his arms, his chin resting gently on her shoulder.

'Shame you're going to uni soon,' he murmured.

'We can still meet up, I'll be home during holidays.'

'Sticking with Environmental Journalism then?'

'Yea, I'm specialising in Analysis and Planning of Urban Areas.'

'Just like your mam, saving the planet. Have you been on any marches recently?' A broad grin spread upon his face.

Maia smiled. 'I've realised now that holding a placard and shouting into the ether won't have as much impact as working from inside the industry, where decisions are made. I'll do my best to join the fight to save our beautiful planet.'

Maia then became coy and was glad Tom couldn't see her blushing when she recognised his gentle goading. They were always great at teasing each other.

'Why do you think I was determined to get a job working here, same reason really to protect the land.' Tom gazed out over the countryside. 'I'll do the work on the surface and you can get inside the powers that be, and together we'll save the world.' He threw his arms wide.

Both laughed. Facing the fire, the flickering orange glow lit up Tom's face. Maia huddled into his warm body, and she felt the infatuation she always had whenever she saw him. She felt his erection pressing into the small of her back, the same thrill she felt for him years ago in the cinema. She could not resist this man.

Maia turned to face him, 'we shouldn't be doing this, you are with Fiona and I'm also seeing ... someone.'

'Doing what?' Tom shrugged, he held his arms wide again, with a questioning smile, 'you always did have that effect on me.'

Little did he know Maia's hormones were raging with a desire she had never felt for any other man. She trusted him. If he promised nothing would happen, then it wouldn't, but it would be heart and body-achingly difficult to resist.

'It's fine Maia, don't worry, I'll go and make up the spare bed. Or I may sleep out here, I often do.'

Maia caught his hand as he stood and pulled him towards her, with clear intentions. She didn't want to sleep separately. Tom was her Achilles Heel, her muse, her first love and this moment would never happen again, as she was moving away in several weeks.

'Are you absolutely sure Maia?' he whispered.

She nodded, and ran her forefinger across his mouth. He responded by gently kissing her fingertips.

They lay on the rug facing each other and pulled it over their bodies in a warm, sensual cocoon. He kissed the side of her neck as his hands gently caressed her. It was all so easy and comforting. He unzipped his jeans, and discarded them along with his t-shirt. Maia lifted her dress up, over her head, and flung it aside. They laughed together. They held each other lovingly and stroked every part of their familiar bodies. As soon as they began to make love, she felt the rhythm of his body, and it wasn't long before she felt the pulsating waves of passion inside, perfectly in tune together.

Wrapped in the blanket, the infinite starlight perforated the black sky, and the embers of the fire were their only light. After they dozed for a while, entwined, a cool breeze prickled their bare skin, so they headed indoors.

Maia recollected now, how she ruthlessly dumped the 'someone' she was with, soon after her night with Tom. She got up from the sofa, poured a refill and as the ice clinked into the bottom of her glass, she wondered if she would ever feel that way with anyone else. She certainly hadn't with Ryan, or the handful of other lovers she had over the years.

The following sunny morning in 2004 at Tom's cottage, she'd woken up in his arms. They had a warm embrace, then she had to leave. Over coffee, they chatted as if they had never been apart, and as if they were never going to be. Both sadly knew it was time for Maia to leave, and that's when she took the photo of him. She was eighteen and had her whole life ahead of her, she couldn't stay. They walked together, his arm around her shoulder, hers around his waist to the car which was left in the pub car park overnight.

'Won't anyone see us together like this and cause trouble for you and Fiona?'

'I'm used to trouble as you know Maia,' Tom offered his endearing crooked smile and shrugged.

After one last loving hug, and a brief but meaningful kiss, Maia got in the car and drove away. The image of Tom raising one hand in a goodbye gesture, the other hand in his pocket was as clear in her mind as if it was yesterday. But he was gone now, forever. Maia took a long sip of the cool sharp herbal drink and felt it soothe on the way down. That was one of the last times she saw Tom. She placed the photo back in the bundle with the others in the box and replaced it under her bed. She knew she had to get on with her life now, but first one last task, she must figure out what the locations in Northumberland were all about.

8

Northumberlandia, April 2015

A FEW DAYS following the revelations about the Northumbria locations in Tom's notebook, Maia woke early feeling refreshed. She prepared a large bowl of cereal with soya milk for breakfast. The cereal packaging advised the contents were full of riboflavins, whatever they were. It also claimed to being fortified with vitamins and iron, which she hoped would give her lots of energy for the day ahead, or the placebo effect of a healthy breakfast would, at the very least. In truth, Maia felt the potent coffee she made for her flask may probably prove more effective.

Maia read the list of locations identified following the meeting with her siblings, and thought, today is where this begins. If there was anything troubling from these locations that would offer clues to Tom's demise, even his state of mind perhaps, it may help Pauline's anxieties ... or potentially, add to them. Maia was taking a day out from her work research, which would do no harm as it had been very intense lately. She'd planned her route, calling in for fuel, before heading north eastwards to the first location on the coastline.

The location, as near as Andy was able to determine from his precise diagram, was an empty, almost derelict car park, where Maia parked up. It was 8 am so not many folk were up and about. The car park faced the sea front, she parked at the end bay, got out and looked around. A few dog walkers, runners and cyclists passed with a hardly discernible nod or, 'morning,' directed her way. She could see a curtain of rain approaching from the flat horizon as another spring storm looked imminent.

Maia loved how the weather was its own mistress. Mother Nature didn't care if you wanted a sunny day, if she wants to pee down upon humans she would. The sea began to agitate, it would be rough in twenty minutes once the distant storm arrived. There was nothing of significance that Maia could detect from the location. It was an ordinary, neglected parking area, with hardly discernible faint painted lines to separate the bays, however, still attracted extortionate fees as it faced the sea. A good place to park up and eat your sarnies, with windscreen wipers sweeping back and forth, on freezing sleet-full days, when it's too cold to leave your vehicle.

She walked around the perimeter, then spiralled her way to the centre, ground-gazing. Nothing. She stood, becoming aware of a few glances her way, and feeling conspicuous, she rubbed her earlobes for the benefit of any passers-by, who would conclude she'd lost an earring. There was nothing of note. She wasn't sure what on earth she hoped to discover, but this was a big fat zero.

It had been a while since Maia had visited the coast and was reminded of a time she went sea-swimming with

Rosa, one late October day last year. She got into her car and headed up toward the Northumberland countryside, reminiscing about the swim. Thankfully the temperature had been a mild eleven degrees that day for her inaugural sea-swim as an adult. She had paddled in the Baltic temperature-level North Sea as a child. The sensation of painful pins and needles, ice-cold feet, and numb lower legs had apparently left her memory, as she stepped into the water some twenty plus years later.

Despite the numbness however, it was a joyful event. Rosa and a small group of swimmers gathered regularly for a therapeutic dip. With trepidation Maia followed Rosa into the water. Rosa was chatting away with her fellow, Wild Sea Women, and there were a number of men around too. Never before had Maia imagined she'd be walking into the North Sea in October, wearing only her swimsuit, rubber wet shoes and gloves and a bright blue bobble hat.

Once over the sharp intake of breath as the sea gently lapped her midriff and she eased her shoulders quickly under the water, it was lovely. Floating about in the sea watching the sparks of eastern sunrise through the clouds was delightful. The feeling of connection to nature was tangible. Apart from the sound of gentle waves and light chatter, it was blissfully quiet away from the road, cars, shops and people. Rosa was an experienced sea-swimmer, complete with orange float, and Maia was aware she was keeping a check on her throughout. She recalled her words. *"We mustn't stay in too long as it's your first go."*

Maia acknowledged she was ok, as her chattering teeth

calmed and her breathing regulated, but remembered the tops of her arms went completely numb.'

Rosa had laughed. *"Seems to freeze the bingo wings first."*

Once they were out of the water, dressed in thick warm clothing, Rosa poured them both a hot coffee from her flask. They sat on a rug on the beach looking out at the wonderful sun-rising scene. Maia became aware she was daydreaming gazing out over the wild waters as spots of soft rain blew into her face.

Maia drove away from the coastline, alighted from her car at the next location some fifty minutes north west, inland towards Northumberland National Park. She inhaled the earthy, damp-wood air of forest. The second of Tom's locations was a short walk from a visitor car park. Maia followed a footpath as near as she could to the specific location in the diagram Andy had kindly prepared for her. She looked around, it was a clearing in a wood, nothing more. She retraced her steps back to the car park, then walked back along the footpath to the clearing, taking her time, sweeping her searchlight vision from ground to tree-tops, but what was she looking for?

She zig-zagged along the path using her boot to rummage in the undergrowth if something caught her eye, which turned out generally to be selfish tourist detritus of confectionary and biscuit wrappers. Ever watchful for dog-owners who'd gone before, and thought it acceptable to leave huge dollops of their beloved pets' unexploded dog-shit mines for others to step, or worse, slide into.

Nothing of note appeared to Maia, so she headed to the third location, this time hundreds of metres from the nearest tourist car parking area. Maia walked to the location along a footpath, again carefully following Andy's graphics, and referring to his old compass he'd used in his orienteering days. This area was open and sparse, nothing looked particularly spectacular, or unusual.

Looking at the ground she wondered what SSSIs looked like, and hoped she hadn't trodden on, and squashed any rare plants. She spotted an old small crumbling building in the distance. There was so much history here, she felt a sense of ancient settlements, fierce battles, and of course hordes of Roman soldiers stomping in synchrony along the wall a few miles from where she stood. If she listened carefully, she sensed the echoes of their ghostly rhythmical steps, and the wind brought the faint remnants of fighting and war cries to her ears. A cold wind shot through her, causing a shiver as if those ancient spirits still lingered. It was eerie and very beautiful.

She gazed at the vista, the grey structure in the distance looked lost in the vast wild landscape as far as the eye could see. 'No wonder you loved it here Tom.' And with that comment, she turned and walked back to her car. She would come here again, soon, for this ethereal connection.

The last place, another half-hour drive, was a large, flat, nondescript area, toward the Scottish border. It was used as car parking for open-air events; farm shows, car rallies and festivals. As Maia perused the area, again nothing particularly stood out. However, the realisation she had no idea what she was looking for, rendered her naively disheartened, believing something would jump out and connect the dots.

Maybe the places were some protected wild creature conservation areas, where Tom would sit for hours making observations. No doubt he would've fiercely protected the environment, also any waning colony of bugs or birds. She couldn't help but smile at his devotion to the cause, bordering on the obsessive and inwardly thanked him.

Maia was now fatigued; her legs ached; this exertion was different to running along the flat, urban riverside area. She'd used muscles that had lay dormant. She thought of Tom striding around these places with consummate ease, she considered his fit, lithe, but muscular body, the tone of his skin. She'd never met his parents, however he must have inherited the skin tone of a mid-european heritage, he was not a Northern pasty-white. She felt so close to Tom, she could almost feel, hear and see him gazing into the distance beside her. Maia could suddenly sense his arms around her, so familiar, the scent of him, his green eyes. She wept openly, standing alone in the middle of nowhere. An intermittent spring downpour caught her attention, she'd be soaked soon, so turned and marched back to the car, to head southwards and the comfort of her city. Why had she come here? She was momentarily annoyed at Pauline, what was the point of all this? Tom was dead, nothing would bring him back. She'd return his notebook to Pauline reassuring her of the conclusion, which she was trying to convince herself, the locations were merely of natural interest.

Maia stopped off at Northumberlandia, the vast community park in acres of land, located ten miles north of Newcastle City. She wandered around the gentle rolling contour paths of the human landform sculpture, of a reclining female body some four hundred metres long. Maia climbed to the pinnacle of Northumberlandia, the Lady of the North, at her highest point, thirty metres at the tip of her breasts. Another smattering of rain was on the way. Maia had a moment to herself in stillness, looking all around and thought, how much she truly loved this magnificent area.

She made her way to the visitor centre cafe, bought a coffee, sat outside, and pondered uneasily as the vapour rose from the hot drink. For a final time she considered, no way would Tom have needed map references, his internal GPS would've been able to pin-point these areas. Maia finished her coffee, as bundles of people arrived; couples, families and full-on weatherproofed walkers and cyclists were in abundance. The weather wasn't great, drizzly, dull and uninspiring. The search for answers was over, time to go home. Though exhausted, Maia put thoughts of Tom aside, and spent the evening proof reading her proposed article for Earth Chart, also booking train tickets for her trip to see Craig in York at the weekend.

The following morning, Maia met Harriet Cooper off the train from London. Harriet had a day in the North East visiting her son who was studying at Newcastle University, which tied-in nicely for a brunch meeting with Maia. Harriet was pleased with Maia's initial verbal proposal they had discussed, profiling key personalities in Northern business. The focus was to research those who were leading the way in environmental good practice. Maia also had, a naughty list, of those failing to maintain even minimum standards.

'Would you consider extending your research to cover Scotland?' Harriet asked, 'maybe a separate article about Scottish businesses?' Maia confirmed her interest, she could hardly refuse the suggestion. Harriet identified two companies she felt would make a good start. Once she left to meet her son, Maia felt a little overwhelmed at the expectation placed upon her, however she had to be up for the task. There was some time-consuming hard work up ahead and she needed to get on with making contact with senior figures in industry, but it was never easy getting time with busy people. She'd need to use all of her powers of persuasion to convince them she was worth their time. Maia was feeling the pressure, however this is what she wanted, wasn't it?

9

York, April 2015

ONE HOUR AND ten minutes on the train journey from Newcastle to York offered a palate cleanser from stress, for Maia to put work aside, gaze out of the window, listen to music, and look forward to some fulfilling social time with Craig. She walked through the city across the cobbled Shambles and arrived at Thomsons Bar. She ordered some lunch and sat at what was their regular seat, a velour, pink patchwork sofa. A huge gilt framed picture of the actor, Rik Mayall as his character 'Lord Flashheart' in the, *Blackadder* series was placed above. Maia surveyed the décor, it was an unusual bar, and a frequent haunt when she and Craig were students. It had retained its unique, quirky style, it felt nostalgic and cosy. The walls were covered in a kaleidoscope of former tourism posters, and ads for various movies, and music concerts, old and new. Maia arrived at the bar thirty minutes before meeting Craig and had time to enjoy a coffee and a light meal of rustic bread, pâté and marmalade chutney. She took a few photographs out of her bag and settled down to look through them.

'What's a nice girl like you doing in a place like this?' the familiar sound of Craig's voice was a joy to hear.

'Is that the best you've got, Pedrick?' Maia looked up, rolled her eyes and stood, arms wide open to hug her glorious friend tightly, which he reciprocated. They hugged for an extended time. Craig got a beer and they sat catching up for over an hour about the ridiculous times they had at university together. There were times when Maia couldn't catch her breath for laughing, listening to events she had completely forgotten about. Out came the photographs.

'Dear me Maia, look at those Christmas photos, death warmed up.'

'True, more like a Halloween grim reaper. Not a good look.'

'But you're looking great now by the way.'

'You too, obviously kept up the rowing, you look as fit as a butcher's dog.'

'Yep, not competitively any more, but I'm coaching and need to keep in shape, and be on my best behaviour so I can hang on to the wonderful, Luiza.'

'It's great to hear you're happy. I've not met, Mr Right yet but I'm in no hurry, not got time with this new position, seems it'll be demanding, which is great, I'm up for it.'

'You will meet someone Maia and he'll be amazing.'

They smiled warmly at each other.

Another photo revealed more memories. 'I remember your great singing voice and the karaoke nights, you'd be up at the drop of a hat everywhere we went,' reminded Maia.

'I was a bit of a tool wasn't I?' Craig shook his head,

'we went to a few decent gigs and festivals though … great times.'

Maia's recall was in overdrive. 'What about the time we wanted to be more cultured and booked to see a ballet. I couldn't stop laughing at you whispering comments about the anatomy of the male dancers. I was really trying to concentrate and enjoy it.'

'We left in the intermission, ended up in here drinking … yet again. You forget how immature we were, just daft kids really, but we worked hard too.'

Maia took a long look at Craig as he flicked through the photographs and enjoyed his laughter. He hadn't changed much, a few more lines around his eyes and he had broadened out as men do, during the transition from twenties to thirties. Craig had a large muscular frame with a broad barrel chest and was prone to weight gain. Maia recalled he could be sensitive about this and would up his activity levels to slim down. His mid-brown hair was neatly cut and his grey-blue eyes were ever so slightly too far apart across the bridge of his nose, but it suited him. His square jaw completed the picture of this physically and emotionally robust man. It was a beautiful, determined, friendly face.

He was a joker too, a quick wit, always taking the mick out of their peers at uni, but never to the detriment of anyone who couldn't take the flack, as he inevitably invited it upon himself, and welcomed it. Maia bet her life he was the same with his police colleagues. Craig also appreciated quality things in life, decent clothing, liked a good watch, an upmarket car, he'd worked hard to secure this lifestyle, as he'd come from quite an impoverished background.

If there was a fault, it would be Craig was prone to trying to control situations. If he thought he was right about something, it was difficult to sway his judgement, and he could sulk if another option was chosen over his, for a while at least until he came around. Maybe he's mellowed, Maia thought. Ever the optimist, Craig would try to seek positives and quick solutions, a problem solver, exactly how he'd helped her in the past when she was at her most vulnerable. She truly loved him and their special bond would never be torn apart.

'Tell me about Luiza?'

Craig spoke warmly of his partner, who was Polish, she'd studied as a teacher in Poland then moved to the UK and joined the police force where they met. Craig described her, 'she is a PC on a neighbourhood beat. She's really bright with a positive approach to life and a hard worker. She is also beautiful, tall and athletic, a good middle-distance runner. We're enjoying the lifestyle with no big plans to marry or have a family as yet, but you never know. We've bought a house together recently, and it's all going great.'

'Sounds like you've met your soul mate, I'm so happy for you Craig.'

'I have. Now we need to work on you. I know some great single fellas in the force if you're interested?'

'Yeah ... maybe ... why not?'

They then got around to discussing the circumstances of Tom's death. It was good to offload the burden and Craig offered condolences. Maia explained the misgivings about the circumstances surrounding his death, and asked what a police investigation would entail. There was doubt it was suicide, and a notebook indicating locations, which she'd followed up, revealed nothing ...

He advised the police would have made some inquiries but if there was no solid evidence of third-party involvement, the coroner was likely to rule it an open case.

Craig wondered whether the police had any information from Tom's mobile or laptop if they were available, however he reiterated if there were no signs of illegal activity, it was unlikely they would explore those avenues. Craig also stated if she sensed something is a little bit off, it may be worth speaking with those who knew Tom well. He sensitively warned Maia not to expect too much. 'Sometimes, unfortunately these events do remain a mystery, especially in cases with no suicide note. But, if something comes to light or there's anything else I can do to help, I will.'

After a moment or two, Craig picked up a photograph of him and Maia in a bar, changing the subject, he tentatively asked, 'do you think about her?'

'Every single day.' Maia felt forlorn, near to tears, but fought them back.

'Hey, it's fine,' he said softly, 'though ... you were a bit of a nutter at the time.' Craig diffused the emotional situation with their mutual humour. 'I knew something serious was up that night.'

'Call yourself a detective Craig Pedrick. I was nearly eight months pregnant!' jibed Maia.

Craig laugh-snorted. 'Just thought you were stressed out with uni work and shifts at the restaurant. Though I did wonder why you were so spotty, sickly, knackered and depressed all the time. Zero fun Maia. Your dress sense went right out of the window as well, with all the dark, baggy clothes and pale skin, I thought you'd gone all Goth on me.'

Maia laughed. 'Charming! Anyway, you're a bloody good mate and I love you to bits for all the support and organising ... well, you know... stuff.'

'Yep, you owe me big time mate. How old will she be now?' said Craig trying to work it out.

Immediately Maia said, 'she was ten years old on …'

They said simultaneously … 'the twentieth of March.'

'The day of her father's funeral, would you believe,' added Maia.

'Tom?'

Maia nodded, it was the first time she had revealed the information to anyone. 'The day of the eclipse too.'

Craig had been sitting opposite and positioned himself beside Maia, with an arm around her shoulder. 'That's a bloody tough one Maia, no wonder you're trying to find the truth of what happened to him.' After a moment or two he asked, 'did you get around to writing the letter. I remember you saying, you could do it anytime, and they'd keep it for her when she was older.'

'I've actually started to write it a number of times but it's so difficult to know what to say. What would she possibly want to know about me?' she said with a shrug.

'That, the woman who gave her life, is a wonderful person who made a difficult decision, which she sincerely hoped would offer her child the best opportunities in life,' suggested Craig.

Maia smiled weakly. 'It does prey on my mind at times and I torture myself, desperately hoping she has a wonderful family and she is happy and healthy. You live your life wondering if you did the right thing. I question myself all of the time, and I fantasise about whether she looks like me or Tom.'

'You absolutely did what was right for her and you at the time Maia. She would have been placed with a lovely family I'm sure, who maybe couldn't have a child of their own perhaps ... I'm here if you want to discuss the Tom situation again, let me know if there's anything I can help with.'

'I'll speak with Pauline, think the inquest is soon and see if anything arises from that.'

Craig nodded.

Maia sat upright, inhaled deeply and said she will consider trying another letter soon. 'The longer I leave it the harder it gets to write anything, she has her own life now.'

Craig sat by Maia on the sofa and hugged her until she was calm. There was nothing in the world that worked as well for Maia, as a Craig bear-hug for keeping it together.

After an emotional, yet fun afternoon of catching up, they parted with a warm embrace. Maia suggested it would be lovely to meet Luiza and ... maybe some of his cop friends too, with a wink.

'I'll filter out only the very best for you Maia. Hey, there's a thirtieth birthday celebration soon if you're up for that. It's on May Bank Holiday weekend, so it'll be very lively in York city centre. Actually, it's a Star Wars Bank Holiday too.'

'Star Wars?'

'May the fourth'

'Sorry?'

'C'mon Maia, keep up. May the fourth be with you, May The Force be with you, get it now? ... dhurr.' Craig pulled an imbecilic face.

'How are we even friends Craig Pedrick?' Maia retorted. Craig laughed.

'Poor Luiza.' Maia shook her head and rolled her eyes.

Maia did have a sense of her life running away with her, and said so. 'Over the last month or so, I've been to my daughter's, father's funeral, I've got a new demanding career opportunity, I've moved home, and been wandering around Northumberland looking for clues from a mysterious notebook,' she paused, 'but, it has all brought me back here, to York, to Thomsons ... and to you.' She smiled warmly at Craig, and he reciprocated.

'And in a week's time, you'll be having a rip-roaring time with the bunch of reprobates I call my colleagues. There's a big group going out on the town, and Luiza's going too, so you could meet her then. What do you think?'

Maia wasn't necessarily the impulsive type, but given she'd had a rough time recently and felt she needed some light relief, said, 'okay, why not?'

10

THE FOLLOWING MORNING after her York trip was Saturday with no commitments to do or think anything in particular. Maia made a huge pot of coffee and warmed up a large crescent croissant, she'd brought from the express shop on her way home from the station. The combination of fresh coffee and the baked aroma of buttery, puff-pastry filled her apartment, it felt indulgent and soothing. She bit into the light brittle flakes, and as tiny petals of featherlight pastry floated onto her knee, she reached for the photo of Christmas 2004 that prompted Craig's question, *"do you think about her?"* On closer scrutiny of the image, her demeanour and the expression on her face shocked Maia. She would've been six months pregnant then and looked like a wafer-thin version of herself, about as robust as the croissant she was eating which could crumble into bits at any moment. Wide eyes, gaunt face as pale as the cold winter moon. She looked terrified. Maia had questioned pregnancy in late September after realising she had possibly missed two or three periods since the night with Tom. She was so distracted and incredibly fatigued from a mix of conflicting pressures; organising the move to York, sorting finances, coupled with trepidation and excitement, plus the emotional goodbye celebrations of embarking on independent living. She thought at the time the sickly feelings were that of a nervous stomach.

Looking back now, on how her brain adapted to a new belief system. She was eighteen and had created a new truth for herself. A phantom, which if dismissed, would go way. She hoped she would miscarry or the problem would somehow magically disappear. She couldn't believe her naïveté now, having lived in that fantasy world, ignoring her body and purposefully buying dark, oversize clothing to conceal the transformation. She was too terrified to bring herself to tell anyone. She wondered how she sustained a baby, having lost a lot of weight with worry, with academic commitments, and working in a restaurant; plus erratic hormones, poor nutrition and morning sickness didn't help. She hadn't been drinking once she discovered the pregnancy, at least that was something she always felt she got right.

In more lucid moments, Maia knew a baby would ruin her future life, she could barely look after herself. Tom was definitely the father, she hadn't slept with the, 'someone' or anyone since their night of passion, but Tom may not have wanted to know either, and would run a mile. He was with Fiona, and had a lovely lifestyle. A baby would've ruined his life too, and definitely crushed his relationship with Fiona. Maia wanted him to be happy.

She studied the image again of Christmas decorations in the restaurant where she worked which reminded Maia she'd missed the family trip to Iceland. She offered a legitimate excuse to her family, explaining she was working and didn't want to jeopardise her student job in the busy Italian restaurant. She stayed overnight at her parents before they left, and guessed they believed she wanted to stay and party with her new student friends. They gave her beautifully wrapped gifts and a food parcel as she looked so drab and unwell, though she vehemently reassured them she was, *"fine, just tired."*

Reflecting back, Maia wondered why she didn't tell her parents, at least her mam? It would've been okay, they would do anything for her. A swift tsunami of emotion caught her off guard and prompted tears pricking her eyes as she gulped down her coffee. Maia's denial rendered the situation too late to terminate the pregnancy. When the stressful secret overwhelmed her, she finally told Craig several weeks before her due date. Craig took arrangements in his stride, or seemed to. She really loved Craig, he was one of the closest friends she knew and she vowed to never leave it so long again, before seeing him.

Maia recalled lying in her bed with Craig at her side thinking of baby names. He had gently encouraged her to consider a name as it was evident she didn't want to become attached, and always used the simple term, *baby*. They laughed at comical derivatives of popular names, also rock stars and actor names. Nothing was decided that night as Craig cradled Maia all night as she slept. The following morning Maia recalled she had thought about the importance of naming her child. As she and Craig were walking to their respective lectures, she remembers their conversation.

"So many boys names are religious, which is just not me. For a boy I like Dale. The Nordic version, Dalur, means valley. A valley can be peaceful, and I'd like him to have peace in his life. There's usually a river running through a valley, and rivers are full of life too. They are strong, and flow for a lifetime. And ... for a girl, Freyja, which is the name of the Norse goddess of love and beauty. It also means, noble woman, and that's what I want for her, to be good-hearted and feel brave. But I'll spell it without the j in the middle, don't want her going through life having to constantly explain or correct her name. Life can be tough enough without little complications ... so, Dale Hewson or Freya Hewson it is."

Craig had nodded, put his arm around her shoulders, and nothing further was ever discussed about the baby's name, or the identity of the baby's father.

Maia looked in the photo box again and found a small plain white envelope with the scan photo of her baby. She had attended a few pre-natal clinics who organised the scan, making excuses to her fellow students of her whereabouts. She also found a polaroid photo a nurse took on the maternity unit. Maia hardly recognised the frail, frightened young woman looking at the white bundle she held, with a little pink face peeping out.

Maia thought about her daughter's birth, seeing Craig brought it vividly back to her. In the early hours of 20 March 2005, Craig took her to hospital when she was in labour. Maia didn't want him in the delivery room. After a textbook birth, she was handed a healthy baby girl. Maia recalled the warmth of the little bundle, the feel of fresh new skin on her face and the smell of her tiny daughter. She kissed her fragile, damp head and plump cheeks, she gazed adoringly at the tiny perfect fingers and toes.

The baby was restful, but for a small flicker of her eyelids, which allowed Maia to look briefly into her navy blue eyes, to tell her she loved her and named her, Freya. She had no recall of how long she was on the maternity unit in a separate bedroom off the ward. She fed and held Freya, and the time came for the little bundle to be gently taken away by a social worker and foster carer, who Maia could only vaguely remember. Both reassured her, she could visit Freya when she wished and write a letter to her. Maia didn't want any fuss, she couldn't bear a prolonged goodbye. Craig came into the room and held her together as she crumbled. He never stopped holding her together throughout university and beyond.

Tears rolled down Maia's cheeks as she gazed at the images, drinking Freya in. Sometimes it didn't seem real, that she was a mother. The desolate emptiness she felt after leaving the hospital, and leaving her baby behind was like losing a limb. She hadn't wanted to visit Freya's foster carers, she'd had a goodbye kiss and told her she loved her. It was all too painful.

Sobs came with the regret of not telling Tom about Freya, maybe they could've stayed together as a family, and maybe he wouldn't have died if things were different. She and Freya could have saved him, the visceral pain within was astonishing. Resolutely, she grabbed a handful of tissues from the box on the table, wiped her eyes and dripping nose. She held Tom's pendant and thought about the circumstances of his death. Was Pauline right to have suspicions?

She gripped her coffee cup. 'If someone has somehow caused you pain Tom, or caused you to hurt yourself and take you away from us, I'll find them and make them pay Tom, I will.'

11

York, May 2015

MAIA TRAVELLED BY train to the celebratory night-out in York on Friday morning, 02 May. The Star Wars bank holiday weekend as Craig put it and she grinned at his, *"May the fourth"* comment. She felt buoyed, watching the landscape whizzing by, enjoying the rhythmic click-clack of the train track. Summer was looming; the weather had warmed and she could feel some heat through the window, glad she had remembered to pop those sunglasses in her bag at the last minute.

Maia did a mental inventory of the contents of her weekend bag, her favourite summer dress, and elegant but comfy sandals in preparation for a heady night-out with lots of walking on the proposed pub crawl. She abandoned the thought of her crop denim jacket, in case it turned inclement, she did go out in Newcastle after all, York and anywhere else for that matter would be a breeze. All of her toiletries and cosmetics were packed and she had meticulously twirled her thick shoulder-length dark brown hair into relaxed tresses. Tom's rune pendant, as always, adorned her neck.

Maia was staying over at Craig's, and on arrival at their home, after only ten minutes chat with Luiza, she knew they'd become good friends. She was bright, relaxed, and wonderfully welcoming, exactly how Craig described her. They took a taxi to the police social club and met others there, before going into York City. Craig, as promised, had men lined up for Maia, it was comical. Throughout the night, whatever bar they were in and when new people joined the group, she'd hear Craig's voice bellowing, 'Maia, Maia! come and meet …' Kev, Rich, James, John, Dave … loads more names. She could take her pick.

Being with Craig again drinking in York was a blast from the past and they were indeed blasted by the end of the night. Luiza drank alcohol in minimum quantities, but she and Maia laughed the whole night at the mad antics, the rivalry and camaraderie of the usually disciplined colleagues, enjoying some release from their stressful work.

Maia was mostly interested in, and attracted to Shaun. It was partly the accent, partly the devilishly attractive hazel sparkling eyes, darting about making sure he was being noticed, but mostly his quick-witted sense of humour. His dark auburn closely cropped hair suited his angular face. He was tall and athletic and clearly loved the attention. He made a beeline for Maia as soon as he saw her. Within minutes he had his arm around her, chatting away and keeping her amused all night. Shaun made her feel really special, ensuring she was okay and had a drink, with many compliments using his roguish charm.

At Craig's house, nursing a hangover the next day, Craig reminded Maia, 'you're meeting Shaun for lunch at Thomsons.'

'Oh, am I?'

'That's what it says in my text message.' He slumped into the sofa, with a cushion over his face, suffering badly.

Luiza kindly drove Maia into York where she met up with Shaun. He was obviously more subdued, but still retained his charm. It worked; she was hooked. He'd had a few girlfriends he told her, but no-one special since he moved to York with his family in his teens from Ireland. Maia felt she was ready for a new experience.

Their long-distance relationship worked well over the few weeks since they met. It never went farther than staying over at each other's houses at weekends. However they did take an impromptu overnight trip to Berlin with Craig and Luiza for a beer festival, and a gig by a brilliant new indie rock group, all of which was excellent fun. Maia was content, she was in an amorous relationship and enjoying a new friendship group. It was all about going out, having fun and laughing a lot. Shaun wasn't one for sitting cuddling on the sofa watching a movie, or having a romantic meal at home, but that was fine.

On one occasion when they were lounging at his apartment, he suddenly decided they should go for a meal at a new upmarket bar-restaurant called, *Zanders*, that had recently opened north of York City.

'The guy who has this place used to own a successful club in Newcastle in the early two thousands, called erm … Euphoria or Euphoric, or something.' Shaun mentioned this presumably to spark some interest for Maia.

'I wouldn't have been going out clubbing then, I'd only be sixteen or seventeen.' Maia had felt quite cosy and wasn't bothered about going out, but at least she was distracted from thoughts of Tom, and more recently Ryan, with her new relationship, and the work she was doing for Earth Chart.

Shaun was a physical guy, and had to have the next challenge planned; cycling, hill-walking, rock-climbing, kayaking, even go-karting, primarily to show off his prowess, which could be tiresome at times Maia admitted to herself. She was, thankfully, really fit and healthy and could keep up. His approach extended to his bedroom prowess too, also athletic and full of fun.

Maia was catching up working on her Earth Chart proposal and needed a few days hiatus from the frivolity. She finally sent an updated draft to Harriet well before the deadline. Shaun kept in touch mainly with texts and photos via social media, of him on a night out surrounded by women, obviously, smiled Maia, and photos of him zip wiring whilst camping in Wales with his colleagues. He was never still. They had been dating for a whirlwind few weeks and Maia felt pretty good about it, though wondered and hoped, that their relationship over time would strike more balance between the hectic and spontaneous, to peaceful and predictable.

Maia's recent meeting in London with Harriet at Earth Chart was not good. She had travelled by train for the meeting returning the same day. To her utter dismay Harriet wasn't impressed with the proposal, the basic research, or the outline for the article. The initial concept had been impressive, but as Harriet advised, it lacked impact and didn't seem to be up to Maia's expected standard. It wasn't good enough to be published, unless she applied more forensic evaluation. Maia was devastated, she had let Harriet down. She took the criticism constructively, it was, in essence a great concept, but not executed well enough to hit the required benchmark. Maia returned home, but headed straight to her parents' house, explaining the situation. They supported and encouraged her to put more effort in, and did remind her she had maybe been less than attentive these last few weeks. She accepted their comments, she had to, they were all true.

'We're going to Iceland if you want to come for a break and get your head together. There should still be plenty of snow up north in Dalvik to get a bit of skiing in, for us, but your dad may not be so keen,' Katrin said in Phil's direction, 'and it won't be too busy.'

Maia impulsively said, 'yep, why not?' She was becoming accustomed to spontaneity. 'A change of scenery will do me good, and I'll have some quiet time to work on my report too.'

'We're leaving the day after tomorrow, so get your snow gear sorted and we'll arrange the flight.'

'Going whale-watching if you fancy that too?' shouted Phil as she was leaving.

'Definitely up for that!'

Maia retrieved her snow gear from the depths of her wardrobe in the spare bedroom, and clambered into bed intending to pack in the morning. She went to bed in a terrible funk and did not sleep well. She emailed Harriet first thing in the morning;

To: Harriet Cooper
From: Maia Hewson
Date: Thursday, May 28, 2015 09:15:33 EST
Subject: Leading the Urban Environment

Hello Harriet. I'm going to be truthful, because I believe you will appreciate my honesty. I admit I've had my eye off the ball recently with personal matters that should in no way affect my work. I'm taking a short trip to Iceland with family and will focus my energies on my work while I'm there. Please keep your faith in me. I wholeheartedly apologise, and I'm big enough to admit when I've made an error of judgement. Do give me the deadline date for the next edition and I'll be back on track well before then. I'd be most grateful for this opportunity.

Sincere regards, Maia.

Harriet responded thanking Maia for her honesty and integrity, whilst reminding her there is a lot of competition, so she knows what she has to do. Harriet promised to forward dates to meet and confirm the next deadline soon. She ended by wishing Maia an enjoyable break. Maia was pleased she had been up front with Harriet and felt better about the situation, whatever the outcome. Honesty is the best policy after all.

Maia checked the replies from several businesses she had made contact, with the intention of arranging interviews for a lucrative article in Earth Chart. So far, she had positive expressions of interest from Beatrice Cowan, the owner of, RecyClothing, David and Adrian Harper of, Pure Organics, and Alexis Leventis, owner of the Apollon Group. All brilliant, however the latter would be her ideal candidate. The Leventis family owned one of the most luxurious hospitality and leisure groups in the north, and not only would it be her pinnacle, Maia was genuinely interested in how a high-end organisation manages environmental issues with financial effectiveness. If these three confirmed interest, she'd have some excellent plans to offer Harriet. Now to get packing.

The Hewsons were going through the departure gate at Newcastle Airport when Maia noticed a text from Craig, she hastily replied. As the plane lifted into the air, Maia felt a lightness inside; she would indulge in some great Nordic hospitality, skiing, communing with nature, and enjoy time-out with her parents and her Icelandic family. Maybe she'd even catch sight of the aurora borealis. She would contemplate how to vastly improve on her work plans, thinking time would be good. Not thinking of Pauline and the Tom situation, also taking a short break from Shaun's constant activity would be positive to get her equilibrium back. She intended to simply and figuratively chill in the, Land of Ice and Fire.

Craig was at work closely observing an interaction between Shaun and a young female police officer he was mentoring. They seemed to be having a disagreement and he got the distinct impression it was personal, rather than professional. Craig caught up with Shaun before he left and asked what was up. Shaun replied, 'it's nothing, but some people can be a complete pain in the arse,' and walked off. He was in a foul mood, very unlike him. Craig saw the girl, who seemed upset, talking closely with another female officer. The women got up from their desks and left the room together.

When Craig got home, he told Luiza of Shaun's odd behaviour and actions, mentioning the girl.

'Well … actually.' Luiza had a concerned look on her face, 'I was going to tell you this tonight. There are rumours Shaun is having an affair with a married woman. A police officer too.'

Craig turned to look at her stony faced, his heart sank. He immediately felt, apart from anger, a protective instinct towards his good friend Maia.

'I know, I know,' said Luiza calmly, looking at the expression on his face. 'I'll do some digging just to be certain. Rumour has it they've been having an on-off affair for ages, and she wants to leave her husband, but Shaun doesn't want her too. This is what I've heard today. He's a bloody rat if it's true!'

'No!' exploded Craig, 'he won't want her to end her marriage for obvious fucking reasons, he's got a gorgeous girlfriend already.'

'Exactly!' said Luiza, 'listen, let me be sure of what's going on before you fly off the table.' Sometimes Luiza's phrases were slightly off, but Craig knew what she meant, and he was right. No point creating a storm unless there was hard evidence.

Sure enough, the rumours were found to be true as they came to fruition via Luiza's messages with colleagues.

Craig wanted to see Maia and explain the situation to her personally, not via text, or in a phone call. If he ever got hold of his so called mate Shaun, he'd confront him about what the hell he thought he was playing at.

'I'll bloody kill him when I see him!' he seethed under his breath, he tried Maia's phone, which went to voicemail. 'I'll ask her to get in touch, not going to break this news by text.

Luiza nodded in agreement.

Craig's screen lit up with a reply message from Maia, *Quick decision, off to Iceland now! Will be in touch when home. M x*

12

AS MAIA'S FLIGHT to Iceland was underway from Newcastle Airport, in another part of the city a young woman was standing at a window contemplating her future, watching a far distant plane cross the sky. Gayle Mortimer's eyes then caught sight of Matthew Surtees as he left the room. She breathed a sigh of relief as she heard his footsteps descending. Moving toward the top of the stairs, she heard the welcome sound of the front door closing. She returned to her position at the window, and from the lofty height of the spacious converted attic, could see him getting into his BMW and speeding off. She stared out of the window, hoping he was leaving to visit the recently opened family restaurant in North Yorkshire. He'd not be back until very late, or, she hoped, would stay over at his parents or his brother's house.

Gayle continued to stare towards the horizon across Newcastle city's built-up rooftops, and St James' Park, the home of Newcastle United Football Club. It was a vacant silent stare. She'd attended a few hospitality events there with Matthew and enjoyed watching the football. Not a hobby shared with him as he ignored the sporting activity, and seemed to want her to simply stand beside him, look great, and charm other businessmen in the exclusive corporate suite.

Gayle returned to her former position, slumped on the adult-sized beanbag and flicked the TV screen on. A celebrity chef was cooking on a morning show alongside a television personality, she switched off immediately, in no mood for the banal chatter of two celebrities today. She looked down at her perfectly even-tanned legs, and began circling her ankles. Her hands rested on her knees, as she tried to relax her shoulders with a deep breath in and then out. She stared at the recently gelled, diamanté-encrusted stiletto nails, and wondered where on earth she would go if she left. Matthew was right, she had no job, no qualifications, no prospects ... or money of her own.

Gayle recalled the last phone call with her estranged family. She recalled her mam's words; *"Sweetheart, we ... well ... we feel he's a little too old for you, and you're always at his beck and call. You seem to have changed, you haven't spoken to your sister for weeks. We never see you, and your friends are always asking after you. Your dad's really worried. Get in touch hun ... please."*

Gayle had rebuffed her mother's anxieties with a dismissive response, reassuring her she was fine, but now felt guilty at the untruth. Gayle scrolled her phone contacts saying, 'Michaela,' under her breath. Michaela's number was still there. The only people she'd really known since being with Matthew, were two couples they met socially, Allan and Evie, and, Frank and Michaela. Michaela was lovely, they got along great, but should she really ring her, now, after *that* night six months ago?

Gayle extended her long limbs and as she rose, caught sight of the framed photo she had hung on the wall in the early, happier days. She had found Matthew attractive at first; black hair cut in a contemporary style, dark brown eyes, neat goatee. He wore designer clothing, and suited the hardly noticeable Cartier frameless glasses required for myopia. Matthew presented as sophisticated and mature, being fifteen years older than her twenty three years. She flung her phone on the sofa, deciding she shouldn't ring Michaela, and questioned why had she bloody stayed with Matthew Surtees? He never made an effort for her now, she saw an averagely non-descript man, who was always drinking, and boring, and gaining more weight every day.

Gayle wandered down the sweeping stairway to one of the huge living rooms in the spacious Georgian terraced house, located in a prestigious area north of the city centre. It was owned by his parents, of course, which he constantly reminded her of, and frequently referred to all the land they owned in Yorkshire too. Matthew's family seemed polite and she was impressed when she first met them. He was the eldest of four children. The two middle sisters, Charlotte and Jacqueline, more commonly known as, Charly and Jax, attended a girls-only school, and they were really nice and kind to her, even though she was very different to them. Matthew and the youngest brother Alexander were boarded-out from a young age, maybe seven she thought she heard him say.

Gayle moved in with Matthew within a few weeks of their meeting. He offered her a great lifestyle, it was exciting and far better than being stuck at her parents' three-bed semi in a boring suburban town ten miles from the city. She kept a copy of the modelling portfolio Matthew made for her and flicked through the professional classy, yet just-revealing-enough images. He did have a good eye for a photograph, and a beautiful woman he could impress with his money. Sometimes she can't believe she fell for his, *"have you ever thought about modelling"* line. But she had, and her online portfolio did actually get her a series of photo shoots for sports and swimwear promotions. She was impressed with Matthew's influence, they could get into any restaurant, club or bar with ease, never having to queue, and he seemed gentle, intelligent and socially acceptable with his well-spoken, polite manner.

Gayle didn't need to work; she left her retail job almost instantaneously at Matthew's suggestion after they met. He could be generous and liked people to see him flash his cash. It was quite the champagne lifestyle which offered her security. But ... she was so sick and tired of him, realising she was merely arm-candy he could parade around, and they had little in common. She lounged in the bay-windowed living room on a sumptuous sofa making a call to the model and promotion agency who circulated her profile. She asked for her agent.

'Hi, it's Gayle Mortimer, is Jenna there?'

No, Jenna wasn't there.

'Can you ask her to call me please,' she repeated her name for impact, 'it's Gayle ... Gayle Mortimer. Jenna had some work lined up in the next few weeks that I may be perfect for.'

Vague response.

'Okay, do tell her I called and I'll try her again soon.'

Gayle knew Jenna wouldn't reply, and may not even get the message. It didn't take much to drop out of favour with the agency. There was always someone bonnier, thinner and younger who would do photo shoots for peanuts. Gayle had been really missing her family lately with no-one to chat to, or laugh with. Matthew wasn't exactly a conversationalist, all he wanted to do was play on stupid violent computer games, or watch similar movies involving world annihilation. The only time he was animated was engaging in immature sexual innuendo with his, 'mates', the young impressionable lads in bars who he could communicate with easily on their level.

Phone-in-hand, Gayle was about to call her mother, but first walked into the vast but empty echoing, contemporary tiled kitchen and made a coffee. The environment matched her mood as she contemplated what to do with her life. She left the coffee on the bench, grabbed her designer silver puffer jacket, put on her ridiculously expensive trainers, and went for a walk. As she walked along the tree-lined, ostentatious street, she often felt she didn't belong there. Memories replayed of Matthew recounting times when his wealthy parents would constantly bail him out, like it was some sort of triumph. They were imprinted upon her brain given the, shocking to her, impact of his youthful misdemeanours.

"I was about eight and broke into a neighbour's house as a dare from an older boy in the village. I stole two expensive looking watches, a cheque book and some money from a kitchen drawer. The

police were not involved as my father returned the items and paid the family compensation. He explained it was merely high spirits as I was bullied into it by others ... but I wasn't bullied, I wanted to do it."

Matthew bragged about incidences like these as Gayle recalled another exchange when she first met Matthew's brother Alexander, Xander to friends and family, who hero-worshipped his older brother. They spoke of the accident in the farmyard where they lived when they were young. The memory still unsettled her.

Xander was laughing loudly, turning to Gayle, *"You do know he's a murderer don't you? He killed a dog. Yea, he was thrashing the quad bike to its limits in the farmyard and ran over a puppy from the litter one of the farm dogs just had."*

Matthew guffawed claiming, *"I didn't see it!"*

"No-one believes you Matt! Especially not our sisters, but you got away with it," accused Xander,

"No. It didn't help that Charly and Jax were bawling their stupid fucking eyes out."

Gayle remembered he was clearly irritated his sisters had caused a fuss, and showed no remorse or apology about killing the defenceless animal. She loved dogs, and missed her family dog, Ruby if she was honest with herself.

On another occasion Matthew seemed amused when explaining he had to make reparation to a neighbour when he crashed into their garden wall.

"I said the car skidded on the wet road. There was some truth in that, it had been raining, but I was hammering the car's limits and was actually as high as a fucking kite at the time."

Gayle realised after a fairly short time in their

relationship, Matthew would embellish events from his youth, to impress her, or so he assumed. She would later disregard many of his comments, and latterly wasn't even listening to his bloviating nonsense. But the drugs worried her, by association. She didn't like the effect, but had tried different ones offered at Matthew's suggestion convincing her they were recreational and non-addictive. She started refusing to use any, to Matthew's irritation, deeming her, *a pathetic bore.*

In reality Matthew nurtured his drugs career during his education, mainly dealing in cocaine. He was very open about this and told Gayle recently he became a key figure in distribution at school, but was never associated with the activity. He was persuasive to less robust younger boys and they often became his fall guys. Matthew seemed to delight in explaining one occasion when two school chums were expelled for distribution, yet when questioned made no reference to him supplying the drugs in the first instance. Gayle often wondered why they didn't, and once asked Matthew, who suggested he held information … and maybe pictures, they would not want their mummies to see.

Gayle was fairly broad-minded, or so she thought, yet some of Matthew's sexual preferences unnerved her. He had a need for total submission and pain. She felt uncomfortable taking the aggressive, domineering role he desperately desired. He did maintain control however, directing their sexual activity. It was different and exciting at first, but not an equal loving partnership. Gayle had three previous enjoyable sexual relationships; however, Matthew led her to believe his was the way of sophistication and that everyone was into swapping partners, group sex, and some techniques bordering on the dangerous practice of sexual asphyxiation. He never suggested it between themselves, but it sickened her anyway. At the very least, he made her feel embarrassed that her previous experiences had been boring, unadventurous and immature.

That dreadful night of debauchery six months ago, invaded her brain again as she walked along the street, her pace quickening as her mind raced. The loss of control, the humiliation, the recklessness of that night … all of it now consumed her. She felt trapped and a choking sensation gripped her. She unzipped her jacket to free herself from restraint and glanced up at the tree tops, now abundant with pink blossom. She breathed in as deeply as she could, trying to calm down.

After several moments and some long breaths, Gayle messaged her sister, her lovely twin, the other half of her, asking if she could call in to see her … *would that be okay?*

An immediate reply said … *of course! Are you ok?*

Gayle had some change in her pocket, she jangled it, and counted it; there was enough for bus-fare home. Decision made, she walked with purpose into the city centre, to the bus concourse. With a serene smile, she'd be in time for Friday takeaway at her mam's house. It was a bank holiday weekend, her twin would be off work, and there'd be time to catch up with the family she'd missed so much. She couldn't help but think of her mam's Sunday dinners, with her speciality roast potatoes and homemade Yorkshire pudding. As she walked, with a skip in her step, she dropped the house keys down a roadside drain, and never once looked back, Gayle was going home.

13

'GAYLE. GAYLE!' MATHEW Surtees was yelling up the stairs. There was no answer. He'd returned from a weekend visit to the family farm in Yorkshire for a discussion about expanding a new restaurant venture, his brother Xander was managing. Matthew wanted a more significant role. He was uninspired about having to visit the hotel leisure outlets he managed in the north east that afternoon; irritated by having to go to work at all. But, Matthew had promised his mother he'd earn a living to prove he could be trusted and involved in the family business after the financial debacle he'd caused. He couldn't wait to leave the bloody job at the Apollon Hotel and Leisure Group, though it did have its unrelated lucrative side.

It was one of the more annoying requirements of his employment as Area Manager of the, Signature Apollon Spas that he had to periodically oversee the venues in person. The places ran themselves, he could get away with ringing one or two, but Alison, the stuck up tart who managed the most luxurious and popular hotel leisure club, would be checking up on him. She wanted his job and he wasn't going to fucking-well hand it to her. He hated her. He was well in with Gregori, one of the owners of the company, so his role was pretty secure, especially considering the information he had on Gregori. He had to start being meticulous with those bogus orders for supplies too, and the inflated costs which were being syphoned away from the company to his own anonymous account.

Gayle wasn't responding to Matthew's calls. He huffed up the second set of stairs to one of the spare bedrooms they sometimes used when there was acrimony, and they, or rather Gayle, chose to sleep separately. He swung open one door, then another three to the spare rooms, assuming she was in one of them, but she wasn't. He stood in silence, he couldn't hear a shower going. 'Where the hell is she? Stupid bitch,' he muttered. She was always just ... there.

Matthew went into the bedroom ensuite, and looked at his reflection in the bathroom mirror. 'Won't be long until you're in charge again.' He tottered downstairs with a self-satisfied smirk, he couldn't wait to hand in his notice at Apollon. He'd persuaded his brother to enter into a partnership to fund, *Zanders,* the new upmarket venue in Yorkshire. Matthew had to acquiesce over the name choice, a derivative of his brother's full name Alexander. They agreed the spelling needed to be uncomplicated for the more ignorant, uneducated customers who may question the pronunciation. Also Xander was the main shareholder after all, and as Matthew suspected, Xander had only agreed to him having a limited partnership in the venture through pressure from their parents. Matthew had failed businesses previously so there was naturally doubt about his managerial skills and financial acumen. It would, however get him away from the Greeks who owned Apollon and he'd be able to retain his dubious business activities on the side.

Matthew reached the kitchen, he hadn't been in there since arriving home. He saw a spoon and coffee cup on the bench, which looked like it had been standing for ages as a skin had formed on the liquid surface. He touched the cup, stone cold. He noticed Gayle's house keys were missing off the hook, where had she gone? She rarely went out anywhere on her own. He rang her number and was confused to hear it ring briefly, then click as if going to voicemail, there followed three sharp pips and a message, *this number is no longer in service.* He glared at his device. Had she blocked his number or something or was she playing games because he'd been away all weekend? More likely the stupid cow had dropped it down the loo again, or broken it, and needed a new phone. He knew Gayle was becoming increasingly despondent, avoiding him, especially at night. She'd also taken to going for long walks in the dene nearby, or tucking herself away in the TV room in the attic space, but at least she kept the domestics going and provided his food and clean laundry. He felt the coffee cup again, looked at the empty key hook, and tried her number, same response, it rang briefly, clicked, then three sharp pips and, *this number is no longer in service.*

'She's fucking gone!' He violently swept the coffee cup off the end of the bench which smashed against the wall, spattering dark brown stains running to the floor. He'd have to get a cleaner or housekeeper now. Glancing at his watch, he huffed upstairs again cursing, 'little slag, pissing off like that. I'll fucking kill the ungrateful bitch.'

He went back to the bedroom, and couldn't find a clean ironed shirt anywhere, and picked out the least crumpled one. Looking in the mirror to sort out his tie, he needed to appear at least presentable for sodding Alison. He thought about his next business deal which would bring in some decent revenue. He grinned at his reflection. 'I'll never have to lay eyes on that skanky slut Alison again soon and the fucking cops are useless, they wouldn't see a deal being made right under their stupid noses.'

Matthew's career began as an estate agent in Durham on leaving University, he was relieved to be rid of parental philanthropic instruction, to work in the community during summer breaks. No more kids or old folks homes for him to suffer. His parent set up the business and he managed the premium property portfolio from North Yorkshire to Northumberland. He lost interest after a few years and yearned for the bright lights and celebrity lifestyle of managing bars and clubs. In 2003 he was twenty eight, and persuaded his parents to fund his business plan for, Euphoria, an ambitious night club project in Newcastle, the party city, promising them a lucrative return. No expense was spared during the conversion of a dilapidated building, which had formerly been a bank. He constantly went to his parents to keep the funds coming.

Matthew was going to be top dog. He wanted the club to be the exclusive best in the north of England, and it certainly was for a period of time. Because of its high-end reputation, it became one of the key night spots in the city, attracting local television celebrities and sports people, also national and international customers. It was on three floors, housing different functions, with the exclusive casino and club lounge on the top floor, hosting topless dancers, with customers openly indulging in drug-taking. He was top dog indeed until his lack of business acumen, and crossing the wrong people, came to light, so he plummeted to obscurity, losing everything. He never got over the humiliation.

Matthew paused, wondering if he had time to watch some, *adult entertainment,* as he put it. 'Thank fuck you can download anything these days if you know where to look.' He glanced at his laptop, then his watch, and decided to go for a drink at the cocktail bar instead. He kicked some shattered remnants of Gayle's coffee cup aside, and stormed out of the house. It was eleven in the morning, he had to meet Alison at 2 pm. Matthew entered the cocktail bar he often frequented, one of a number in the high-end neighbourhood.

'Alright there?' he asked the barman who was busy preparing the bar for the day ahead, though obviously Matthew wasn't bothered at all, if he was alright or not. He was absolutely livid about Gayle leaving.

'Bit early isn't it, even for you,' jibed the young man who recognised him as a regular, 'the usual?'

'Actually, I'll have a Bloody Mary, at least it's got breakfast juice in it ... you do know how to make that properly don't you?'

'Yes, I certainly do,' replied the barman, just popping to the kitchen for some celery.'

What Matthew wasn't aware of was the barman retained his smile, all the while thinking, you condescending twat as he went into the kitchen and said to anyone who would hear, 'that Billy-no-mates ponce is in again. What a prize knob he is, really thinks he's a cut above asking me if I know how to make a Bloody Mary, that's brekky today apparently.'

'That tosser,' added the chef who was preparing brunch orders, 'he's always trying to strike up a conversation with anyone who'll listen to his drivel about this fantastic place he's opening. Never see him with anyone, apart from that beautiful young lass sometimes.'

'I switch off when he starts. He had the nerve to say it would be way better than here ... what a fucking dickhead. We all know why a gorgeous girl like her would hang around with him, not for his looks or personality. He gives me the creeps if I'm honest.'

The barman and chef's eyes met with a knowing look. Then the barman said, 'hey, have you got any celery for that knob's drink?'

'Celery eh? ... will this do for the sad fucker?' The chef held out a wilted, bendy piece of celery, and as the leaves flopped over, he burst out laughing.

'Perfect!' said the barman grinning. He could hear the chef still chuckling as he tried to stifle his own outburst heading back to the bar.

Sitting at the bar with his Bloody Mary, the wilted celery constructively propped up with crushed ice, Matthew was itching to blether about his new venue, Zanders, in North Yorkshire, but the barman made himself completely scarce, busying around the tables in the restaurant area. Bored with no-one to chat to, Matthew's thoughts turned to Beth from his club years ago. He often thought about her, she was one that definitely got away from him sadly. It was a shame she disappeared like that, he had really liked her; she was one of the dancers, very petite and looked so much younger than her age. He invited her out for dinner, which she graciously accepted, he was after all the charismatic nightclub owner.

Once they had ordered, sitting opposite each other in a cosy corner, Matthew took Beth's right hand in his left hand. He turned her hand palm up, to expose her inner forearm. He leaned toward her and recalls constantly stroking the soft smooth, pale flesh of her skin with his right forefinger and index finger. At first Beth seemed to appreciate the warm gesture, however, she did seem to try to release her hand after a while, but he kept hold, stroking her arm. It was such a nice feeling for him, using just enough pressure so she couldn't withdraw it, and it would look obvious to nearby customers if she tried to yank it away. He was only being playful. When Beth had relaxed, Matthew told her about a recent funny experience he had, looking directly into her eyes. He described having sex with his cousin's wife in a secluded outhouse at a family wedding, but as he'd known the woman since childhood, he asked Beth, with a chuckle, if she thought it was a little incestuous. At the time she didn't answer, just smiled a little awkwardly, but she seemed to be happy listening to him talk about his night club success; the inside scoop on which celeb was shagging who at the club, and who was on what drugs. He was very up front and informative, revealing intimate details of people's secrets.

Anyway, it must have been the mussels or something, because she went to the ladies and didn't return to the table. A waitress came over and politely told him his date had to go as she'd been ill in the bathroom. To himself Matthew reflected, 'that's the trouble with these uncultured types, can't manage exotic cuisine, when they're only used to Greggs fucking pasties.'

He took a long drink of his Bloody Mary, then sent a message to Gregori Leventis, suggesting a meeting about their, 'other business'. They had known each other for some time, as it was Gregori who set Matthew up in his current role at Apollon Leisure, after he lost his fortune in his Euphoria night club. Matthew had been good to Gregori during his night-club, and subsequent bar management years, he was offered an incredibly good service of all that was on offer. Matthew tolerated his job but vehemently despised cow-towing to Gregori's older brother, Alexis, who was most definitely the boss. As Matthew sipped his blood-red cocktail, he thought about Alexis Leventis, and said under his breath, 'what a self-righteous prick he is.'

14

Iceland, May 2015

MAIA AND HER parents travelled to Reykjavik, then took another connecting flight to Akureyri, the capital of the North of Iceland, which made it a tedious day. They eventually settled into the cosy, upmarket holiday cabin, owned by Katrin's sister. The next day, Maia and her parents took a walk around the beautiful city and along the waterfront. It felt like her second home … it *was* her second home. They met family for dinner at a favourite restaurant. It wasn't long before Maia recalled how easily she could lose the thread of Icelandic banter, as the thread unravelled away from her. The family would transfer to spoken English at times which offered some relief. Phil was virtually fluent as he had lived in Iceland, teaching English to primary aged children for a while until Katrin finished her Masters in Environmental Coastal Development.

Maia felt tired, and the worry of her rejected article was weighing on her mind. She left her seat to go to the ladies, grabbed her shawl and headed to the open terraced area, overlooking the beautiful snowy distant hills. She would never tire of absorbing the stunning views. The constant barrage of conversation-collisions was drumming in her head and her high concentration level was generating a headache, as she stared trance-like at the view.

A male English voice from behind her asked, 'are you okay?'

Maia turned. A man was standing in the shadow of the light behind him, which sheltered his face.

'Yes, fine thanks.'

'Keeping concentration is tough sometimes isn't it?'

She nodded. He walked forward from the shadow and she saw a pleasing face. Brown hair, a few days growth of facial hair gave him a rugged look, with broad shoulders, his athletic frame was in silhouette. He was somewhat taller than her, which didn't take much at her, not even eleven Wispas height. He had the most striking bright blue eyes. Maia didn't have the strength of resistance to fend off advances, should he try to make any.

'I'll leave you if you want to be alone,' he said softly.

Maia didn't know if she did want to be alone or not. She felt flat emotionally and put it down to fatigue. 'Sorry, I'm feeling quite tired from the journey.'

'Hey, no problem.' He put up his hands. 'I'm Ben, here on a bit of an expedition. Anytime you want to chat in English, I'm in here ... quite a lot actually.'

'Thanks Ben, but I'm ok really, might see you around.'

As Ben was about to turn and leave, the pair were interrupted by the onset of an emerging green and pink curtain of light above the distant hills. The swathe of aurora lights flowed to and fro, then billowed and retracted, shimmering for three whole minutes. A few more people wandered onto the terrace to witness one of the most dramatic, spellbinding displays nature has to offer.

The volume of people caused Ben to stand closer to Maia, their arms almost touching. 'I'll never get tired of seeing that.' He turned to walk away and said, 'enjoy the rest of your evening.'

Maia felt his warmth leave her side and as the wondrous lights faded, she returned to reality and with a jolt said simply, 'beautiful.' Forgetting her manners, she called, 'Ben. Sorry. My name is Maija by the way.' The influence of the evening's Icelandic conversation rendered her naturally recounting the correct pronunciation of her name.

'Lovely name.' He stepped back into the well-lit room.

Strange, she thought, had he been watching her. She returned to the table and received a knowing nod from her dad. He said he was tired and was heading back to the cabin as he wanted to be up early for the whale-watching trip the next day. This was met with friendly jeers from the family group. He patted his stomach indicating he'd had enough, then in Icelandic saying something like he had to watch his figure, so his wife won't have to. Maia made her apologies and left too. She glanced around the room and thought she saw Ben sitting at a corner table with his back to her. He didn't turn around, so she wasn't sure if it was him, but he had piqued her interest.

Maia lay in bed and thought about Shaun. She did enjoy her time with him. He was fun and energetic, but neither of them seemed to want to invest too deeply in a partnership. She recalled a recent night out in York. He was called over to a table with a few young women sitting around and was enjoying the attention, and she did question whether there was any reason to believe anything was happening, however, a mild uneasiness hit her. One of the girls had stopped Shaun on his way to the men's room. She was tall, blonde and attractive Maia recalled. They seemed to be having an in-depth conversation, though his body language suggested he was resistant, and non-committal to the dialogue.

Maia asked him, not in an overbearing way, what was it about. Shaun seemed genuine telling her a PC from his shift wasn't happy about a situation at work and, *"she needs to grow a pair if she wants to get on."* Odd words, thought Maia. She observed the attractive girl back at the table with the crowd of friends huddled together, making non-obvious looks across to them. Maybe they were having a good old gripe about his supervision at work or something.

Maia wished she could chat with Rosa, about Shaun and her disaster with Earth Chart, but it was too late to call, as she'd be getting the little scrumptious cherub, Anthony bathed and ready for bed. Rosa could always put things in perspective. It wasn't too late, however, to ring Shaun, but she never wanted to come across as possessive, and definitely not have to monitor her lover's every move. She sent him a text. *Hi, wondering what shift you're on? All fine here in the white wilderness. Call me when you're free xx*

There was no reply. By the following evening, she sent a further message. *In case you didn't get my message, signal isn't great here sometimes. Let me know if all ok?'*

She realised as she read it back, she was giving him excuses. Of course, now he could agree, and claim he hadn't received her first text. Maia sent it minus the usual, *xx* ending, for which she felt a little guilty because Shaun could be extremely busy at work perhaps. There she goes again, offering him excuses. Now was not the time for her to be piling more emotional stress on herself, worrying if her boyfriend was shagging around.

Maia wondered why was she such a failure at relationships? Everyone else seemed to manage things so easily. Maybe her missed chance for a lifelong relationship was, Tom. Maybe if she'd been more patient, and paid him more attention when he was going through his rough patch. She should have helped him, not made things tougher. They could be together, with Freya. But this could now, never be. She lay in bed feeling a deep sadness engulf her being.

The whale-watching trip the following day was glorious, though it was some time before they did actually see one. Maia had been before as a young girl and though it was exciting, she didn't appreciate the majestic beauty of these creatures. The power of the whales crashing into the water was overwhelmingly emotional. It was worth the rough seas for the vision of Katrin watching with awe and reverence. Thankfully sea-sickness pills were available too. It was a beautiful shared experience, and she was so glad she came on this Icelandic trip.

The family rounded the day off with a meal at the restaurant again, showing off their social media images of the whales, and the puffin colony. Maia felt quite disappointed Ben wasn't around. Later she examined why her interest had piqued; was she flattered he made the first move? Was it that she liked the look of him? A bit of male company never goes amiss and he was attractive. Was she a little bored? Was she getting back at Shaun, but for what she didn't know? She still hadn't received any messages from him.

Maia had to consider whether her relationship back in the UK was slipping away. If it was, why hang around waiting to find out whether Shaun was unfaithful. When would she ever learn not to get too distracted from her own path because of a relationship? She had almost quit her job because of Ryan's jealousy in a past life, before she came to her senses, realising he was the problem, not her male work colleagues.

This time, she could have put her career back years if she lost the contract with Earth Chart by taking her eye off the ball, for some full-of-himself crazy cop. Lesson learnt! In fairness there was no evidence about Shaun's infidelity from what she knew. She would see him upon her return and was fairly sure, things would be okay. However, if she was happy with Shaun, why was she so distracted by Ben?

Another day passed, and Maia felt a sense of anxiety about Ben. Maybe she had put him off with her disinterest, or he could have left the area? It would be weeks before the temperature got into double figures, and she walking to the store for supplies during a completely enveloping white-out blizzard. A group of four men, head-to-toe in bulky weatherproof clothing walked by her, one of them stopped as the others carried on.

'Hey! Maia. How you doing?'

It was Ben! Her heart skipped a beat. This was ridiculous, she was unfeasibly pleased to see him and it showed. Quickly, she masked her over-enthusiasm with surprise saying she thought he was someone else she knew. 'You can't tell who anyone is in all this gear?'

'True,' he agreed with a lovely smile, 'you ok?'

'Yes, and Ben, I'm sorry if I was stand-offish in the restaurant. Going through stuff at work, needed a break and where better to come.' She gestured towards the beautiful scenery all around.

'Why here?'

'Mam is Icelandic, she's from Dalvik.'

'Lucky thing, wish I had family connections here. I really do love this place, in fact this whole country.'

'Are you working here? Is it temporary?' Don't sound so bloody desperate Maia thought.

Ben pulled his hood back so she could see his face as the weather was clearing. The clean light of sun and snow reflected in his azure-blue eyes. 'I'm working near Kárhóll, surveying the land for a new scientific observation centre, 'got another four days, then back to Blighty.'

'Where in Blighty?'

'I'm originally a Lancashire lad and based back there now, but I've lived all over. You?'

'I like to think of myself as an Icelandic-Geordie.'

'Great combo.'

This guy was totally attractive in the cold light of day, and there she was, hair scraped back in all her bare-faced, squint-eyed, lip-chapped, ruddy-cheeked glory. Hope he's attracted to the ultra-natural look she thought. He seemed to be. There was a moment when they looked into each other's eyes, and rogue snowflakes floated downwards and one landed on the tip of Maia's nose. Ben took off his glove and lightly swept it away as if it was the most natural thing in the world.

'If you'd like to go for a drink or meal somewhere, it would be great? Not had a decent conversation with any lovely company for quite a while.' He laughed, nodding to the men who had walked off in the distance.

Maia accepted Ben's offer. What on earth was going on with her? She felt a sense of familiarity about him. It hit her, there was an outdoorsy resemblance to Tom, even in the tone of his voice, which shook her a little. She had never met anyone else like Tom, and accepted she never would. Maybe it *was* the Tom-factor which unsettled her, but she forced herself to desist from comparing Ben already to Tom. They agreed to meet in the same restaurant that evening.

Katrin was overjoyed when Maia announced a date with, 'a nice scientific type,' and Phil was fully on board too.

'You'll have your phone with you, you're a sensible girl, just ring if there's any trouble,' said Phil.

'I'll be fine Dad, I'm nearly thirty and not daft. You two watch too many dark Scandi murder series. You know, that one where the woman was found naked, frozen in a lake with an ice-pick in her eye.'

'Maia … for goodness sake!' retorted Katrin.

Maia and her dad grinned at each other.

15

GETTING READY FOR her date, Maia wanted to get the balance right. She'd go for casual chic; black jeans, fur-lined ankle boots, a soft duck-egg shirt, and a charcoal grey cashmere flowing cardigan seemed to fit the bill, with obligatory weatherproof coat atop. She changed her ear-rings for the neat silver Celtic-style pair she'd bought in the jewellers yesterday, and of course her rune pendant set the outfit off nicely. Understated but classy, and most of all, warm.

It was a definite, no-no, in these parts to be over-dressed or over made up, just the way she liked it. She was happy in her skin. Maia didn't do dressing to please others any more, whether professionally or personally. She was always respectful and dressed appropriately for every occasion, but it was liberating not to be too bothered about others' opinions, her possessive ex-boyfriend Ryan for one.

Kissing the pendant, she said, 'wish me luck,' and smiled at her reflection in the mirror.

Maia received a lovely welcome from Ben, waiting outside the restaurant. A brush of a kiss on her cheek. She patted his arm, as he removed his coat, purposefully aiming for his well-defined bicep. She felt relaxed and calm. There was a lovely frisson to add a spark to their meal. They ordered a beer and agreed on the wine and food after a browse through the menu.

Maia's phone rang, 'oh excuse me, I'm so sorry! Should've switched that off.' Shaun's name came up on the display, she had totally forgotten about him. She cut the call and silenced her phone, he can leave a message, she thought, but somehow knew he wouldn't. Turning the volume off, spoke volumes to her.

Maia and Ben had a great evening together. They were at ease with each other. He was interesting and modest, with a sharp dry humour. More the quieter type than she was usually attracted to. Her mind strayed wondering if he had a girlfriend, partner or even a wife at home. Ben was going out to Kárhóll the next day to update the detail from his survey. It was about half an hour's drive away, and he invited her along, which she was thrilled to accept.

They spent two full days and two evenings together after the trip to Kàrhóll, as Ben had taken a break from his duties. He met her parents briefly in a café for a hot chocolate. They told Maia later they were impressed with him, her mother particularly because of his knowledge of the local area, and his interest and respect for Icelandic culture and trying out the language.

Her dad hinted they were visiting friends out of the area the next day, so the cabin would be free for Maia to, 'entertain', he said tapping his nose. She laughed. Katrin gently thumped his shoulder and suggested he was forcing them together. He was merely suggesting Maia could demonstrate her expert culinary skills and cook him a meal, then broke into raucous laughter, knowing this was the least of her skill-set. Maia crossed her arms and smirked at him.

Maia invited Ben over. Katrin had made a wonderful stew which they could share with fresh warmed bread and beer. The evening was wonderful, it was good to be relaxed at home instead of meeting in a bar. He was staying in digs with his team, all men, and it definitely was not the place for her to visit. He asked when her parents would be home, he'd like to say goodbye as he was leaving the day after tomorrow.

'They're staying away tonight, actually.'

He looked at her and smiled. They both smiled. There was a strong magnetic physical attraction between them. They had kissed gently and willingly after their first date and the feelings gained momentum from there. Any excuse, whether they were walking together, in the car, or sitting somewhere, whatever, there was a desire to be close, touching, hugging and kissing, ever since they met.

Ben leaned towards her, 'I'd love to stay,' he said enthusiastically with a grin. 'If you're absolutely sure?'

Maia knew Ben's intentions to stay were definite, however thought his question very sweet, almost honourable. 'I'm sure,' she confirmed and kissed him.

The passion between them was rising. His hands stroked her back and gently he held her buttocks pulling her towards his groin as they lay on the sofa. She felt him pressing against her willing body.

'Shall we?' she asked, looking towards the bedroom.

He nodded smiling.

They went into the bedroom and he undressed watching her all of the time. She was down to her underwear and sitting on the bed. Ben knelt in front of her and she could see the anticipation in his face and in his boxers. He parted her legs and kissed her belly, slightly above her knickers. Fleetingly she thanked herself for packing some decent undies. She slid her bra off and Ben continued up her body to kiss her breasts. She held his face as he slid her knickers down, slowly taking in the vision before him. He caressed her gently between her legs. She slid her hand down his toned stomach and pushed his boxer shorts down his hips, being naked together felt really good.

Maia felt an overwhelming sense this is where she was meant to be, in her body, mind and soul, within this perfect connection. They made love and it was as natural as it could ever be, as they moved in harmony with each other. She adored his body, his hands, his face, his hair, his scent, the sound of his voice, his maleness, everything. They made love twice again, once in the blackness of the night, and later as the dawn emerged through the shutters. It was a sensual, mutually satisfying night.

Maia was making coffee as Ben took a shower, he had to leave for work soon. As he walked into the room, Maia knew she wanted to have this guy in her life, for definite. Not only the great sex, the ease at which they connected, the fun they had, and they seemed to share the same values in life.

'Where do we go from here?' He asked as he sat close beside her, sipping his hot coffee, 'I'm leaving in a day. Are you with anyone? I haven't asked and maybe should have.'

'No-one special,' replied Maia and she realised, there wasn't anyone special.

'Me neither, I'm divorced, I hope that doesn't put you off.'

Put me off?... she rejoiced internally, halle – fucking – lujah! Then switching off the glee, said sombrely, 'sorry to hear that, doesn't always work out does it?'

They had already exchanged details, but talked more practically about how and when they could meet up. Ben worked away a lot and commented it may have had something to do with his marriage breaking up.

'I'd come with you if I could,' said Maia, 'I'm quite adventurous and love travelling.' Which was absolutely true.

His face lit up. 'Really? Sounds great.'

The time remaining was spent together, as many minutes as they could. Though Maia knew Ben was special to her, it still surprised her how bereft she was when they said their final goodbye. As he got into the hefty 4WD heading for Reykjavik, they shared a tearful kiss. When the vehicle was out of sight and she was alone ... she sobbed. There were times when there was so much loss deep inside of her, Maia was rendered utterly broken.

The remaining time in Akureyri was enjoyable. Maia and Katrin enjoyed a day skiing in Dalvik. Maia welcomed the freezing rush of air on her face as she zipped down the slopes. At first she felt wobbly, but like riding a bike, you never forget how to ski and she soon got used to the unnatural angle and clamped feeling of ski boots. They stopped frequently to absorb the scenery, side-by-side listening to the complete silence of pure and perfect nature. Katrin was an accomplished skier, she taught her children from being tiny on their regular family trips to Dalvik.

Maia and Katrin enjoyed the après ski too, sitting in the sun with a drink, gazing at the high-definition scenes all around. No amount of 4K technology could replicate the vision. The piercing sunlight bounced off the white snow all around, with a covering of glittering ice, giving pinpoint accuracy to the vista for miles. The clear crisp sounds of voices rose up and disappeared into a stunning jigsaw-blue sky.

Katrin recounted tales Maia had heard many times, from when she was a young woman working in this ski resort; also her university days in Akureyri, before she moved to the UK to start her life with Phil.

'Do you know why the red traffic lights are heart-shaped in Akureyri?' Katrin must have asked this question a dozen times over the years.

' g geri Mamma, but do tell me again,' Maia, without thinking, often used her hybrid language.

Katrin smiled. 'It was after the financial crash of 2008. There was a desperate need for positive thinking, so the authorities took steps to capture the imagination and focus on what really matters ... love, even sitting at traffic lights.'

'That's Icelandic positive thinking for you.' Raising her glass, Maia congratulated the positive vibes and pristine panorama offering up a, 'skál!'

Katrin visited twice a year when she could to keep in touch with family and Maia couldn't blame her. She felt privileged this land was half of her, she adored it. She held hands with her Mamma. Sitting on lounge chairs, looking toward the mountains, with sunshine glinting off their sunglasses, they didn't need to speak.

Back at the cabin, Maia waited for Ben to contact her in the evenings. She kept her phone close by, even taking it into the bathroom, constantly checking it around the time he should be ringing. She tried so hard to be nonchalant, but Katrin and Phil recognised her disquiet. Her parents were relieved when Ben called her. The lovers called each other every evening and spoke for ages. It was like falling in love again as a teenager, Maia thought, but with the realism and hindsight of being more mature.

'Have you any idea how much you're going over your phone allowance?' Phil asked, 'it'll cost a small fortune.'

'True love doesn't come cheap,' said Katrin.

'Don't I know it? I was virtually bankrupt flying over here to see my gorgeous lady, when we were courting.'

It was lovely to see her parents hug and appreciate each other now, after thirty-five years of marriage. Maia could visualise this with Ben already, but not with Shaun. Oh dear, the Shaun issue, and there was the guilt. She had sent a text explaining the signal had gone haywire and it was difficult to call. She sent occasional text messages, never when Ben was around as she wanted to maximise her time with him. Shaun wasn't prolific in contacting her either.

Her good friend Craig had introduced them, so she did harbour an added element of guilt about the fact she had fallen for another man, whilst in a relationship with Shaun. Although, it had never really felt like an exclusive relationship, and Craig's comment about Shaun, needing a calming influence in his life, stayed with her. This would not be her role in a relationship.

Maia held Tom's pendant after she finished the call with Ben, 'this could be it Tom,' she said to it … to him. She wondered if, and when, there would come a time when she didn't tell Tom what was happening in her life. On the flight home, she had a seat all to herself and chose this moment to take out her journal and write more about Tom. None of the entries were easy, and this one, she knew was going to be the most difficult. She cast her mind back to recall his words in as much detail as she could, and could visualise him, unable to look at her.

Returning to the UK meant dealing with … stuff! What a contrast to the fresh feeling of relaxation and joy in Iceland. She kept looking at the few photos she had of Ben on her phone, and his LinkedIn page; Ben Lasek, Freelance Surveyor, he looked older and a bit boring in his formal picture, she preferred his rugged outdoor look. She'd read his bio a few times; experience in polar and arctic region surveys, and so on. He had a great CV, but we all embellish she thought, she'd find out if he lived up to the hype no doubt, but she felt good about the situation so far. Maia hoped he was as good looking as she remembered, FaceTime calls are okay, but it's different seeing the person in the flesh. Maia felt their connection wasn't simply a holiday fling, or a rebound thing. She hoped he still liked her as much too, and not simply attracted in the moment and in the surroundings of wild, snow-topped landscapes, hearty stews, beer and crackling-fire log cabins.

Maia recalled Craig's message at the airport, she sent a text saying she was home. She didn't get a reply. Then her phone rang with an unknown number, it was Luiza.

'Hi, lovely to hear from you. Is Craig ok?' suddenly becoming concerned.

'Hey Maia, ya he's fine, don't worry, but he asked me to call you if you got in touch. He's in court all week on a big enquiry, so has no idea when he'll be free.'

'Okay, what's up?'

In her lovely accent Luiza said gently, 'it's about Shaun, there is some news you may not know, or not want to hear.'

'What is it, is he okay?'

'Oh, he is certainly okay Maia! Apparently he has been seeing someone while you were away, in fact, may have been seeing her when he was with you. I'm so sorry he is a complete twat!'

Luiza fell quiet, what Maia couldn't see was her mystified face at the sound of Maia bursting out laughing.

'Are you okay, did you hear me properly Maia?' said a confused Luiza.

'Oh, that's great news and hearing you say, complete twat, killed me Luiza, sounds so pretty when you say it. I've never heard you swear or say a bad word against anyone.'

Luiza laughed too.

'Thing is,' continued Maia. 'I've met the most wonderful guy while I was on my trip in Iceland, and I'm going to see him next week'.

'Yay!' yelled Luiza down the phone, 'we've been so worried about telling you and didn't want to spoil your holiday.'

'It's all fine, let Craig know as soon as you can, I'm okay. I'll tell you all about Ben when I see you, and by the way tell Shaun he's dumped!'

'With pleasure.' Luiza told Maia about the circumstances

surrounding Shaun's infidelity and it didn't surprise her one bit, her suspicions were right.

'I've had a blast for the time it lasted, spending time with you and Craig has been great, it was just what I needed. Seriously though, for now I need to focus on my career, but I'll never be too busy to see you and Craig, let's make a date to meet up, and thanks Luiza, for the good news.'

It was very good news indeed, as Maia didn't have to go through another relationship break up, but she did wonder whether she was capable of sustaining one which endured. She lay in bed getting used to city noise again, listening to the piercing pitch of emergency vehicle sirens rise and fade; she recollected her love-hate relationship with the sound. They reminded her of her trip to New York and the unceasing night-time noise; she loved the vibrancy and excitement of living in a city, but inevitably those sounds meant someone, somewhere was in trouble.

Her thoughts drifted to Ben's smile, then her hormones fluttered around her torso, resting in her groin in particular. Maia longed for his conversation, his dry humour, his body, in fact his whole being, she hoped she could keep the faith this time, and she would make it with Ben.

To distract herself, Maia decided to be proactive and make contact with the business leaders she needed on board for her article. She would begin with Alexis Leventis, he was the main challenge. If she secured his interest, many would follow. She tapped the business contact number she'd been given. 'Good morning, it's Maia Hewson from Earth Chart, could I speak with Mr Leventis please?'

Tom Cassidy, in his words 13.09.2002

Most of the staff and the kids at the home were okay, but this is why I ran away to Pauline's. One worker used to come into my room at night, and just the sound of his footsteps along the hall at lights-out terrified me. Then it seemed an age when the whole place was quiet, my door would open and I couldn't move. He grabbed me, turned me onto my stomach and pushed my face into the pillow, I could hardly breathe. He pulled my pyjamas down and I felt the sudden pain, like a scorching knife rip into me. He whispered to shut the fuck up or he'd kill me and no-one would ever know or care. He never said anything else. The stench of him was disgusting. I knew he was going into Jordan's room as well and I used to cry for him 'cause I knew the same thing was happening. That's why me and Jordan were so close. It wasn't worth telling anyone, no-one ever listened, least of all our parents. They'd say I was attention-seeking as usual. I got used to being called a liar.

Eventually, I told Pauline what happened, but said I couldn't remember the name of the worker who abused us, or anything about him as he was only there a few weeks. I know she didn't believe me, but she wouldn't push it. She reported what I said, they have to, but nothing came of it, never does. I couldn't even tell her his name, still can't bring myself to say it, I've tried and tried to forget all about him and make him not exist. His stupid fucking face and sickly sweaty smell, it's making me feel sick even now. He's probably out there doing the same to other children, I really hope someone has stopped him. If I saw him again now, the bastard would be dead.

16

Edera Cottage, Northumberland, June 2015

MAIA WAS DISAPPOINTED with the news Ben had to return to Iceland, and he couldn't confirm when he'd be back home. So she was glad to see Craig and Luiza, who made a flying visit from York to see her. Craig needed a break away from working on an horrific and complex murder, he hadn't slept well for weeks from stress and never-ending shifts.

Maia met them at Café Dalvik, where Sophia spent the evening entertaining with her wit and hilarity; resplendent in a muted, but classy diaphanous magenta two-piece outfit of palazzo pants, with a long jacket covering an ivory silk top.

Luiza had an opportunity to inform Maia about Shaun's personal troubles at work. His affair with the married officer, while he was two-timing Maia, had come to a head, and a huge argument erupted in the staff canteen one day. He was being cited as the adulterer in the divorce case, and he was not taking it well.

Nik whisked Luiza away, being interested in gleaning

details about making traditional sweet and savoury Polish Pierogi, which she had thoughts of serving as a lunch option at the café. Nik and Luiza went into the kitchen, while Sophia was busy with other patrons.

Craig was full of apologies to Maia about Shaun.

'Hey, I had a fabulous time honey,' Maia said grabbing his hand. 'Don't be sorry, we had a hoot for those few weeks did we not. I don't think Shaun is the reliable partner type somehow.'

'True.' Craig agreed. They looked into each other's eyes. There was such respect and fondness between them.

'Luiza is the most wonderful person. I love her, like I love you, you're well-matched and the best friends anyone could have,' said Maia.

Maia ordered Craig another single malt Laphroaig, neat with ice. He smiled broadly finally relaxing, 'can't wait to meet your fella, Ben.'

'Can't wait to see him myself. We managed a couple of days together last week, but he's off to Scotland soon, and I've got lots of appointments for work myself. Got a good feeling about him Craig, really have. He seems honest and down-to-earth, certainly not the cheating kind.'

Craig asked, 'have you thought any further about the situation concerning Tom?'

'Sure, but I've not had any time. Once I've completed the next stage of my article I'll get back on it,' she was pensive. 'That reminds me I must contact Pauline. I don't like leaving it too long, but she knew I was off to my half-homeland.'

Luiza returned, they chatted, and finished their drinks, then said their goodbyes. Sophia was insisting the couple stayed overnight, but Luiza and Craig wanted to travel back, so they could have the next day chilling out at home. Maia was tired too, but content. She thought of Ben on the drive home, but tried to diminish her yearning for him or she'd never get to sleep.

Craig's comments about Tom's death inspired Maia to contact Pauline the next day, they discussed the situation and Pauline offered her the owner's details for Edera Cottage. Pauline had signed the rental agreement as guarantor for Tom when he moved in some years ago. As soon as Maia finished her call, she rang the proprietor, Ivy Tomlinson, who was happy to meet with her and chat. She said the police had interviewed her about Tom. Maia felt it would be good to get away from her laptop and breathe in some fresh air, so agreed to drive up to Northumberland and meet Ivy at the cottage later that afternoon.

Ivy was a petite lady around eighty years old who was waiting outside the cottage, she offered a warm, but brief greeting. It was approaching mid-summer and a warm wind breezed through Ivy's wispy white, candy-floss hair. Ivy had the tough weathered look of a woman who had spent a lot of time outdoors. Mugs of tea were already prepped as they stepped inside the small dwelling, and Ivy explained she was living in between the cottage, and her other home a few miles away. She poured the hot drinks and told Maia she was using the cottage as an artist's studio for the time being. Ivy was known locally for her landscape paintings of the area, and had made her living over the years from selling her artwork, and renting out properties.

As Maia entered the main room, she noticed the faint smell of oils, turpentine and a foisted dampness. There were a variety of canvases in different sizes propped up along the walls, some barely started, some almost finished, all craggy countryside images. One in particular was beautifully bleak, and truthful in the depiction of the wild landscape all around. There was a large dining table in the centre of the room. On the table was a mass of small and tall glass jars, with assorted brushes in them. There were paint tubes and palettes; scissors, pencils, sponges, cloths and rags, stained with varying amounts of coloured paint adhered to them. There was a larger glass container, which may have had thinners in it, Maia thought, for cleaning brushes. None of it seemed to be organised.

'The name of the cottage is unusual,' Maia began the conversation once they were settled with their tea, and obligatory bland biscuits were placed on a delicate floral China plate.

'Edera. Yes my husband named the cottage when we bought it. It's a translation of Ivy in Italian. He did have his romantic moments.'

The women chatted for some time. Ivy was a humorous, fascinating person, who had led a full life, and didn't suffer fools gladly. She was an expert on the local area and still led some low level rambles for visiting tourists. Ivy was candid about her own life experience and to Maia's astonishment, revealed a romantic moment that she only ever had one orgasm with her husband. She is convinced it was the night she conceived her only child, a son. Maia thought it best not to ask whether she had any orgasms with anyone else.

It was extremely emotional for Maia being in the place where she and Tom had spent the night together in 2004, and where they conceived Freya. As she was sitting in the tiny two-room dwelling, she looked out of the large window to the garden where she and Tom had sat under a starlit sky with a blazing fire, overlooking the landscape. It was probably one of the most romantic nights Maia would ever have, she thought ruefully. At least she had more orgasms than Ivy did, it seems.

Ivy had really liked Tom and Fiona, and was hoping Fiona would return to the cottage, but Tom died while she was away visiting family in Devon, and she hadn't come back. Ivy continued to recount anything she could remember from the few months leading up to March.

'Fiona rang me once a while ago to explain the rent would be delayed. I wasn't concerned, they were good kids, possibly going through a rough patch. The last time I saw Tom was a few weeks before his death. He did seem a little tired but was always a pleasant young man, nothing amiss. I had a clear out after he died, and gave all his belongings to his mother Pauline; lovely lady. Then Fiona came to collect a few of her own personal items on the day of the funeral, including Tom's phone which had photos on it. She didn't spend much time in the cottage as she was so upset. I'm sure she really loved him.'

Ivy's words were a great comfort to Maia. They sat in silence for a few moments, when Ivy nimbly leapt out of her seat, raising her hand acknowledging a thought. 'Oh, I found a rucksack! It was right in the back of the cupboard beneath the kitchen sink, all rolled up and tucked in behind the pipes.' She handed it to Maia, 'you may as well take this. I am so sorry about Tom, he was a lovely lad and he really cared for the countryside. I have Fiona's number if you want to ring her, she's a nice girl, I'm sure she won't mind.'

Maia thanked Ivy for her time and asked if she could visit again with Pauline, as she may like to see her paintings. Ivy agreed this was a good idea. She would make it a special occasion and make some of her, homemade concoction, winking at Maia, she suggested not to bring her car next time. They hugged and Maia left.

Maia returned home slightly reeling from the distinct memories of Tom, but was content at the thought of meeting a warm, wonderful woman in Ivy, and knowing Tom was loved. She made a coffee and, holding her phone, said, 'may as well strike while the iron is hot, as they say,' she rang Fiona's number.

A soft voice answered. Maia took things gently, explaining who she was and why she was calling, hoping it was okay that Ivy passed on the number, commenting, 'Ivy is quite the character,' which put Fiona at ease.

Fiona was calm, and agreed it was okay to talk about Tom. Maia thought Fiona's voice made her sound much younger, and the lilt of her Devonshire accent was charming. She became upset feeling guilty, because if she had paid more attention to him, it may not have happened. Maia gently halted her flow and empathised with her, saying she felt exactly the same, agreeing that lots of people shared the sense of guilt and grief too. Fiona briefly explained she had met Tom at a festival near her home in Devon. She moved up North to be with him, but spent some time away with her family regularly to keep in touch. Maia winced at her sudden lightning strike of guilt, was Fiona visiting her family when she and Tom were together. She had to brush that aside.

Fiona referred to Tom's vulnerable behaviour, 'he would sit up late at night, or I'd hear him go out in the work's van at all hours with no explanation. He fell behind with some of the tasks at work once, which was most unlike him, and his supervisor had to chase him up over it. He could become distant from time to time, and drink a bit too much, but most of the time he was fine, those phases were all to do with his background.'

'I know about that Fiona,' said Maia softly.

Relieved Maia knew, Fiona became upset explaining Tom would occasionally sit out in the garden staring into the countryside during the night and cry, 'it was always after he'd spoken to someone he knew in the past called Jordan, who he occasionally met up with. I haven't returned to Northumberland since attending the funeral, but I should do soon, to see Ivy she was so good to us both.'

Maia thanked Fiona for talking with her and reassured her no-one could have prevented Tom's death. It was a comfort to her knowing Tom had confided his early experiences to Fiona, more proof he was cherished.

Maia sat back and pondered over the details she had received. It was confusing. Was Tom simply going through anxieties and depression from his early abuse, or was it something else? She was absolutely shattered, and fell asleep where she lay on the sofa. She woke with a snort, dribbling onto the cushion. Frustratingly, Maia still had no answers whether Tom's death was an accident, or suicide. Why would he drive into a wall? Maia had a nagging sensation there was something else occurring, though she'd tried to convince herself the locations from his notebook were nothing significant, it played on her mind. Was he driving to meet someone, was someone following him. He had taken drugs in the past, maybe he'd drifted back into that lifestyle. Living in such a remote place would be easy to meet up with ... who? Drug smugglers? She knew absolutely nothing about that world. And, who was Jordan?

Maia plodded to the toilet, didn't bother getting washed or brushing her teeth, whipped her clothes off, dropped them on the floor and clambered into bed to drift into a much-needed deep sleep.

17

MAIA RECEIVED A message from Harriet Cooper at Earth Chart in response to the re-submitted proposed draft for her article, and gave her a date to discuss the progress. Harriet was happy to travel north as she could see her son too. Maia suggested Café Dalvik and arranged to collect Harriet from Durham train station. She asked Nik to keep a private booth for them with plenty of tasty offerings.

Nik was on speakerphone and Maia heard Sophia's remark. 'Ooh I've got a really lovely businessy outfit to wear, it's low key and classy. We want to make a good impression don't we? I'll try to keep a lid on my Tourette's too!' Roaring with laughter, 'we don't want anything rude to slip out in front of your boss … best behaviour … promise.'

What Maia couldn't see was Sophia looking at Nik with wide eyes making a zip gesture across her lips.

Maia was nervous meeting Harriet again, but the trip to Iceland made for interesting and dynamic conversation during the car journey from the train station. They were welcomed at Café Dalvik by a smart-looking Sophia. Her outfit comprised of charcoal grey pin-stripe cigarette trousers, a deep amethyst soft shirt, and her infamous violet patent brogues. Didn't matter what she wore, Sophia carried it off fantastically. Maia noticed she had toned down the make-up, straightened her hair and looked naturally beautiful. She settled them into the end private booth.

Harriet was a softly spoken woman, which belied her unfaltering direct approach to business dealings. She could be silently lethal, like a ninja or sniper Maia thought, though she did admire her. Harriet's style was usually, plain shift dresses with jacket or she'd wear a suit with stylish pumps, always groomed and business-like. Harriet wore her hair down today, how frivolous thought Maia. Her light brown luxurious hair caught the light as it cascaded onto her shoulders. Maia had never seen her looking so relaxed. Harriet wore an olive-green linen dress, dotted with a floral print, with a pale peach short cardigan; the combo looked great on her. She wore low heeled sandals revealing perfectly manicured toenails. It was a really hot day and they enjoyed a welcoming freshly-squeezed iced lemon spritzer in the air-conditioned room. They discussed the way forward and to Maia's relief Harriet was encouraging about her work. She was particularly impressed Maia had secured contact with, Alexis Leventis of the Apollon Group, and confirmed the draft plan for the article had been approved for publication.

Maia inwardly heaved a huge sigh of relief and thanked Harriet for her support. She couldn't tell how old Harriet was. Her face had signs of ageing with slightly hooded blue eyes, and deepening lines around her mouth. It was a hot day, and Harriet took off her cardigan revealing the tops of her arms showing the extra covering of flesh that bemoans women in their middle years. Harriet took to Sophia, but then everyone does, and she enjoyed meeting Nik too, suggesting they could have some corporate functions at Café Dalvik, which pleased them all greatly.

Harriet mentioned a little about her personal life, she was married with two sons in their twenties, but not much more. It was essentially all business. The meeting was successful. Maia felt so much better and motivated about her future with the company, but she needed to maintain those high standards. After Maia dropped Harriet off at Durham station, she drove home passing, The Angel of the North. Rising twenty metres high, the iconic rusted sculpture, with wings outstretched, longer than a Boeing 757 jet, stood at the helm of the North East watching over the land. It was a sight to behold and always made her feel she had arrived home as soon as she spotted it's welcoming wings. Maia became overwhelmed with tears of relief, but there was something else. She took stock, making a mental list of the last few months as she drove;

> Work demands had taken their toll, however this meeting went well.
> She was fatigued from the Iceland trip, even though it was lovely.
> She had a recent broken relationship.
> She had started a new long-distance relationship.
> She had reunited with Craig, which was great, but brought back emotional trauma.

> She was still having unsettling thoughts about the issues over Tom's death.
>
> She felt under pressure to solve remaining questions for Pauline.

Then there was always, Freya, the precious little girl quietly growing up in the back of her mind. Maia played gentle music in the car and took her time driving home. Taking her foot off the accelerator felt good; nowhere to be right now, and she had some space in her head to devote to thinking about Ben.

It was early evening when she arrived home, and she sat with background music on, and a cool gin, relieved her life seemed back on track. She stroked the soft sheen of a cushion beside her as she sat on the sofa. Her eyes fell upon the beautiful watercolour above the sofa opposite. The abstract sky, in blue, lemon and pink was a perfect background for the purple hot air balloon featured in the centre of the frame. The angle of the balloon and the stream of small triangular flags in bright colours trailing from the basket, gave the impression the balloon was actually floating. Her good friend Daphne was indeed a gifted artist, as was Daphne's partner Zain. She must catch up with them soon and visit his new studio.

Gazing at the painting she said, 'stunning,' Maia loved it. As she got up, something dark caught her eye on the floor by the side of the sofa. She retrieved the small navy rucksack Ivy had given her from the cottage. Lifting it, she thought it appeared too heavy for the lightweight fabric, which she hadn't noticed when she was at the cottage. She sat with it on her knee, unzipped the front pocket; nothing there, but she felt the weight of an object on her thigh. Opening the main zip, there were two small internal pockets halfway down the bag. One was zipped, she opened it, inside was a small black mobile phone. Maia looked at it. She simultaneously felt a heightened sense of nervous energy, and a heavy sinking feeling in her stomach. She took it out, pressed the on / off switch at the side knowing nothing would happen.

Warily, she placed the mobile on the coffee table and stared at it for some time. It felt like something alien infiltrating her home, silently beckoning her to explore its secrets. Maybe it wasn't Tom's, she tried to convince herself it had nothing to do with him. She put it back into the rucksack, which she bundled into the bottom of her utility cupboard in the kitchen. Overnight Maia couldn't get the mobile phone out of her mind, did it hold secrets? Was it connected to the notebook and the numbers? She felt angry at Tom for leaving this mystery and confusion behind, would she never be able to just let it all go?

Maia awoke in the early hours, and had to force herself to stay in bed and not rise too early to deal with the phone, even look at it. She refused to get up until 6am. Flinging the duvet off, feeling annoyed she was forced to get out of bed, she retrieved the rucksack, which, she was dismayed to see hadn't vanished overnight. No, it was real, so was the phone, which she placed on the coffee table; small, dark and menacing … taunting her. She made a coffee and sat directly in front of it. The style reminded her of an old-fashioned Nokia mobile. She'd never heard of the make, Alcatel which was shown on the front of the device, she had no idea what to do next.

18

THERE WAS AN ulterior motive for Maia to arrange to meet Pauline at Café Dalvik. If Mike was around, they may not be able to have a free and open discussion. Maia decided her next course of action was to access the mobile phone. She'd asked Pauline to look for a phone charger in Tom's belongings, and to her credit, Pauline did not question why, simply acknowledged the request and said she would see Maia when she picked her up at 11 am.

Sophia's exuberance was contagious, she was so welcoming of Pauline and couldn't do enough to make their lunchtime a special occasion. She was in a turquoise, bronze and lemon paisley patterned maxi length dress, with ringleted hair flowing, she looked like someone straight out of the 1970s. Maia complimented the look.

Sophia commented, 'I've gone all retro-boho today!' spreading her arms and doing the obligatory twirl.

'And you look fabulous with it,' said Pauline, 'I had a dress similar to that years ago. Paid a fortune for it from my Freemans catalogue account. Still have some of my old stuff, it'll be fashionable now. You'll have to visit and have a rummage Sophia. None of it fits me these days.'

Sophia said with glee, 'fabulous idea darling, definitely up for a rummage!' She left them briefly and returned from the kitchen to their table with a tray festooned with an array of small, savoury and sweet treats. Café Dalvik's chef was trying out some new recipes of lunchtime bites, including the Pierogi Luiza had suggested. Sophia suggested Pauline and Maia be the first to try them and give feedback. Nik brought out a coffee as she was taking a break and they all sat together enjoying the small offerings, chatting and giving marks out of ten. It was a lovely indulgence for Pauline. Maia promised to bring her and Mike back for dinner some time.

Sophia and Nik had returned to their tasks, as Maia and Pauline were having a final coffee. Pauline reached into her bag and surreptitiously handed over a phone charger without a word. Maia briefly explained the circumstances leading up to why she asked for it. She did not want to upset Pauline, and downplayed the fact that the phone found at the cottage, could be Fiona's, or left by a workman, or a recent guest, which she knew was unlikely.

'What happened at the inquest Pauline?' Maia asked tenderly.

'There was nothing that looked suspicious from the police enquiries. The coroner made a decision to leave it an open verdict, as there was no note or other indication of suicide. They said it was likely he would have been unconscious from the head injury as a result of the collision and died from the internal injuries. I just hope my boy didn't suffer.'

'Oh Pauline,' whispered Maia looking down into her coffee cup, not wanting to think about Tom's battered body.

'Mike is still really struggling, he misses Tom so much, he was his son in every way. I sometimes feel we failed him, maybe got some things wrong. You can't help but blame yourself when you don't protect your child from everything.' Pauline, leaned forward, in a suppressed tone, 'the toxicology report showed borderline amounts of alcohol in his system.' She became animated, 'what on earth was he doing driving if he'd had a drink? I'm so angry with him Maia. He would never deliberately do anything like that, would he?' She shook her head, 'even though he had a reckless side when he was younger. You know when he came from that care home, he didn't know where he was … or even who he was. He was a frightened little lad. Goodness knows what went on in his family and in the children's home, apart from what we know about … Pauline shook her head. She then smiled, 'but he really settled down. Tom had such a lovely nature.'

'The alcohol could have been from the night before,' Maia suggested, 'alcohol stays in your system a while. Maybe if he was having a drink in the evening, then driving quite early.' She gave a little shrug and looked deep into Pauline's eyes, 'I can't believe Tom would knowingly take the risk, or … do anything deliberate either.' Maia told Pauline about Fiona and Ivy and reassured her he was loved and was never lonely or suffering.

Pauline seemed flat when talking about Tom today, naturally there was still a lingering shock present. She looked quite sternly into Maia's eyes and said, 'there must have been something going on for him personally I think. He seemed really content with Fiona, she is a lovely girl, we met her a few times. I trust you Maia, I know you would not do anything to harm the memory of my son. Please find out what happened. Mick can't get over it, thinks someone was after him and ran him off the road or something.'

'If I can establish anything that would help us understand what happened, I will, but we can't be certain of finding anything out.' She slipped the phone charger in her bag, and took Pauline's hand to reassure she would do her utmost.

Pauline told her something strange happened at Tom's funeral, 'Would you believe, Tom's sister Abigail approached me, she knew who I was. We had let the parents know of his death via Social Services. Abigail said she wanted to pay her respects, and indicated she would like to know more about her brother. She briefly mentioned that she doesn't really get along with her parents. So, Abigail gave me her telephone number and invited me to meet for a coffee. I couldn't believe how much she looked like him; a very bonny girl.' They both smiled.

'Well ... he was absolutely gorgeous,' said Maia.

'You're still wearing his pendant, that's lovely to see,' Pauline smiled. 'Do you think I should ring her.'

'What is your heart telling you?'

'She seemed genuinely interested. Quiet, nothing like him.' Pauline chuckled.

'Then go for it,' suggested Maia, 'if it becomes too demanding or upsetting you can stop contact. Make the call now while I'm here if you like.'

'Would you come with me to meet her, if Mike doesn't want to?'

'Of course!'

Pauline rang Abigail's number; it went to voicemail so she left a brief message saying she would be happy to meet. 'Yes, Maia, that feels like the right thing to do, and any excuse to talk about Tom, and maybe find out more about his … his … I know I shouldn't say this, but his bloody parents.'

Maia returned home after dropping Pauline off, with a wave to Mike as he opened the door. 'She's still in one piece,' she reassured, he smiled and waved. 'Joined at the hip those two,' she mused.

Maia plugged the charger into the phone once she returned home, it fit perfectly but nothing happened. She left it for a while to charge, and began writing in her journal, then checked after an hour. Maia touched the on / off switch at the side, hoping nothing would happen, but it sprang into life. She had the same sense of thrilling foreboding when she first discovered the phone. She assumed it would be password protected, however on pressing the centre button, the last calls actually showed up on screen. It was a simple, old, unsophisticated device, obviously from pre-security days.

Her hands were shaking as she realised Tom would have been the last person to touch it. 'What happened Tom?' She wanted to call someone, but knew it would be better for her to look through the data herself. Maia sat with the small device in the palm of her hand, as apprehension, fear and a little excitement flooded her brain. She scrolled down the last few contacts. The list revealed incoming calls from random mobile numbers, no names. She made a mental note of the last three digits of some as they passed, but the numbers all seemed to be completely random, only one or two seemed to match with any others.

As she continued to scroll she was thinking this wasn't getting anywhere, then she stopped and quickly had to scroll back up, because a name appeared as one of the contacts, *JD Pica*. Maia opened and read the messages which referred to a coded name, *Cuntrylad*. The texts were very brief, indicating times, dates and seemingly cryptic locations perhaps. It wasn't difficult to ascertain who, Cuntrylad was; the spelling being a piss-take moniker for a ranger. It must be Tom, but who was JD Pica? Strange surname, Maia thought.

She contacted Craig to seek advice and explained about the phone's data. Craig suggested, 'sounds like you have a burner mobile on your hands, the random numbers could suggest drug activity or stolen goods contacts.' This was surprising as Craig would have no knowledge of Tom's past behaviour. He continued. 'Regarding the name it would be tricky to determine JD Pica's identity. Unless it is a surname, though very unlikely, they wouldn't use anything identifying. Local police probably won't be interested in the information as it's isolated from the road traffic accident, and not current. Whoever's numbers are on there will not be identified, as the recipients' devices with be in landfill, down a drain, or at the bottom of the River Tyne by now. Without any CCTV, or tyre marks suggesting Tom was run off the road, there's no proof of third party involvement. Sorry Maia, really difficult to move forward with it. I'll keep thinking and if I can suggest anything else, of course I will.'

'I did ring some numbers, but the lines were all dead.'

'Maia, I'd strongly advise you not to delve too deeply, or ring any more of the numbers, and never, ever meet with anyone. Do you know if Tom had any dealings with … and sorry about these questions, stolen goods or vehicles on a large scale, drugs, or any sort of criminal gang activity, even people smuggling. I'm sure he hadn't but that's the sort of thing a burner could be used for.'

Maia was silent for a moment, she wondered if Tom was into something criminal, maybe connected to drugs, when he briefly associated with the biking fraternity in his late teens. She heard Craig say something, but was distracted.

He repeated, 'Promise me you won't meet with anyone, please promise. Or at least, take bodyguard Ben with you, but even then I wouldn't advise it.'

Maia was grateful for Craig's thoughts and genuine concern, 'promise I won't do anything daft, honestly. Haven't said much about all this to Ben, but it's all going really well, we're meeting up soon and I can't wait to see him.'

Maia read the text exchanges for what seemed like the hundredth time between Cuntrylad and JD Pica. She stopped scrolling and decided to put the name into an internet search, maybe she had missed something, but JD Pica didn't exist. For Pica alone she found; the Perth Institute of Contemporary Arts. Pica also referred to a medical condition where someone compulsively eats non-food items like crayons, hair, chalk, paper, and even pooh. 'Nice,' said Maia, there were further entries including pictures of birds, but she was getting nowhere.

19

The Laseks

BEN AND MAIA had not managed to meet up since Iceland, as Maia had to focus on her work, and Ben had been recalled to Iceland to oversee a few technical issues with the installation he was working on. Before he took the flight he visited his parents, he had something playing on his mind. He had lied to Maia, he was still married, though separated from his wife. He questioned why he'd stated he was divorced, and not quantified that. It would've been fine had he been honest and said the divorce was near completion, apart from the fact … it wasn't.

It was a beautiful June morning and Ben's enjoyment of another bright day was marred by thoughts of approaching his wife Shona to get his car back. He wasn't sure his cheap run-around would make the journey to visit Maia in one piece, it had been temperamental recently. Shona had made no effort to replace her car which had been repossessed, and was using Ben's.

Ben considered Shona, his current, not yet, ex-wife, to be a bloody nightmare with her demands. He'd found it easier to walk away from the arguments, not that he saw Shona much these days. She still resided in their marital home, and was not going to give it up easily. On many occasions Ben often ended phone calls abruptly when he was getting nowhere. He hated arguing. Discussions had become more acrimonious lately, especially about finances.

Ben rang his mum Lorraine, 'gonna pop through tonight if you and dad are free?'

'It's about time you paid us a visit, I want to hear more about this girl you met in Iceland. You are still in touch with her aren't you?'

Ben sensed the anxiety in his mother's voice. Was her thirty-three year old son lonely since his marriage had broken down six months ago. Would anyone ever take him on again?

He said frustratingly, 'yes mother. But we both have work commitments so it's been really difficult to arrange time together. I'll see you around six-ish. Will dad be back in?'

'Should be, you know what he's like on fishing days, he doesn't know when to pack up and come home.'

'Never understood the attraction, unless it's to get away from you, Mum.'

'You'd better watch it if you want dinner! I'll see if Helena can make it through as well, it'll have been a while since you laid eyes on your little sister.'

'Good idea, if she's free, be great to catch up with her.'

Ben arrived at his parents' cosy home, they downsized a few years ago from the large four bedroom semi that was his childhood home. They loved this ancient stone cottage which retained many of its old features, also the open aspect overlooking the countryside at the rear, with the curved slab of, Pendle Hill in the far distance. The tiny street of five terraced cottages came with a reasonable slice of land over the back lane, which they had nurtured into a small allotment. At the end of the extensive garden, they had a decked area with comfortable garden seats and a table; the area was strewn with candles, and lights for sitting out in the evenings watching the sunset.

'I'm absolutely starving!' Helena had arrived.

Ivan was standing at the fridge getting bottles of beer for the guests, 'you want one darling?'

'Can't, I'm driving Dad thanks. Just food for me, soon as … ' She leant over to kiss his cheek, 'Dad I'm sure you're shrinking.'

'It's those high shoes you wear.'

'No it's not,' came Lorraine's comment from the garden, 'he's shrinking, it's his legs they're getting more bowed as the years go by.'

'Ay, he couldn't stop a piggy in a ginnel wi' 'em,' said Ben in his broadest Lanky-twang.

Helena chuckled. Whilst his dad said, 'I could still take you on at footy son.'

'True Dad, you certainly were a better player than I ever was.'

When they were all seated outside on the small patio area off the back kitchen, Helena was devouring a huge portion of home-made cottage pie, and was clearing the vegetable sides, then asked if they could, 'pop some chips on to go with it, I'm still hungry.'

Ben said, 'don't know how you stay so slim, must be the nervous energy in court.'

Helena, muttered something inaudible with a mouthful of food, but her nodding head, showed she agreed. Once she drew breath, she asked, 'so, who's this lovely Nordic lass then?' Then immediately stated, quite vehemently, 'don't worry, we'll keep shtum.' Gesturing zipping her mouth closed. 'You really don't want Shona getting wind you've got a girlfriend, or she'll claim adultery.'

Ben grimaced, and knew Helena was right. He explained how he'd spotted Maia in the restaurant and thought she looked gorgeous. 'She is how she looks, friendly and full of fun, but she's definitely got a classy edge and interesting personality. We had really good fun together,' he smiled. 'Her family seem great too.'

'So, nowt like Shona then,' said Helena curtly.

'No, not quite.'

'Still having bother with her, Ben?' asked mum, Lorraine.

'She's giving me a hard time for no reason.'

'She still got your car and the house?' asked Helena.

The family had liked Shona a lot, as the younger, bubbly blonde tornado seemed good for a stoic Ben. She brought him out of himself, Lorraine would comment, but soon, they saw another facet to her personality since they separated.

'You do need to sort it out son, it's hard but you can't go on like this,' commented Ivan, with gentle fatherly advice.

'What happened with the divorce petition?' queried Helena.

'Says it's still with her solicitor.'

'She's not signed it yet then?'

'Not yet, but it's a formality.'

'A formality that needs completing. It's June now, so it's been, what, four months since the meeting to sort everything?'

'I know!' Ben stood abruptly and went into the house.

'Probably enough Shona-talk for one evening,' said Lorraine.

'I've told him I know some great family solicitors who'll sort her out,' said Helena holding up her hands. 'Okay, I know, I understand him dragging his feet, so she'll sign and not be even more bloody awkward. I've told him to get, The Terrier to represent him.' Both parents looked bemused. 'You know, Terri, my colleague, best divorce solicitor in the North,' Helena said with a grin. 'Shame Shona can't find another sucker to fund her lifestyle, then she'll move on.'

'Helena, that's not nice,' said Lorraine.

'Probably true though,' said Ivan.

'Definitely true,' said Helena, 'she almost bankrupted them, and lied about massive online loans. How she kept that info about the legal judgements from embezzling her former business partner at the beauty salon I'll never know. I mean, it *was* years ago, but I felt so sorry for Ben when he discovered what she'd been up to. All innocence and light, until the true Shona revealed herself. Leopards and spots. He must've felt quite stupid … and he really isn't, he's just a lovely, trusting guy.'

The conversation changed and they all brightened up as soon as Ben returned to the table.

'Maia sounds great Ben, much more your type, interested in all that environmental malarky,' Helena said with a smile, 'got a photo of her? It'll be nice to put a face to the name.'

Ben began scrolling his phone. 'I'm ringing her tonight to sort out a trip to Newcastle, to spend a couple of days together, before I head to Scotland.' Ben thought about Maia's attractive face, her voice, her body, but he'd better not think about that too much. He was really looking forward to seeing her. He felt light-hearted and positive inside and she was on his mind always.

'She's busy with a really demanding article she's writing for an environmental magazine. I admire her, I really do.'

'Oh yeah, admire which bits?' asked Helena tilting her head with a questioning smile.

Ben laughed. 'Here she is,' he enlarged the profile picture of Maia's smiling face and showed it to his family.

'She looks lovely,' approved Lorraine.

'Phwoar, nice one son,' said Ivan comically giving him both thumbs up.

'Dad … really?' admonished Helena.

The family sat in the glow of the summer sunset and chatted, greeting the neighbours who were also enjoying the red and gold vision of the setting sun beyond the undulating landscape. The strings of solar lights ignited as darkness eventually swept over the land. The temperature cooled, the sun finally dipped, sliding under the black blanket of the distant horizon. Helena had to leave to drive back to Manchester, as she had a busy day in court the next day, not before a gentle word with Ben about, The Terrier, and a meaningful hug for her older brother. Ben hugged his parents promising to report on his trip to see Maia the minute he was back.

It was a decent walk back to his rented place along the canal, he played his Icelandic playlist of Nils Frahm, Olafur Arnolds and Nanna Bryndis Hilmarsdóttir. The haunting music reminded him of the calming whiteout scenes he had seen for months in Kárhóll and Akureyri. Whilst he was looking forward to returning to Iceland, he'd prefer to be back in the Land of Ice and Fire with Maia.

20

Pendle, June 2015

IT WAS A late Friday afternoon when Maia leaned back into her office chair in the spare bedroom, now transformed into office space for freelance writing. She peeled her back from the chair, it was stifling. She stood, stretched her arms up and arched her back to allow her body to fully extend, then got ready for a run. Following days of relentless research, writing, editing and evaluating her report, Maia decided all work and no play was not something to which Maia Hewson subscribed. She was missing Ben and looked forward to seeing him on her visit to Pendle on Sunday when he was home from Iceland.

Maia had been neglecting family visits, and wanted to spend time with her scrumptious niece and nephew to squeeze the living daylights out of them. Maia closed her MacBook, collated all of her handwritten notes and placed them, along with her work mobile, in the slim desk drawer, then messaged her brother Andy to arrange a visit in the morning.

As Maia pulled into the driveway of Andy and Jen's

home, she saw her niece Kate at the window waving furiously to her. Kate's face animated into one of utter delight, then she disappeared and within seconds the front door was flung aside and Kate ran onto the driveway shouting, 'Aunty Maia, Aunty Maia!' Fortunately, Maia had the sense to put her bag down as Kate, took a flying leap with both feet off the ground into her arms. She wrapped her legs around Maia's hips and, goodness she was getting heavy, almost unbalanced her.

Jen's voice was heard, 'steady on Kate, you nearly knocked Aunty Maia flying.'

'She's fine,' said Maia as the two crumpled into each other, Maia caught a whiff of vanilla cupcakes. Kate grabbed Maia's cheeks and had to use all of her resistance to prevent squeezing really hard with excitement. Maia burst out laughing. Kate threw her head back and bellowed a hearty laugh too. This was the tonic Maia needed, a child's laughter ringing out and the exuberance of a three-year-old's affection.

Nathan gave her a chubby grin, at seven months old he was beginning the stranger-danger stage and coyly looked away, burying his face into his dad's shoulder. He came around in a little while and she got many hugs and snuggles with him. The soft skin of a baby always drew Maia's mind back to her own experience of becoming a mother. She was used to the emotional trigger now. Nathan smelled of freshly puffed baby powder, and his features were the image of Andy, a tiny mini-me.

Maia had the most fabulous afternoon playing in the garden, catching up with Andy and Jen, and admiring their gorgeous expansive new home with the repaired grass and hedge from the volleyball night. Maia had the privilege of reading Kate's night time story, and once the children were tucked up in bed, the three settled to more adult conversation. She talked lovingly about her trip to Iceland and meeting Ben, complaining they had little time to connect, but she was leaving for Lancashire the following day to visit with his family, and hadn't even thought about packing yet. Andy and Jen showed huge interest in Maia's love life, and her work.

In a quiet moment, when Jen had gone to bed, Andy asked about Tom and the notebook situation. Maia gave him a brief run down as she didn't want to burden him with the added mobile burner phone detail, in truth, she didn't want to talk about it at all and it would worry Andy. In true older brother style, he consoled her suggesting nothing may come of it and for her to be careful, with a stern look.

'You get more like dad every day.'

'Oh, great, thanks Maia!' he rolled his eyes as they sniggered together.

They agreed to book a weekend away with the children and all the family soon. Aunties Nikky and Sophia were also planning a family gathering at the café. 'That will be brilliant,' remarked Maia before heading to bed. It'll be in my calendar once we get a date fixed, wouldn't miss it for the world.'

The following day Maia made the two and a half hour journey to Pendle to spend time with Ben who was returning from Iceland. She was trying to visualise him; his height, his face, his body, even though she'd had a pretty good look at him all over. She could only visualise snapshot images of him in her mind, a perception, that's all, it was weird. She hoped to discover more about the area and meet his parents too.

When they met, she enjoyed seeing his smile, and hearing his voice; all so familiar and lovely. She'd forgotten how striking his bright blue eyes were.

'I've organised a trip for Summer Solstice on 21 June at The Water Meetings, it's a walk from Barrowford village at midnight. We might catch naked witches dancing, and if we're really lucky, witness a sacrifice.'

'Looking forward to that, do I need to wear any specific clothing for a sacrifice ... a hooded shroud perhaps?'

Maia and Ben enjoyed a whole day and night together before they embarked upon meeting his family. She was delighted to discover Ben's parents were welcoming, yet she felt a slight resistance from his mother Lorraine. She wasn't overflowing with charm, as Maia's own mother Katrin would have been, meeting her child's new partner. Each to their own, she thought, maybe she's a little apprehensive meeting a new girlfriend, however Lorraine said little. It was Ivan, Ben's dad, who spoke for the most part and he was hilarious. Diving straight into a conversation, offering to show her the garden immediately.

Lorraine admonished him, suggesting, 'the lass an't even had time for a brew.'

'We can drink it outside,' he implored. 'Ben tells me you're into the environment, come and look we have recently had solar panels fitted.'

Maia was genuinely interested and would've been happy

to go straight outside, but Lorraine insisted they sit around the kitchen table in the traditional dark wood surroundings of the kitchen to talk first. There was an old-style stove which was central to the family home. The general chat was pleasant, with Ivan breaking into a traditional Czech song as he poured the tea and stamped his feet.

'I'll teach you this song and the dance, its good!'

Lorraine, rolled her eyes and Ben laughed, shaking his head, 'you'll get used to him.'

Maia already liked Ivan a lot. Throughout the day, she felt a reticence from Lorraine, who looked quite dour at times. What was that about she wondered? Maybe it took her a while to warm up, maybe it was her personality. Maybe, she was worried her son had met another woman who wasn't quite right for her boy, it was a little strange. Ben and Ivan went outside and they were left together. Lorraine didn't instigate any conversation, so Maia set the ball rolling.

'We had a lovely time in Iceland, did he mention my mother is Icelandic?

Lorraine nodded, 'oh yes, that's right, he did say.' There was no further curiosity.

Maia continued to explain a little about her trip; about skiing in Dalvik, whale-watching, the lovely restaurants and shopping, and visiting Ben's worksite in Kárhóll. Lorraine remained non-committal, nodding and an occasional, *hmm*, in acknowledgement. Maia asked about Lorraine's work, knowing she was involved in hospital administration for the National Health Service for years, and reached a senior position. Again, it was stilted, not much information was divulged to enable a fruitful conversation. Maybe she had really liked Shona, and wasn't happy with the divorce? Things fell silent. Maia had enough, thinking she's not even meeting me half way, I shouldn't have to try this hard.

'Better go and check-out Ivan's solar panels,' Maia said looking outside.

Lorraine said nothing and got up, allowing Maia to walk through the door ahead of her. Ben put his arm out to welcome her and asked, 'do you know all my secrets now?'

Maia, felt like saying, blood out of a stone doesn't yield much, but replied smiling, 'not yet.'

The afternoon went well, Maia busying about with Ivan, looking at all of his plants and asking questions. She could see herself coming to help him here, it was a lovely, open environment. Later, Ivan brought to life tales of Demdike, Chattox and Alice Nutter, the Pendle Witches, where ten people were hanged at the conclusion of the trials. It was eerily spooky listening to his engaging voice with silence all around. Maia was transfixed, as daylight faded into evening, looking across to Pendle Hill in the far distance. Sunshine was annulled by a passing dark cloud, and the low whistling hum of the wind drifted toward them over the hill. All was quiet, when the garden solar lights were extinguished by a burst of long low rays of a setting sun, and the back door clattered, which startled Maia.

Helena arrived in a flurry, striding up the garden path. She grabbed Maia's hand to introduce herself quite formally, she then sat beside Maia, leaned over and grabbed her for a hug saying, 'I might get a sister-in-law with some brains this time!'

'That's not nice Helena,' said Lorraine.

Uh-oh ... maybe the previous daughter-in-law was closer to Lorraine than Maia believed. She had a slight uncomfortable feeling.

Helena brushed Lorraine's comment aside, and with enthusiasm said, 'tell me about Iceland?' It was well after nine, and they were all ravenous waiting for Helena to join them, after being delayed at work.

Ben, Helena and Maia were chatting in the front room whilst Ivan and Lorraine finished preparing supper in the kitchen. Helena asked if Ben had any contact with Shona, Lorraine suddenly emerged from the kitchen, taking an interest in the conversation. Maia had the impression the family had agreed not to discuss Shona in depth in her presence, fair enough, and she had to stop questioning Lorraine's motives. She felt excluded from this family situation as if she was intruding.

Maia tried not to keep glancing at the wedding photo of Ben and blonde-bombshell Shona in the multiple photo frame, thinking, he's gone for a completely different type with me, and surely they need to change that photo. She felt an urge to wait until they were out of the room, remove the photo, draw glasses, a moustache and black out some teeth on Shona's image, and replace it. She wasn't usually prone to envy and childish actions, but it made her smirk inwardly.

Maia spent time with Ivan in the kitchen, helping to stir pots for the traditional Czech meal he was making, and she helped with the table settings. Lorraine became more animated, but seemed fatigued, and Maia noted she didn't touch any alcohol during dinner, maybe she was teetotal?

Ivan had Maia in stitches with his random tales of working as a tree surgeon. He was never afraid of heights whatsoever, and delighted her with his extraordinary tales and re-enactments of near misses from plummeting to his death.

'He embellishes for dramatic sake,' said Helena turning to Maia, rolling her eyes.

'I do not,' he retorted and said something like, 'little rostak!' translated as, rascal, for Maia's benefit. After a lovely evening, apart from Maia's apprehension about whether Lorraine like her, Maia and Ben returned to his place. It was really getting late and she was tired. Tomorrow maybe she'd glean something about Lorraine's relationship with Shona. Then she broke into a broad smile, 'your dad is a complete hoot!' Maia enjoyed her stay and did feel welcome within the family. Lorraine's guard came down and she softened somewhat, though Maia wondered if they would ever really nurture a solid relationship. Maia and Ben trekked over Pendle Hill, and enjoyed the beautiful Lancashire countryside during the rest of the trip.

The following weekend, Maia was sitting at home not knowing where to put herself, as Ben was arriving in half an hour or so. The apartment was spotless, she'd even cleaned the balcony glass frontage and the large glass doors. She was spotless too, she kept checking herself in the mirror, feeling strangely nervous about him visiting her in her own space.

'For goodness sake, you're fine, your home is fine, stop fussing,' she started this dialogue with herself, and got up off the sofa to straighten the cushions. Clicking her tongue with self-annoyance, she mused whether the place looked too pristine, this wasn't her natural habitat. 'Should I chuck my bag on the floor, and mess up the cushions on the sofa? ... He's really not going to notice Maia.' She laughed at herself, and put some music on, 'it's all fine, calm down,' she said floating her arms downwards and blowing out gently.

It was nerve-wracking. Maia never felt like this when Shaun was due to arrive, maybe there was more at stake this time. She said loudly, 'oh shut up Maia, it'll be fine.' Her phone rang and startled her! It was Ben on hands free, 'think I'm nearby, I can see the bridges and my Satnav seems to know where I'm going.'

'Great let me know if you get lost and I'll guide you.'

'Okay, see you soon, Maia pet.'

She laughed at his Geordie-ism. He'd picked up a few since watching old re-runs of, *The Likely Lads,* series. Her Lancashire, Lanky-twang accent was coming along fine too. Ben arrived, and Maia felt a rush of warm excitement as they hugged and kissed at the front door. They settled down side by side, had a coffee and she offered him a snack, which he didn't want.

'My stuff is in the car, I'll get it.' He returned with his weekend bag and a lovely bunch of flowers, light blues and brilliant white. Not too ostentatious, but beautifully presented. These were no last-minute buy from a service station.

'I went for the most Icelandic colours I could find,' he flushed slightly.

It was thoughtful, she received them gratefully, saying she'd try not to kill them as her record on the domestic front was rather iffy, glancing at the surviving Peace Lily plant. She was sending him a message not to expect domestic heaven, with lavish home cooked meals either, or any meals in fact. Mental note, she must get that stew recipe from Katrin they'd enjoyed together in Iceland. She was not going to suggest Café Dalvik tonight, she'd wait before inflicting Sophia on him, as they'd never get away.

'The culinary world is at your fingertips in this city, just choose a country of your choice. Bacon butties are on the menu for breakfast.'

'Perfect!' he said mimicking a chef's kiss.

Maia retrieved two Einstök lagers from the fridge and had a brief moment, looking at the utility cupboard door, with the secretive phone inside the secretive rucksack. Should she tell Ben? That would mean having to allude perhaps, to nefarious activity, explain who Tom is, and why he is important to her, which inevitably links to Freya. Her mind raced for those few moments, when she snapped them away in an instant, and made the firm decision to not say anything at all.

Maia handed an Einstök to Ben. She had enjoyed her trip to Pendle and was keen to understand more about Ben and his family.

'My grandfather moved to the UK to find farming work in the late 1940s, to send money back to his family in Czechoslovakia, as it was then. He ended up in Lancashire and met my grandma at a local dance. At the time she was training to be a nurse. When she graduated, they got married and had five children, so I have a large extended family, cousins all over the place.'

Maia found the story enchanting, but was keen to

ascertain any detail about Shona, and her relationship with Lorraine. 'Pendle is lovely, but you lived in Liverpool when you were married, have I remembered that correctly?'

'Yea, where I went to uni, and based my home there for a while. I was married far too young.' He said no more. They'd have to talk about past relationships another time it seemed.

He pulled her toward him, 'it is so good to be back with you.'

They lounged on the sofa and she felt his excitement match hers.

'Shall we?' he asked.

She looked into his eyes, 'why not?'

They made love and lay in bed most of the afternoon, chatting about a million different things, mostly the Iceland trip, it was great, but time flew by. Later, they wandered along the Quayside, had drinks and chose where to dine. The three days they spent together were glorious. It was so easy to be together, going for walks by the river, a coffee here and there. They ended up having a bar meal on Saturday in a cosy corner of a traditional pub where a band set up to play, it was a perfect evening. Maia took Ben for a drive to show off the beautiful north east coastline too, where they walked along a pristine unspoiled beach off the Northumberland coast.

Maia felt she must inflict Sophia upon him at some point, so he knew what he was getting into with her family, so a Sunday afternoon at Cafe Dalvik was arranged. Sophia was on top form, and wouldn't leave him alone, stating to Nik, 'I could turn you know, with this one.' Giving him fake lascivious looks. They had lots of fun and laughs, interesting conversations, and romance. For Maia, it was perfect, she couldn't be happier.

After a lovely weekend, driving home, Ben wondered when he would feel comfortable telling Maia about his troubling divorce situation. He was worried in case he had misled her … no question … he *had* definitely misled her. Ben was aware he deftly avoided any in-depth conversations about his marriage and divorce proceedings. He hoped Maia hadn't noticed and he felt some guilt for deliberately not going down that route. He would explain the situation definitely the next time they met, not over the phone. Would she trust him once he told her he wasn't legally divorced yet. Maybe he could pressure Shona to sign, so it was done and he wouldn't have to lie.

Ben felt queasy about the situation. He had a brilliant time with Maia, and their relationship was strengthening all the time. He said aloud, 'think I'll ring my little sis and get, The Terrier on board.

21

Newcastle, August 2000

IT WAS THE August summer bank holiday weekend in 2000, the year of the millennium. Jordan was eighteen years old, and he did not want to be here, at the crematorium. He was desperate to be back in the bar, not drinking, but working. After a few destitute years, he had finally got work at a great place, The Water's Edge, a large lively pub on the Quayside. He was really pissed off at having to take a break from work, to stand here paying respects.

Respects, you've got to be kidding, he thought. Jordan couldn't care less about his father's funeral. An older sister had managed to track him down and insisted he attended for their mother's sake. He couldn't wait until it was all over and he could get back to work. A number of his siblings and half siblings were sitting together in the front pews of the crematorium. The oldest sister was sitting next to their mother, who was in a wheelchair. His mother looked completely out of it, she was grey and haggard, not long for this world either, he observed.

Sitting in the last row of seats, Jordan looked on at the

rag-tag small bunch of misfits attending the service. He would make for the door the minute it was over. He wasn't even listening. Nothing good could be said about the rotting carcass lying in the coffin. Good fucking riddance, he thought. Jordan couldn't be bothered with the sycophantic messages from people around him, extolling the false virtues of his violent, alcoholic father.

"Great bloke, had some wild nights," and, *"oh aye, he definitely liked a pint or six, ha ha, was great crack that fella."* These were some comments he heard before the dishevelled congregation entered the building. Jordan stood around a corner out of sight, to deter anyone from starting up a conversation with him. In reality, his dad had gambled and pissed all the family income up the wall so they had no food, heating, or decent clothing. Jordan lived an impoverished, dull, frightening existence as a young child. Some of the younger siblings didn't feel, or witness the full force of that bastard's fists as the father became older and more frail, but Jordan did. He was the eldest boy and the punch-bag, trying to shield the younger ones. His mother did fuck-all to stop it, she hardly could anyway, and bore the main brunt of the assaults.

Jordan was trying to make it on his own, alone. He couldn't wait to get out of there and re-start his shift. He was losing money being here. His hourly rate would be deducted, but as it was a sunny August bank holiday weekend maybe the tips would make up for it. The miserable musical dirge began, and the curtain went around the wooden box being rolled away. The instant the first person began edging out of the seats, he turned and walked out as fast as he could, not before ensuring the eldest sister caught a glimpse of him as proof he'd turned up. He took a last look at the shell of a woman that was his mother; he wouldn't be seeing her again.

It was great to be back on shift at, The Water's Edge, he busied himself getting stuck into serving drinks, zipping all around the pub clearing tables, and taking orders for food. There were some gorgeous women out wearing next to nothing, way out of his league of course, but he could look couldn't he? Jordan knew he had a vulnerability which many women picked up on. He was polite and attentive, so he got a lot of attention in a, cheeky-chappy way. He loved working there.

Out of the corner of his eye, he thought he recognised a bloke at one of the far tables, but couldn't be sure as it was so busy. The music was banging, it was late-afternoon and the alcohol had the punters rocking on their feet, actually rocking from side to side. The cacophony of voices was immense, as everyone sang along to, Robbie Williams' *Rock DJ*, and of course, *Millenium*. Jordan had a keen eye for trouble the millisecond any aggression looked likely. Though small and weedy, Jordan could really handle himself; he had to all his life and would defend anyone. He didn't want work on the doors; why would he want to invite trouble? He'd had enough of violence as a kid. Today, he promised himself, was the last time he would ever really dwell on his childhood, or the violent bastard who was dead.

"*Hey Jordy-baby!*" a bunch of girls who had befriended him were waving cash at the bar to get his attention to serve their drinks.

He winked at the quieter, pretty one with dark hair and shouted, 'okay, you're next.' The women cheered as he handed over bright, colourful, festooned cocktails of all shapes and sizes. The pretty girl smiled right at him, and made his day.

Later, Jordan was collecting glasses and recognised the guy he'd spotted earlier. With a horrible seething ball of anger and nausea gripping his stomach, he realised it was Matty, the guy from Linden House who had abused him. He was dressed in a smart suit, and sat with some other businessmen. As their eyes met, Jordan saw the hint of recognition, but Matthew quickly looked away. Jordan waited until Matthew went to the toilet and though he was terrified, he needed to challenge him, he was so sick and tired of being scared all his life. Jordan walked diagonally towards Matthew knowing they would meet at a quiet area by the stairs leading up to the gents. Matthew wouldn't know he was being followed.

As he approached the stairs, in a fierce, whispered voice, which made Matthew stop and turn, Jordan said, 'I know what you did. I know what you are, you perverted fuck!' said Jordan, trying to hold it together.

Matthew shrugged and acted as though he didn't know Jordan, but before he walked away, his eyes scanned almost 360 degrees around the room, and he leaned in toward Jordan, 'if you say anything, or speak to me ever again, photos of you and that other kid will be all over the internet. In fact, I know Robby the manager here really well. He'd be amazed to see what his bar staff got up to a few years ago. It's amazing what sort of gay porn spam you get in your emails these days.' Matthew paused and said, 'scumbag,' as he walked away, and smiled as if they had exchanged pleasantries.

Jordan was shaken to the core as vivid memories came into his mind. There was a familiar scent of Matthew-breath which made his stomach lurch. It didn't occur to Jordan that should Robby have received that type of email; he may not recognise the boys in the images, and would either delete it, but maybe he'd report it to the police saying he'd received unsolicited child pornography. Jordan couldn't fight the feeling of complete powerlessness, and faded away into the background, as he always did. Memories of his dead father, and his dysfunctional family, the pain of physical abuse, and the humiliation of sexual abuse were all too much. Whilst the world of bouncing, young, vibrant people were socialising and enjoying their lives, Jordan returned to a dark, dank desperate world filled with anxiety and dread.

After his shift, Jordan left without doing his usual look around to make sure everything was clear in case he came across Matthew again. He went back to the digs he shared with a few others; he was on the housing list to move to another area in an attempt to get away from this crowd. He didn't go into the main room where a few were gathered smoking heroin, there was tin foil strewn about the floor. He walked straight by, despite some encouragement to join them. He sat on his bed and started shaking uncontrollably.

The fast, rhythmic banging base music caused ringing noises and light sparks inside his head, and Matthew's sneering face appeared with every flash. Pressure was building in Jordan's brain with a vengeance. He curled up on the bed and pulled the pillow over his head and face, pressing it into his ears to drown out the piercing noise and visions in his mind. Jordan's father may be dead, but it wasn't the death of all his demons. He got up and trudged back into the main room, desperately needing to block out these feelings and rid himself of the memories at any cost.

Jordan lost his job at The Water's Edge a few weeks later. He began turning in late and was fatigued and unkempt when he did turn up. On the fourth time he turned up late for his shift, the manager told him he had lost his job, *"you were a good worker Jordan. Dunno what's going on but I've no capacity for time-wasters here. Three strikes and you're out I'm afraid,"* were the actual words. Jordan fully understood why and was powerless to counter the statement. He was devastated, spiralling his descent further into a reliance upon drugs. Jordan was tracked down by Matthew after he saw him in The Water's Edge. Because of Matthew's far-reaching network, it didn't take too long before he discovered where Jordan lived. Sol, one of Matthew's associates, did a good job in recruitment. It wasn't too challenging, they were all drug or alcohol addicts; they were malleable, and as long as they turned up for runs, they could earn, and get their fix. Sol was persuasive and able to get people to do his bidding. He would've made a great salesman in another career.

Jordan was ripe for the picking, at first he didn't know it was his abuser, Matthew who was the leader in distribution in the area, as he only communicated with his associates Sol and Baz. Jordan only had one conversation with Matthew subsequently, in which Matthew glared through him, saying he still had the Polaroids. Jordan didn't care as long as his addiction was being fed. There were so many times over the years when Jordan tried to free himself. He would destroy his mobile, move to different areas of the city, and once tried a drug rehab scheme, however his vulnerabilities kept drawing him inside Matthew Surtees' destructive network.

Five years later, in 2005, Jordan had been clean for a year, he had successfully returned to working in bars. He was appointed head barman at a small traditional pub on the edge of Newcastle. He was learning the ropes of how to order, and complete stocktaking tasks, also running staff rotas with a view to managing a small bar himself someday. He was reliable and healthy, and had acquired a council flat in a rough, but friendly area to the east of the city, and he shied away from any trouble.

Leaving the bar after a long shift, he cheerfully said to a colleague, 'off out with Chantelle tomorrow, going to take her for a nice meal and all that, you know, treat her like a lady.' Jordan met Chantelle when she took a summer job working at the bar. He was besotted with her. She was studying at college and he worshipped the ground she walked on. She was bright and pretty, and he wondered what on earth she was doing with him.

He noticed a neutral look on his colleague's face. 'Um ... I'm not sure about her Jordan, mate.' His mate didn't look up to face him.

'What does that mean?' Jordan was rightfully defensive.

'Look, I'm just going to say it. I saw her with a lad a couple of weeks ago, didn't think anything of it, then saw them together again ... a few times. They go to that bar over the High Level Bridge, seen them a few times. Really sorry mate, thought I'd better tell you.'

'Well, it might be a college friend or her brother, or something?'

'Definitely not her brother the way they were acting.'

'Nah, she wouldn't do that to me. Prove it.'

'I'm finishing now, have a walk over with me and see if they are there. Would hate to see you get hurt mate, if she is a player. She knows when you're on shift; she's well in with you, and you cover for her when she's late, and do her extra shifts, and the cleaning she's supposed to do ... and ... other stuff.'

The two men walked over the bridge and entered the bar, sure enough Chantelle was sitting with another man who had his arm around her. She was nuzzling into him as he was making her giggle. The vision absolutely broke Jordan. He walked away, knew where to get hold of some decent stuff, took the stuff, went to his bed, and never returned to work. The destructive pattern repeated. Jordan couldn't trust anyone or anything, and was powerless to resist association with Matthew's network again. He defaulted to the old ways, it was the only way he knew how to survive, and get through another day.

22

Newcastle, August 2015

MAIA AND BEN worked out a plan of how, and when they would see each other over the next few months, as Ben was working away much of the time. Maia continued to focus on her work and was expediting tasks for final approved for her Earth Chart report, *Leading the Urban Environment,* having made appointments to visit the designated businesses.

Maia called Pauline regarding the mobile phone Ivy had given her at Edera Cottage, omitting any hint of Craig's suggestions of suspected criminal activity. Maia asked Pauline if she recognised the name JD Pica. Pauline knew no-one of that surname and the only reference she could think of was that JD may refer to their neighbour's son, James Donkin, who Tom often played football with when they were young. After some thought she mentioned a, Jordan, who was the only person apart from Aimee, Tom ever mentioned from his past. Pauline wasn't sure of Jordan's surname, so she offered to contact another carer who Jordan had stayed with temporarily before he moved to Linden House. The name resonated, as Fiona had mentioned Jordan too. Maia had also written about Jordan from Linden House in her journal. The name was becoming significant, but without a surname, it was meaningless.

Pauline said, 'I'd like to see Jordan again if you ever catch up with him. You often wonder how they turn out.' She reminisced about the night Tom turned up, 'like a little waif and stray. It didn't take him long before he put some beef on though, he had quite the appetite!'

She recounted tales from some of the children she and Mike had cared for. They remembered every single one. Aimee definitely stood out in their memories, she had stayed at Linden House for some time too. Maia heard Mike in the background at the mention of Aimee,

'Eh, Aimee Bancroft, like a whirlwind that one! She was here a little while, and Tom knew her from the home. Her attitude will certainly have helped her in life.'

Pauline added, 'what a character, not afraid of anyone or anything. Of course, it was all a front, it always is, they're frightened little chicks inside, no matter how they act out in front of you.'

Pauline rang Maia that evening to confirm Jordan's surname was, Davis and he often worked in bars, in the main, the Corner Tavern on the outskirts of Newcastle city centre. She was also aware he had periods of homelessness and living in hostels, and he was Newcastle United's biggest fan apparently, *"absolutely mad about them,"* in his foster carer's own words. Maia thought, needle in a haystack time, however advised she would keep Pauline updated if she found out anything further.

Maia was wondering whether to bring the whole

business to a close when a flash of inspiration hit her. She grabbed her mobile and began tapping in the letters, p, i, c, a, and with a self-satisfied smile at the results read out, 'Pica pica, is the medieval Latin name for the bird, Magpie.' With a wry smile, she said aloud, 'nice one Tom.' Pica simply had to be Jordan, his friend at Linden House and a Newcastle United fan, The Magpies.

Maia did obvious traces on social media platforms, maybe a guy with the same name, Jordan Davis, of similar age in nearby locations might come up; and she could make sensitive inquiries at the Corner Tavern too. The electoral roll would be no use if Jordan had a transient lifestyle, she doubted he was permanently or temporarily registered anywhere. If he was sofa-surfing, or homeless, and drifting in and out of dwellings, it could be impossible to trace him, but there was no harm in trying.

Maia rang Rosa, explaining what she'd discovered, or 'deduced' in true detective style. 'Fancy a trip to the Corner Tavern for a few beers, whenever you're free?'

'Great work, Vera! You've caught me at a good time, just finished work early and Steve is around,' Maia could hear Rosa's raised voice saying, 'I'm sure my brilliant husband will be more than happy to babysit our darling cherub for a few hours.' She also heard Steve's muffled affirmation in the background.

Rosa added, 'and I need info about the new beau immediately, every squelchy detail.'

'Ok pervy-patsy.' Maia laughed. 'Full disclosure, see you soon.'

They met up at the Corner Tavern within two hours. It

was a warm sunny early, Friday evening on 8 August, with a smattering of clouds in the sky. The pub was a large traditional bar, which was popular with families, and locals for live sports, and basic home cooked meals. The bar area was full of men standing around enjoying a pint. There was a family area which led out to a beer garden and play area. Maia and Rosa took their drinks outside.

The two friends chatted and Maia filled in the detail about Ben.

Rosa commented, 'this chap sounds as though he has something about him, not like the one-dimensional Ryans or Shauns of this world eh?'

'We've rented an apartment to spend some time together in Scotland where he's working, as he has a few days off soon.'

'S'pose there may come a time if you both want to make more permanent arrangements, maybe?' Rosa said hopefully.

'You old romantic, it's early days and maybe things will fall into place over time.'

Rosa clinked her glass to Maia's and said in all seriousness, 'I'm sure it will all work out, he sounds perfect for you.'

After lots of reminiscences and chat, there came a point when Maia decided she would reveal the information about finding the phone and showed Rosa the data on it. Maia had alluded to allegations of abuse at Linden House recently. Rosa had a long career in social care, so none of it would surprise her, and Maia needed someone to share the emotional burden with. Rosa, as expected was in tune with Maia's anxieties about the phone contacts, however remained pragmatic about what could be achieved. She cautiously suggested it would be difficult to find anything out about Jordan, if he was indeed, JD Pica, as he had left care a long time ago.

'There are so many retrospective child abuse allegations. It's horrific to think children suffered at the hands of abusers who were supposed to be keeping them safe, then getting away with it. There's a process for reporting historical incidents, but without Tom being around, and no name of the shitbag ...' Rosa lowered her gaze and with damp eyes, said softly, 'poor Tom.' After a short silence. 'When I'm back in the office, I'll ask if anyone worked at Linden House, or knew anyone who did,' said Rosa.

'That would be great, let me know if anything turns up.'

They scanned the men in the bar when they went through to the toilet, on their mysterious Jordan-watch. They'd no idea what he looked like, but for Pauline's description from years ago. Rosa asked a young glass collector, if he knew someone who worked there, or was there a regular by the name of, Jordan Davis who'd be in his early thirties. The lad said, yes, there was a Jordan, but he was mostly in on Saturday afternoons, as he never missed a Newcastle match. He asked if she wanted to leave a message.

Maia stepped in and said dismissively, 'no, it's okay, he's someone we may know from school, that's all.'

On Saturday 9 August 2015, Newcastle United were playing their first match of the season and there was every chance Jordan would be watching. Maia decided to go back to The

Corner Tavern. She would have to make surreptitious enquiries to identify him, if so, she questioned whether it was right to make actual contact. As she dressed, in jean-shorts, pumps and vest top for the warm weather, Maia did wonder what kept her motivated to carry on enquiring about a possible lost cause. Tom had died, maybe it was a freak accident, he could've been distracted, fallen asleep, or deliberately driven into the wall. Tom was Freya's father, and if there ever came a time no matter how far into the future, she wanted to know about him, Maia would tell the truth. It felt like unfinished business, and she couldn't give up yet while Pauline was relying on her.

Maia arrived at the Corner Tavern, her gaze swept around the packed bar as she headed for the ladies. She recognised Jordan's face immediately! She hadn't realised, but she had actually met Jordan when she was with Tom many years ago, one boring weekend afternoon. They were in the snooker club in Newcastle where young folk would gather as drinks were cheap. Jordan approached their table as they were mid-game. She remembered Tom putting his arms out wide to hug him and introduced Maia. Jordan being painfully shy, simply nodded in her direction.

Maia kept an eye on Jordan from her seat in the lounge where she could see across the dividing hallway into the bar. It was definitely him. There's something unique about the way human beings hold themselves physically, and every little movement or walk is distinctive, and she recognised this in Jordan even though it was years since she'd briefly met him. He appeared gaunt and unkempt, sitting with another man tucked away in a corner who was equally dishevelled. The man must've bought Jordan the drink, Maia assumed, as she didn't see him go to the bar, and had the same drink in front of him the whole time, never taking his eyes from the tv as Newcastle players began their season. She observed the man give Jordan a cigarette at half-time, which he took and headed outside, she followed. Jordan bummed a light from one of the stragglers smoking outside, then he walked to a corner as far away as he could from others in the smoking area.

Maia approached, ensuring no one was within earshot. 'I hope you don't mind me asking, but did you know Tom Cassidy, he was Richardson before that.'

Jordan stepped back, and with narrowed eyes, said 'who wants to know?'

'It's okay, my name is Maia and I went out with Tom when I was sixteen, I'm sure we met you in, The Hustler Club in town years ago.'

'Don't remember,' he mumbled.

'Have you heard what happened to Tom?'

Jordan hung his head, and whispered, 'yes.'

Maia continued, 'it's too awful to think about. Do you remember his foster mam, Pauline, she was asking after you. Is it okay if we have a chat about him sometime?'

Jordan was reluctant but agreed, 'okay, after the match.'

Even though Maia kept one eye on Jordan for the duration of the match, once it finished in a draw against Southampton, there was much activity and when she searched for him, he was gone. She thought wryly he would know every exit and how to leave unseen from the pub. A chance missed. When she was home she read through the notes in her journal.

Tom Cassidy, in his words 13.09.2002

*Jordan stopped talking, he rarely spoke to the workers, only to me and Aimee. He was such a quiet kid, and really skinny, anyway, he got even thinner cos he couldn't eat, sometimes couldn't keep food down. I'd hear him being sick during the night after, you know, we'd sneak his bin to the bathroom and wash out the vomit, so he wouldn't get into trouble. We were terrified when **that** name was on the duty rota. We'd play footy outside or hide in the nearby woods all day. You don't really understand what's happening when you're young, it's confusing and I was petrified. Me and Jordan suffered the same, so we stuck together like glue on the nights he was on duty. We knew it would happen. It was good we had each other. Sometimes one of us would burst into tears when we played in each other's room when no-one was around. I would put my arm around Jordan, but he hated anyone touching him, even me. We'd play on my Game Boy or watch telly and try not to think about it, until the next time.*

I saw Jordan in the city not long ago when he was working as a glass collector in a bar. What a state, poor soul, he'd taken to drugs and was knocking about with some real crackerjacks. I tried to keep in touch, but he keeps moving around. But when we do meet, we always hug, we always have, really massive hugs.

23

JORDAN HAD SNEAKED away from The Corner Tavern before the match ended, to avoid that lass asking him questions. He made his way back to the disgusting accommodation where he had been placed recently, and wondered if his meagre belongings were still there. Not that he cared, he owned very little, and what he had was crap. So if anyone had rummaged through his stuff, they'd gain nothing. What did that lass want anyway, summit about Tom Richardson from the care home, and Pauline ... whatever ... it was nowt to do with him.

Jordan drifted into memories of his friend Tom, the one person he would love to see again. Tom made a point of trying to keep in touch with him over the years, and tears dripped as he recognised he didn't appreciate Tom as much as he should have. In recent years they had lost touch, only meeting occasionally when Jordan was off the stuff. He never wanted Tom to see him when he was in a state. It was always great to see his face, but now he was dead, and he'd never see his face, or hear his voice again. Jordan was devastated by the loss of the only person he trusted since he was a young boy at Linden House. A wrecking ball smashed him into a thousand pieces when he heard the news.

He recalled the last time he saw Tom about a year ago, in the autumn of 2014, and couldn't help but smile at the memory. Tom had contacted him and told him where and when to meet. They were enjoying a pint together in what was their favourite bar, *Reds*, on the Quayside. Tom had come straight from work, wearing his countryside ranger polo shirt, cargo pants, and walking boots carrying a small rucksack. The sun-bleached hair, and strong tanned arms, all a sign of his outdoor occupation. They stood at the bar soaking in the traditional feel of the seventeenth century building with its stone walls and low beamed ceilings. This was one of the better times. Jordan was trying to get clean again, and Tom was happy in his life with work, and with his partner Fiona.

Jordan was facing the entrance of the bar when a face he recognised appeared. Surprised, even shocked to see him, as this wasn't the sort of bar he would usually frequent. The face of Matthew Surtees had entered his world, again. Their eyes met and Matthew headed towards him, looking disgruntled. Jordan knew it was because he had refused to do any more drug runs for him.

Jordan saw Tom look around, he must've noticed the startled look on his own face. Tom froze, pint in hand. It seemed a million thoughts collided, as Tom instantly recognised, and was horrified by, the face he saw approaching. Matthew Surtees glared at Jordan, then at Tom. Tom was incensed by the vision of the man who had abused them when they were terrified young boys in the children's home. Matthew had exploited both of them later in their vulnerable teenage years too, when they engaged in drug-running. Jordan was the main culprit, and would enlist Tom's help to do some deliveries as Tom had his own transport, in the form of a motorbike at that time. They made good money and had a constant supply of drugs. Tom had broken away from the activity when he gained employment as a countryside ranger, and had been clean ever since. For Jordan it was more difficult.

Jordan recalled that Tom stormed towards Matthew who backed away. As they were in a public place there was little Tom could do. He threatened Matthew under his breath, 'if you ever go anywhere near him again,' pointing at Jordan, 'your life will not be worth living.'

Matthew cowered as Tom leaned over him, he had grown into a physically powerful man. Matthew was deeply pissed off, Jordan had been a useful part of his drug-running group on and off for many years. He responded defiantly, 'you can't stop people earning a living.'

'He doesn't want to do it anymore, and if I see you around him ever again, I will kill you.'

'That's a serious threat.'

'I mean it.'

'You better watch your back ... Ranger.' Matthew sneered. 'You have no idea who you're talking to.'

Tom turned on Matthew and almost spat in his face, 'I know *exactly* who I'm talking to, you perverted piece of shit!'

At this point everyone in the place turned their attention towards the two men as the volume had increased. The barman was alerted to the fact he may have to intervene if a fight broke out, and made his way toward the two men.

Tom suggested they spoke outside, but Matthew refused to leave the bar, referring to him and Jordan as, *"scrotes who are not worth bothering with."* Matthew attempted to walk by Tom, knowing he had some protection as long as he remained in the public bar. It seemed Tom felt years of suppressed anger, fear, pain and stress build-up inside from his feet right up to his head, which he couldn't contain any longer. He looked at Jordan who sensed the valve on the pressure cooker was about to release.

'No! Tom, he's not worth—'

Tom punched Matthew hard in the face, before Jordan finished his sentence, imploring Tom not to fight in case he lost his job. Matthew stumbled backwards, arms flailing, off balance, and ended up sprawled flat on his back. There was an audible crack as his head hit the stone flagged floor. Tom nodded to Jordan, then towards the door and they left. Within seconds, Jordan walked back into the bar. Matthew raised his arms to cover his face and head, fearing another assault. Jordan stepped over him to pick up the hoody he'd left behind. He turned and grinned at the sight of Matthew sitting on the floor, propped up against the bar with the barman bending over to help him up.

A sniggering Jordan met Tom outside. Tom said, *"I've a good mind to go to the police about that disgusting nonce!"* then saw Jordan's face, *"I know mate, it could incriminate us in his dodgy dealings and I could lose my job over that piece of shit, but he keeps getting away with stuff, makes me so bloody angry!"*

Jordan was pleased Tom was doing well and had successfully distanced himself from the, Celt Run as they named the deliveries to Scotland; but it was only a few months since he had been involved with Surtees and his associates, and so, would be incriminated if Tom went to the police.

Jordan hated the fact Tom was witness to what Jordan felt was his failure, his weakness, his shame, his addiction. He recalled Tom patting the corporate emblem on his work t-shirt stating, *"if it wasn't for getting this job I may not be here. Totally lost my shit for that year when I was younger. Honestly mate, you need to stay free of that pond life. Let me know anytime you need anything ... anything at all. If he ever contacts you again, I'll be there ... okay?"*

Jordan nodded, then smiled at his last memory of Tom and repeated what he said then, in total admiration, 'that ... Tom .... was the best single-punch KO I've ever seen in my life.'

Tom had laughed, shrugged his shoulders mimicking the style of a boxer ready to fight at the sound of the bell, and nodded. *"Have to say, it felt great sinking my fist into that pervert's podgy face!"*

The two men, with their unbreakable bond of shared history, grinned broadly to each other. They clasped each other close in a strong, prolonged embrace, to the consternation of some curious passers-by.

As they parted, Tom turned and with his distinctive grin that could light up any room said, *"watch what you're doing kidda, see you soon."* He winked and walked away.

This last, clear-as-daylight memory, had Jordan's face soaked with tears and his nose was streaming as he shook from emotion. As he wiped away the warm salty liquid from his face, he desperately needed to get away from the unbearable pain of loss and guilt. He sharply changed direction and headed toward a place, where he knew he could obtain those chemical inducements that ceased the thoughts, and diminished the pain, at least temporarily.

Back in, Reds a customer had retrieved Matthew Surtees' discarded spectacles from under their table and handed them to him. Matthew put them on, however the force of the blow had bent the bridge of the titanium frames, so one of the lenses remained at a jaunty angle to its twin. Matthew became aware there was a large group of young men in the corner enjoying an early evening drink, and the unexpected entertainment. They couldn't help but laugh at the vision of the bloodied, tubby bespectacled man slumped on the floor, who had been completely humiliated and overpowered from the assault.

The barman suggested he called the police and they could give a description of the man who punched him, as he recognised Jordan came into the bar frequently. However, Matthew realised if there was any involvement from the police, it was likely Tom would bring up narcotic involvement, so he declined. He didn't want any interventions into that element of his lifestyle.

Gayle appeared in the doorway, still glowing from the prolonged eye contact she had with the rugged, outdoorsy, hot-as-hell guy outside the bar. She spotted Matthew, and her whole being slumped, he was sitting with his elbows on a table, propping his head up with a large wad of bloodied napkins pressed against his nose. Gayle couldn't help but suppress a smile, which attracted the attention of the young men in the corner, who recognised the look on her face. There were more low-level laughs, along with admiring glances at the gorgeous young woman trying to show sympathy towards Matthew, asking what had happened? However, she guessed he had been obnoxious and rude to someone, and probably deserved a punch in the face.

As they left without buying a drink, Matthew heard one lad suggest, 'she's got to be his daughter, either that or he's loaded.'

Matthew's recovering brain was full of seething revenge, he'd get that fucking ranger if it was the last thing he did.

24

FOLLOWING THE ASSAULT on Matthew, Gayle knew she would have to soothe his incandescence. They'd gone home from, Reds Bar, and she tended to his injury. His nose wasn't broken, but it took a while before the burst blood vessels stopped producing fluid. She gave Matthew an ice pack to hold against his swollen lip and nose. He said his neck was hurting too, probably whiplash she thought. The bruising wouldn't come out until the next day. Fortunately his glasses had reduced the impact of the punch, and she had to stifle a giggle as she gently bent the frame of his glasses back into place from the jaunty angle.

Gayle had seen Matthew like this previously when things didn't go his way. The overgrown, spoilt, man-baby would throw things around and spout about all the wrongdoings everyone had done to him in the past. It all came out, the same gripes again and again. She knew he wanted revenge, and would manipulate a situation to exert power over her until he was satisfied he was the boss again. Once he had calmed he advised, 'I've invited Michaela, Frank, Allan and

Evie over tonight. Drinks first then some supper, let's make a real night of it.'

Gayle was annoyed he hadn't consulted with her at all, but delighted, as these were the only people she saw other than Matthew.

'Great, shall I prepare a lovely supper?' Gayle really enjoyed having company over, she was a great cook, often bored since finishing her job, and loved trying new recipes, however nothing seemed to impress Matthew.

'Nah, we'll just do takeaway. I'll order a load of stuff from that posh new Asian Fusion place. Think that will impress them, and I'll get some decent fizz to, not that cheap crap you drink.'

'Nothing wrong with it, it's fine.'

'Asda's special range, eh?' He teased.

Gayle was disappointed not to have the opportunity to provide her guests with a meal. She imagined chatting in the immense kitchen with a glass of wine with the girls, as she busied prepping and cooking, however it was another of Matthew's foibles, he loved showing off with extravagance, posh drinks and food, with her dutifully at his side.

The couples were invited to meet at the local cocktail bar, then back to the apartment for supper, movies, and for the boys, to play on console games. They had an entertaining evening at the bar, everyone was in good spirits and the drinks flowed frequently. When they returned to the apartment, Gayle noticed Matthew ensured a lot more potent alcohol was consumed, constantly topping up drinks and bringing new and exotic bottles of liquors into the mix.

The women decided to have a sing and dance, having

turned the music volume way up in the expansive front room, whilst Matthew took the boys up to the TV room to play games. Gayle recalls the women listening to Ed Sheeran, Katy Perry, Calvin Harris and repeated renderings of Pharrell Williams, 'Happy,' which they danced around the room to, and sang at the top of their lungs, *"because I'm happy, clap along if you feel like a room without a roof, because I'm happy, clap along if you feel like happiness is the truth,"* and Gayle was happy, very happy when the girls were around. After a while, Matthew appeared at the doorway encouraging the women to go upstairs. They staggered and rolled on the way up to the TV room. On reaching the attic they realised the guys had been otherwise entertained.

'Thought you were playing games up here, not watching porn!' said Evie, as she dropped into her husband Allan's lap.

'Just getting into the mood for later.' Allan ran his hand up in between Evie's legs.

Matthew produced small vials of amyl nitrate, a complete surprise to Gayle.

'Poppers!' Allan exclaimed, 'christ, I haven't had those since the nineties.' He took hold of the small glass bottle and snapped the top, offering Evie the first inhalation.

'Oh my God!' She reeled backwards as her blood vessels relaxed, rushing the supply of blood and oxygen to her heart producing a euphoric sensation.

'Good stuff eh?' said Matthew. He continued his lascivious dialogue encouraging them to reveal their innermost sexual desires and what they had not dared to try before. He initiated a strip game, whilst erotic images flickered across the huge screen in the TV room. He enthusiastically suggested swapping partners. There was little resistance, as judgement was impaired from enormous quantities of consumed alcohol and narcotics. The couples engaged with the momentum of swapping partners in different rooms throughout the night, trying out various positions and techniques, before falling asleep with their respective partners.

In shame and silence Michaela and Frank left the house without a word, early the following morning. It seemed Allan and Evie had already left. They severed contact with Matthew and Gayle. Gayle sent a few apologetic voicemails to Michaela, sounding frail, shaky, and full of remorse. Gayle knew little of the depths her partner, the congenial Matthew, was capable of, and now it was becoming clearer to her. She realised he had perfected the art of breaking down defences, using coercion and expertly tapping into basic unfettered and impulsive human desires.

Corfu 1999

It was a bleaching hot morning in Benitses, Corfu, when Kostas, the owner of the Casa Nostra bar headed up to the mezzanine terrace, shocked to see a young bar worker lying on the floor dazed, and naked but for some torn blood-stained shorts. He asked the young woman gently, 'what happened?' she was not much more than a girl. Kostas couldn't understand, he'd left his bar manager and this capable young bar worker in charge the previous evening. Kostas attended to the girl and comforted her as she cried and began to explain. She was seduced by a British tourist, 'we got along fine at first, and I agreed to have sex, he seemed really nice, very gentle but ... it turned violent and he ...' the young girl cried and cried as Kostas realised she'd been viciously raped.

Following medical attention, the young woman was too ashamed to report the incident to the police, and Kostas was reluctant to advertise the incident officially, and give his bar a bad reputation. Though he did warn his fellow bar owners to be vigilant about the description the girl offered. Kostas did not see her again, believing she left the island.

By the time Kostas had discovered the girl, an English man had taken a taxi to board the earliest available ferry or flight to the next resort smiling to himself. The genial, polite, bespectacled, twenty-four-year-old tourist was never stopped to have his luggage searched. No one suspected he was the culprit of the reports from young women, and men who had been drugged into sexual compliance, and on a few occasions raped when they resisted.

25

AS THE LEAD with Jordan was severed, Maia decided to try one last shot, then she was giving the whole thing up for good, it was pointless. If she felt she had done everything possible to try and find out anything she could that may provide the remotest link to Tom's past and his death, she would be satisfied. She rang Pauline and explained about Jordan's elusive actions, and asked if she knew what happened to fourteen-year-old Aimee after she left her respite foster placement, this was the only other person Maia could link with Tom's past. Pauline had only the vaguest of notions, she may have moved out of the area. Mike recalled her surname was, Bancroft.

Maia half-heartedly decided to make initial enquiries about Aimee, from the information Pauline had offered. She traced a likely selection of, *Aimee Bancrofts*, on Facebook around the mid-thirties age group, as she would be now. There was a profile of an Aimee Bancroft-Dara, and the distinct spelling of her first name and reference to a possible maiden name was enough to take the chance. Maia sent a private message to her via Facebook. She had nothing to lose, but didn't have much hope that Aimee would get in touch, if indeed it was her.

Maia had forgotten about making contact, when out of the blue, Aimee responded several days later with a short message asking directly, who was contacting her, and why were they asking if she knew children from a care home years ago. Maia responded.

Thank you so much for taking the time to reply Aimee. I knew Tom really well when he came to live with Pauline and Mike Cassidy. I am very sorry to tell you Tom died recently. I'm trying to find out as much information as I can from anyone who knew him at Linden House, which may lead to information about his death. It will also help the Cassidys try to come to terms with losing their son. If you have any information, or memories you feel you could share, I would be so grateful, and will pass them on to Pauline and Mike.

Maia hoped the subterfuge of emotional blackmail would work to get to the information she really wanted about the abuser, but there was no further response from Aimee.

Days later, Maia received a message from Rosa, advising there was a reunion of former staff at Linden House who met every year on the date it was closed down. One of her colleagues knew some of the workers and identified, Catherine Morris, who worked there in the nineties. It was believed she now worked as an independent social worker, acting as a Guardian ad Litem in family court proceedings. Rosa suggested Catherine could possibly be contacted via the court offices or may have a professional profile; it was a potential link at least. Following internet searches, Maia found a Catherine Morris on the staff list for Northumberland University where she currently lectured.

It was the beginning of September when Maia rang the university Social Science Department, and staff were preparing for new student cohorts. She left a message on Catherine's voicemail. Catherine called her back the following morning. More subterfuge as Maia explained the circumstances of why she was making contact; she would greatly appreciate any information Catherine may recall about a young boy, Tom Richardson, who stayed briefly at Linden House. She explained he died recently and she was trying to collate some personal testimonies and memories for his parents Pauline and Mike Cassidy.

Cath's ex-smoker rasp responded, 'oh, that's dreadfully sad, the name does ring a bell, but I can't recall Tom right now. Some children stayed at Linden on a quick turnaround for assessment only. I do remember Mike and Pauline well, lovely people, she was a brilliant foster parent, one of the very best.' Cath invited Maia to her office the following week for a chat as she was happy to help if she could, asking her to bring some identification.

Maia arrived at the university building, and was guided by a receptionist to a small windowless room with four, navy upholstered lounge chairs, and a large square low table in between. Catherine entered the room with a tray and two drinks, with milk and sugar in separate pots.

'Hello Maia isn't it? Please, call me Cath. Do help yourself. I took a chance and made coffees, I'm always gagging for a mid-morning caffeine hit.' She smiled and placed the tray on the table. Cath was a striking, bright woman with quite a forceful, direct approach. She wore floral-rimmed glasses, a flowing dark top to cover her ample body with a quirky ornate brooch in the shape of a tree of life pinned to one side. Her hair was cropped, she wore large square silver earrings, and luminous fuchsia lipstick. Cath lowered herself to sit, then just as her backside hit the seat, she shot up without warning, flung one arm wide, fingers spread and the other dramatically slapped to her forehead, as if she was stopping time. It quite startled Maia!

Revelation showed in Cath's face. 'Nearly forgot! I had a dig around my old papers, and found some photos.' She marched out of the room and returned in a flurry with a large brown envelope. 'We were given some personal documents when Linden House closed down and all the children's official records were sent to the archives. I've meant to pass these on, but time goes by, and, you know ... I think Linden House is converted into flats or a business centre or something now.' She poured the envelope contents onto the table, 'I read about Tom's death after you called, terrible accident, it must be so devastating for Pauline and Mike. Such lovely people.'

Maia had hardly spoken, and had poured milk in her coffee while Cath was out of the room. 'Do you want to see my ID?' Maia held it out.

Cath glanced a Maia's official UK Press Card ID. 'Oh bloody hell aye, forgot about that. This isn't for the papers is it? This is confidential stuff about little ones' information.'

Maia noticed a change in Cath's demeanour, she defensively reached across the table as if she was going to pile all the papers back in the envelope. Maia understood, personal information needed to be protected as well as everything else.

'Absolutely not, I'm not here in any professional capacity, purely on behalf of Pauline ... I was Tom's teenage girlfriend and The Cassidys were our neighbours. So, no everything will remain confidential, promise.

Cath softened. There were greetings cards, letters, and what looked like old notices which may have been pinned to a board, also polaroid photos of staff and children from her time at the home. She riffled through, holding odd items up explaining what they were as she reminisced, and that she hadn't been through the stuff for ages. She found a snapshot of two little boys grinning together, Tom with his arm around Jordan. Maia was quite taken aback when she saw Tom. He was a weedy, pale, timid-looking little boy with an empty smile on his face, who she hardly recognised. Though she could see the boyhood face of the man she knew and loved.

'I do remember his little face. You got me thinking about the place and all the children,' Cath stopped and sighed, 'he wasn't there long at all. Tom and Jordan were inseparable.'

Maia knew exactly why.

'There was plenty of fresh air and space for the children to run wild, which they needed.' Cath fell quiet and drifted into a reverie with a slight frown. She picked out a few photos; a clear image showed a group of seven children including Tom, Jordan and Aimee standing outside the home.

Cath clicked her tongue as she recalled Aimee Bancroft,

'she caused us loads of bother, quite rightly, she had a lot in her life to be angry about, and she would take the little ones under her wing.'

There was something written on the back of the group photo in faded blue felt pen; *Summer 95. Matty S, Cath M, Jane P*, then a list of the children's names. Cath peered at the photo.

'Ah, Jane was lovely, my co-worker. It's awful but she died of breast cancer recently, poor soul, only fifty two. Hm ... and Matty S, was it Matthew Sumner or Sturridge or Surtees ... whatever?' Cath's expression changed, 'he was casual summer staff ... completely useless! Totally disinterested in the children's needs; a quiet type, and a bit arrogant if I'm honest. None of the children took to him. He would've instigated taking these photos I'd imagine, though we sometimes did have staff pictures taken with the kids. He had a camera of his own, seemed to have some interest in photography,' Cath vaguely recalled, 'I was glad to see the back of him, bloody useless lump he was.'

Maia took a punt, to ascertain if there were any allegations about Linden House. Cath's eyes widened as she sprang to life questioning why? Maia explained Tom told her many years ago he was abused there. Cath wasn't aware of any investigations while she was there. She worked part-time, was a single parent with little ones herself, and generally worked day shifts with some evening duty.

'Oh no, that's terrible,' she looked sympathetically at Maia, 'if you know anything, you should report it to social services, or the police non-recent abuse team may well be interested? If there's someone still out there who is a risk to children, they should be stopped.'

Maia replied Tom would never say who it was.

Cath nodded her head sadly, looking at the image of Tom and Jordan. 'Those little boys should never have been placed there. It was often the luck of the draw where children were placed with limited foster carer availability. Though Tom was lucky to have lived with the Cassidy family that's for sure.'

Maia explained Pauline and Mike had legal Guardianship for Tom and he changed his name to Cassidy.

'Good for him. I'm glad he ended up with some love and light in his life.'

Cath handed the few photos over of Tom to give to Pauline and Mike, 'please do give my best wishes to them both, if they remember me. I always felt good about placing children with them knowing it was a safe home ... Ah, I'm so sorry about Tom.'

Maia agreed to pass on Cath's good wishes, thanked her for the information and photos and left. She felt terrible for those two little lost souls in the photographs. It made her more determined to find out what she could about Matty S in particular, there something about how Cath described him, she found it unsettling and the dates he worked there tied-in with dates for Tom's placement.

26

JORDAN THOUGHT A lot about Tom since he saw the woman in the pub asking about him a month ago. He was back into his cycle of dossing, getting money where he could to buy stuff and was homeless again. He'd been kicked out of the place he'd lived in for the last year or so, and had nowhere to go. One of his sisters came across him on the streets, but he couldn't bear to have anything to do with his dysfunctional aggressive family, always yelling and fighting. Jordan hadn't ever fully recovered and his will to survive was disintegrating. His descent into drug dependence was constantly repeating.

Slumped against a wall under the Swing Bridge, Jordan felt hungry, but he wasn't sure if it was actually hunger, his stomach ached most of the time, and he felt nauseous. The headaches were worse today. Relentless. He'd lost his balance on a couple of occasions feeling dizzy and disorientated. His malnourished legs could hardly hold his weight. He could hear his pulse pounding in his head, which matched the rapid drumming sensation of his heart against his ribs. The attacks were becoming more intense, more frequent and frightening.

He had to use both hands to drink, eat and smoke, to try and steady the tremors these days. The only time Jordan was at peace was when he was asleep, as long as it was a peaceful, narcotic induced sleep, without the nightmarish terrors that often beset him lying awake in the darkness. Every time he slid into that peace; he never considered the terrifying experience of waking.

Jordan had to get up, and go. He wanted to run away, anywhere away from here, but couldn't. Him and his fellow homeless would be moved on again soon. He stood, shaking and rolled up the sleeping bag he'd stolen last week from the doss-house. He'd taken a severe beating last night, that's why he left, but couldn't even remember what for. He couldn't go back there now. He ached all over.

Jordan trudged west along the riverside to shelter in bushes, before the offices on the Business Park became visible ahead. Trees lined the wide pathway, there was always somewhere to hide. Cyclists and walkers passed by, many giving him a wide berth, or hurrying their footsteps to create distance, and those with children guided them along shielding their view of him. At first he found it humorous that he had such a repelling effect upon other humans, but now he couldn't give a shit, and hardly noticed them.

He settled in some bushes, trying to find a soft bit of earth, always equidistant between benches where working folk would emerge from nearby offices to sit and have a sandwich or a natter. He knew they wouldn't want him anywhere near. He slid his legs into the sleeping bag. The thin fabric was stained and it smelled of the former owner's stale urine. Jordan was so cold, his blood felt frozen in his veins. He pulled the flimsy covering over his chest. He was fortunate to have been donated a thick padded coat from, Family Market, a local charitable agency, which had virtually saved his life. He could sell it, or swap it if he needed to, but it was also insurance for his next fix.

Cooler September days were more frequent along Newcastle's riverside. Jordan was hungry, starving in fact, he couldn't recall his last meal, and needed to go to Family Market, at least he would be warm and fed there. Always soup and a bread roll, but it was at the other side of the city in the east, and he didn't have the energy to get up and walk. Maybe tomorrow. He wondered what was the point of anything, and drifted off to sleep.

On waking, he huddled his face into the foul smelling sleeping bag, defence against one of those random anticyclones that brought freezing Siberian winds from the east, over Northern Europe. The plummeting wind chill temperature was whipping down the river with a force that made his eyes sting. He closed them against the icy blast, he just wanted to be warm, and sleep. He wanted this feeling to end, to end now, he couldn't bear this life any longer. Jordan looked at the steely grey-blue of the river and inhaled the gritty-mud smell from the river bank. He wondered how cold it would feel and how long it would take before he drifted under the water, and whether drowning would be painful. The thought of choking for air as water flooded his lungs prevented him from doing so. He glanced up at High Bridge, some forty metres above the river and thought, you wouldn't feel much when your body slammed into the water, it would be quick at least. He managed to doze on and off curled up through the night under the trees. He woke the following morning and made his way back east, to the refuge under the arch of the Swing Bridge, and the little warmth of the city, hoping someone may drop a few coins his way, or offer some food or drink.

He dropped off to sleep again resting against the and was disturbed by someone saying his name quite loudly. 'Jordan ... Jordan, are you okay?' He was snapped out of this reverie by the voice repeating his name. He turned and looked at the blurred vision of a woman. He tried to focus and look into the face staring directly at him. A woman with dark hair, wearing running gear had stopped in front of him. She had kind, soft brown eyes. She kept repeating his name, but who was she?

27

MUCH TO MAIA'S surprise, Aimee Bancroft-Dara replied further to her private Facebook message, asking for memories about Tom and Jordan from Linden House. Aimee's reply was brief, indicating she couldn't remember much and doesn't dwell on her past, but did remember Tom from Linden. Aimee suggested he was a quiet boy and seemed much happier placed with Pauline and Mike, than in the children's home, and he liked pizza nights at the home. She also remembered his friend Jordan describing him as, *a silent little lad who used to follow me around all over the place.*

Maia was thrilled to have a response, she looked through Aimee's social media profiles. Aimee had been quite the athlete, running middle distances for the county. There were images of her with a variety of medals around her neck from competitive races when she looked around late teens to early twenties. Aimee, it appeared was still heavily into an athletic lifestyle, posting images and workouts from what was her fitness studio in Leicester. She was a glamorous woman who may have accessed cosmetic enhancements, or maybe it was photoshopping; or maybe not, and she was simply a naturally stunning woman. Aimee promised, the next time she was up North, she'd get in touch, and sent her regards to Pauline and Mike who she'd been on respite placements with briefly. Though Maia was pleased, she remained doubtful about this intention, Aimee was probably simply being polite. Maia had, at least, achieved some contact, whether it would lead to any development in her search, was doubtful.

Maia prepared for her run; she often ran along the riverside not far from her apartments and would notice the batches of homeless people under the graffiti emblazoned arches of the bridges she passed. Sometimes she'd buy a couple of hot chocolate drinks and a warm pasty or bacon roll, which she would place beside the rag-tag bodies under the bridges. As she was running by the shabby humans sheltering under the arches, she recognised a familiar face. She couldn't be sure and didn't want to stop and stare.

She'd often pass a woman running in the opposite direction, whom Maia named Iceni Queen Boudicca. She internally repeated each syllable with her every step to the beat in her EarPods; Iceni Queen Boudicca … Iceni Queen Boudicca … Iceni Queen Boudicca … until they passed each other.

Boudicca, with her cropped flame-red, spiked hair and lined face looked battle-scarred and worn, yet tough as nails. Was she an ex-servicewoman, a war-veteran? Maia wondered. The prosthetic lower-leg running blade gave testament to this perhaps, or maybe it was a result of disease or accident. Boudicca's heavily tattooed torso led Maia to wonder about breast cancer too, as scarlet roses entwined across her chest, upper arms and back, which were revealed during runs in the summer months. Maia had eventually cut through the steely determined gaze of Iceni Royalty as they passed. She felt privileged at the first imperceptible nod of acknowledgement as their eyes met briefly. Every time Maia saw her, she felt she should kneel at Boudicca's feet, and give thanks for her survival from whatever trauma that caused her injury.

The next day Maia took the same route. It was an unusually bitter cold day as she ran alongside the grey-brown river which rippled restlessly. No bright blue water or sparkling reflective sunlight today. The freezing wind bit into the exposed flesh of her face. She paid reverence to Iceni Queen Boudicca as they passed each other, was that another imperceptible nod of royal acknowledgement she hoped. Maia slowed her pace under the sheltered area of the arches, and saw the familiar features of someone she recognised amongst the group of ghostly faces as she approached. The familiar ghost was dishevelled and hunched over in a filthy sleeping bag. She stopped and spoke his name, 'Jordan,' then a little louder, 'Jordan.'

Maia could see his confusion and concern, quickly she identified herself, 'it's Tom's friend, we met at the Corner Tavern a few weeks ago.'

He nodded, and seemed to recognise her.

'I'll get you a warm drink, you look freezing.'

Maia couldn't comprehend the difference in Jordan in only a few weeks, his face was almost skeletal. She returned fifteen minutes later; thankful he was still there.

She brought a large warm baguette crammed with fillings, a brownie and two hot chocolate drinks. She encouraged him to drink the warm liquid, which he did very slowly. He was reluctant to engage with her, although grateful for the warm food which he nibbled. Maia asked if she could sit with him, he didn't respond, she crouched down tucking her knees into the crooks of her elbows. It was a little more sheltered and she was fortunately still warm from running, having the sense to wear her bodywarmer, beanie and gloves. It was difficult to start a conversation with Jordan. She drank her hot chocolate as they sat in silence for a long interval. It took ages for Jordan to eat half of the baguette and one brownie. His hands were constantly shaking.

Maia began a conversation, mentioning she had made contact with Aimee, which seemed to interest Jordan, and he responded with a faint smile. 'She was older than us and really brave. She would argue with the workers and stick up for the younger ones in the home. A real handful for 'em.'

'She's agreed to meet me to talk about Tom. Would you like to see her?'

Jordan said, no ... then, yes, but would need to clean up his act first. He held his head in his hands, then made eye contact with Maia for the first time. Jordan's pale blue eyes, looked dry and soulless sinking into the sockets. His gaunt grey face reminded her of an Edvard Munch painting, *The Scream*. Maia felt his resistance to hear, to see, to feel ... anything. The need to block everything out and stop his internal screaming. Maia had recognised it in Tom's face when he was lost inside himself.

Jordan looked ten years older than his thirty three years; his hair was thinning, he smelled awful, his stubble was growing in grey, and he had lost some teeth. It was pitiful. In that moment, Maia appreciated her privileged upbringing and questioned how can this happen to human beings in the twenty first century? Jordan had not made this his life choice. She sat in silence as close as she felt he was comfortable. There was no pressure.

'You don't have to sit here, you can go, don't feel bad, it's just the way it is for me.'

'What would you want to happen Jordan if things could change right now.'

'A shower and a clean, warm dry bed.'

'Okay, you can come to my place to warm up. I'll help you get sorted if it's what you want?'

'Nah, you can't do that.' He shook his head.

'Please Jordan,' she implored, 'I couldn't help Tom, I wasn't there for him, he would want me to treat you the same as if he was here.'

They sat in silence for some minutes.

Jordan said, 'there's a place not far which I've stayed in before, it's a bit of a nightmare, you get robbed and beaten up for your stuff, but ...' he said weakly gesturing to the pathetic sleeping bag.'

'C'mon show me where it is.' Maia made a move to get going, it was freezing.

Jordan gathered his belongings and bundled everything in a carrier bag. He stood, hunched and winced against the force of the icy blast, drawing his coat around him. It would've gone around twice. Maia walked alongside him, it was slow progress. She had an idea, she always had a small wallet with a ten pound note and credit card in the zip pocket of her running jacket. Maia stopped at the entrance to the basic Lo-Motel they were passing. Jordan looked confused. She encouraged him to follow her inside, and checked him in for the night using her credit card.

'I'll meet you tomorrow for breakfast. Don't disappear on me again,' she tried to catch his eye, 'Jordan, please.'

He nodded his head to affirm.

She left him in the foyer, 'I'll be here for 10 am to give you time for a good night's kip and a sort out.'

As she walked away. She heard him say, 'thanks', but when she went to acknowledge him, he had turned his back, room key-card in his hand, waiting by the lift.

Maia was exhausted when she got home. It had been a very emotional day, she took out her journal to make some notes and came across Tom's words about Aimee.

Tom Cassidy, in his words 13.09.2002

I remember Aimee stayed on respite at Pauline's once, after I'd been there a while. She was like a tornado, so bloody loud. I liked her she was good fun and, fearless. Yeh, Aimee shook things up, you know, especially at Linden House, the staff were scared of her I think. She could run rings around them. I remember she was having an argument with one of the workers, and they asked something about why she acted like she did as they were only trying to help. So Aimee said, the only good social worker is a dead one. That shut them up. She came across as really angry all the time, always picking a fight with them, but she had a quiet, nice side. She definitely looked out for us younger ones, wish I'd told her then about me and Jordan, she'd probably have kicked up a right fuss and told everyone about it. Then it might have stopped.

28

MAIA MET WITH Jordan the next morning and, she was pleased to note, he looked more human than the two-dimensional painting he reminded her of the previous day. He'd obviously made use of the shower and free toiletries. They sat in a nearby cheap pub, Jordan ordered a massive breakfast and loaded up on refillable coffees, with four sugars in each mug. He thanked Maia for paying for the room, and began to reveal more about his past after he was full of sausages, bacon, eggs, hash browns, the lot, plus three refillable mugs of coffee.

'Dad died of alcoholism, and he was a violent bastard, so I didn't care. Mam is in a nursing home with dementia, probably from him knocking her about. I went to see her once, but she doesn't really know who I am. I've lost touch with my brothers and sisters, we were all separated in care, so I don't really know them.'

Maia didn't say much, just allowed Jordan to continue, 'there were times I was deein' alreet, even made head barman once and could afford t' gan t' the match once in a while.' He stopped speaking and continued eating.

Maia asked if he knew who, Pica or Cuntrylad were. Jordan froze with his fork halfway to his mouth, and smiled, then a flicker of fear ran across his eyes. Maia explained she'd found a phone, and reassured him there was nothing incriminating on it, and the police didn't know about it. She simply wanted answers.

'Me and Tom used to go birdwatching at the kids' home, it was surrounded by trees and we found an old ripped nature book with all the proper names in for birds, in Latin or summat I think. So when we were running, we gave each other nick-names to make contact. He named me Pica ... Magpie, me being a massive Newcastle fan. I couldn't think of anything clever, so Cuntrylad was just a joke name I thought of.' Jordan told Maia about the drugs runs he and Tom were involved with, Tom only briefly, before he turned his back on it all. In a low voice Jordan confessed, 'I am a user Maia ... an addict,' he hung his head, 'I needed the money and the drugs.'

'But Tom didn't, he was working, he could get money if he needed it from Pauline I'm sure of that?' Maia said quizzically.

'It was before he got the ranger job, and he was knocking about with some real headbangers who all had motorbikes. Tom only did a few runs through Northumberland to meet with some Scottish lad. Glad he never got caught, and got clean or he wouldn't have got that job. Probably did it for the same reason as me at first, they wait until you're at rock bottom,' he sneered. Then he smiled, 'Cuntrylad took my phone off me to try and stop any more contact. He looked after me, tried to anyway.'

Maia realised it was Jordan's phone Tom had kept, and wondered about the relevance of the Northumberland map references in his notebook. Likely meeting points to transfer packages and money she guessed. 'He did have a wild couple of years, I remember Pauline being really worried about him. Was he using when you last saw him.'

'Nah, definitely not. He'd have a good drink Tom, but never touched the stuff. He'd stopped completely. Tom was stronger than me, he got out and walked away from all the shit. I'm glad he was happy.'

Maia explained about the notebook, 'I wonder if he kept it from years ago and your phone for leverage to take to the police for evidence.' She heaved a lengthy sigh, 'we'll never know.' For the first time, Maia revealed her vulnerability to Jordan as her eyes brimmed. His did too, and she gently tapped the back of his hand, as it rested on the table. The moment was over and he finally finished his huge breakfast. Jordan was still, then said one of the last times he saw Tom, they spoke of some photos that were taken at Linden House. Jordan could not make eye contact.

Maia said softly, 'I know about the abuse, Tom told me.' She remained silent.

Jordan looked away in anguish, averting his eyes. Then he recalled sensing flashes of light, as he was being abused, but his eyes were tight shut. 'I didn't really know exactly what it was, and thought it was maybe in my head, as I often get these, like flashes,' he put his hand to his head and splayed his fingers in and out imitating flashing. 'Like even now, feels like I'm going to have a massive epi or summat. Tom said later it was probably Matty taking photos of us together when he forced us to strip, and ... and, em, touch ourselves, but I really can't recall, probably blocked it out, or my brain is fried with all the shit I've taken over the years.' He forced a weak smile.

'Was it a guy called Matty S?'

Jordan nodded and spoke about Matty threatening to show the photos to his boss at the pub where he worked, and how he couldn't bear the shame of pictures circulating and being possibly recognised.

'Maybe Surtees threatened or blackmailed Tom about the photos too?' Maia wondered.

'Could be,' Jordan shrugged. 'Once Tom ran away from Linden House, I asked to be returned home. I lied about the beatings off my dad to workers because at least I knew where I stood ... and, I wouldn't be abused by Matty again. Lesser of two evils,' Jordan looked up, their eyes met. Maia had never felt so much compassion for anyone in her whole life, she was speechless.

'So, I stayed with my shite family as there was neewhere else to go until I couldn't stand it and left home when I was fifteen, dossing about or on the streets.' After a pause, he said, 'that Matty Surtees is a really nasty shitbag Maia, the man is pure evil. That first day I saw him at the Water's Edge, I went back on the stuff and lost my job.' He said in a hushed tone, 'I couldn't risk my boss getting photos of me like that.' Jordan hung his head and began crying silent tears.

Jordan's vulnerability was raw, Maia tentatively put her arm around him, he was so bony and weak, she wondered how long his life would last if he didn't get off the streets, and off drugs for good. 'I promise I will try everything to get that bastard somehow for you and for Tom.' She positioned herself to shield him from the vision of anyone passing by, to stop any gawking at this grown man breaking down with his head in his hands.

A few moments later she said, 'Jordan, is it okay if we get you a few new clothes, nothing special, it'll keep you going till you get sorted.'

He agreed and they walked into the city centre. Jordan refused to go inside the shops with Maia but stood outside smoking cigarettes, she'd reluctantly bought him, needlessly advising they were bad for his health. Maia bought him toiletries, shaving gear, underwear, a pair of jeans, a pair of joggers, some t-shirts, two sweatshirts and a pair of trainers. Nothing expensive, but looked sturdy enough. She handed him the bags, 'and don't let anyone nick any of your stuff, and don't bloody-well sell it, I've paid good money for those.'

Jordan was becoming more relaxed with Maia; they could joke a little, and both loved talking about Tom. Jordan was a real pain in the butt for Maia with his resistance and apathy for the most part, but she got it, she understood why he didn't trust her one bit. She was firm with him but tried not to show her frustration. 'Promise me, you won't lose touch again Jordan. Will you contact the housing team, and think about drug rehab again maybe?'

Jordan nodded, but Maia wasn't convinced of his conviction.

Over the next week he lived up to Maia's promise and kept in touch with her every day on the cheap phone she'd provided for him. He had gone to stay with a younger sister while he was waiting to be rehoused on a scheme that supported drug rehab. Maia offered help with application forms if needed, and reminded him to make health appointments at the dentist and the like. She felt a sort of older sibling affection for him, all related to what Tom would want her to do. She understood the precarious nature of Jordan's emotional stability, which could be shattered at any time. Maia was desperate for more information about Matty S and his nefarious dealings, she couldn't suppress the sense of revenge she felt, but she didn't want to push it, Jordan's trust was essential.

Aimee too, exceeded Maia's expectations and arranged a fleeting visit to meet with her and Jordan. On Friday 11 September, she arrived fresh off the train from Leicester and met Maia and Jordan at Century House; the sprawling spacious bar attached to Newcastle train station. The bar was built into the cavernous arches of the building, with a high-domed, intricate ornate ceiling.

They ordered breakfast, and after awkward introductions, Aimee spoke up to break the ice. 'I'm married to Samiran … well, Sami. We met at a gym and we moved to Leicester to help run his family business when we got together. They are Hindu, a proper family who have been lovely to me.' She paused and revealed and attractively cute dimpled smile, 'I always sneak a McDonalds burger or Greggs' bacon butty in when I'm here though, as they're all vegetarian.' Aimee was naturally beautiful, now in her mid-thirties. She spoke about how they hoped to start a family soon too, as their gym and sportswear business was now well-established. She could be quite forward too, asking Maia, 'have you got a bloke then, bonny lass like you should have.'

'Erm, yea, Ben. Not been together long but he's a good guy, I think.' Maia realised she'd never spoken much with Ben about any of this situation, nor did she feel it was right to ... for now.

Aimee and Jordan recalled some funny incidents at Linden House and both seemed to relax. He was looking much better, he had filled out, was clean-shaven and looked fresher in his new clothing. What a difference, Maia thought.

Aimee had buried a lot of memories of her time in care, however Jordan did bring back recollections of the kids who stayed in the home, the things they got up to, and some of the workers, good and bad. Jordan mentioned Matty, he briefly described him and asked Aimee if she remembered him.

Maia interjected, 'actually I have a photo of him with Tom and you all at Linden House.' She retrieved it out of her bag, 'I got it from Cath, a worker from the home. They both nodded at the recognition of her name.

'Cath was alright really, so was Pauline, Tom's foster mam,' affirmed Aimee, 'that's when things changed for me, staying with her and Mike, I started going to the gym and looking after myself.' Aimee looked through the images and stopped at the group photo and read the names on the reverse. Her true Geordie dialect slipped out, 'urh aye! Matty S ... Matthew Surtees was his name, he was really creepy, and stunk of B.O. He was a big fat, lazy stupid bastard and I wouldn't have owt to do with him.'

Aimee studied the photo. 'D'you know, years later, Matty saw me in a bar in town, and said he'd do a model's portfolio for free 'cos he knew me, and had his own studio. I told him to fuck right off! Wouldn't trust that slime-ball. Though I think he batted for the other side, as he would constantly pay loads of attention to Damien, one of the older lads I knocked around with in the home. He was always asking to take polaroids of him, very dodgy.'

Maia pressed her further asking if she was aware of Matthew doing anything he shouldn't have around the children.

'Wouldn't surprise me, but if he'd tried anything on with Damien, he'd have decked him!' Laughing, 'he was a big lad for his age and couldn't half handle himself.' Aimee noticed Jordan wince, hang his head, and sensed an edgy change in him.

Aimee was a sharp, bright woman who had learnt a lot during her time in business, and her time in care. She recognised the effects of trauma instantly. She stared at Jordan. 'God no ... he didn't! ... did he Jordan?... did he?'

Jordan was about to get up and walk away. Aimee quickly went to sit with him. She held his hand, looked him squarely in the face and whispered firmly and sincerely, 'we are survivors, whatever happened to us as children was *not* our fault. It can make you stronger, you will be fine Jordan when you find your path. I'm here for you, call me anytime. People who haven't gone through what we have, really don't understand at all.'

Much was revealed about Aimee's past in those few words. She leant forward to comfort Jordan and her long poker-straight fair hair fell in silken strands. Aimee's flawlessly made-up face; classy clothing, immaculate nails, full eyelashes, and glossy pout, masked the plump, raggedy, defiant little girl in the photograph.

29

Dunfermline, September 2015

BEN WAS STATIONED north of Inverness for six weeks until late October, completing preliminary surveys of land around the Moray Firth. Meanwhile Maia was getting stuck into her interviews and research for the Earth Chart article. They agreed to meet for a couple of nights near Dunfermline which was halfway between Newcastle and Inverness, but still, over a two and a half hour journey for each.

It would be worth the drive, thought Ben, he only hoped he wasn't called back for anything during his brief break with Maia. As Autumn was nearing its full golden-red glory, he had booked a cosy apartment near the town centre so they could eat out, and spend a bit of quality time together.

He was skirting the edge of the beautiful Cairngorms National Park, bypassing Kingussie and Dalwhinnie, thinking he'd love to visit the munros and lochs with Maia. The thoughts were pleasing, but Ben was fidgety, gnawing at his finger nails, he must face up to telling Maia about his divorce. He banged the steering wheel in anger at Shona still having this influence over his life. The financial issues, were not settled and he wasn't really sure how or when he was going to talk about it. Ben was late getting away and tried to make up time; it was 8 pm by the time he arrived and got showered.

They ate out at a tapas restaurant and Maia introduced her recent involvement in supporting a homeless guy, Jordan. Explaining he was a friend of her first boyfriend Tom, who died in a road accident. Ben observed her melancholy whenever she mentioned the teenage boyfriend Tom. He did wonder why she offered such a high level of time and commitment to an acquaintance from years ago, when she was so busy, but Maia had a good generous heart he concluded. After the meal, Maia asked him if he was tired or whether there were problems with work. He knew she was aware of his unease.

This was his in-road. 'Let's go back, there is something I want to talk about.' He offered a weak smile, 'please don't worry, there's nothing wrong.' It was a short walk back to the apartment. Maia had shopped for some wine during the afternoon and poured them a glass. Ben took the glass, hand trembling, he was terrified in case she left him, in case she felt she couldn't trust him; this was awful, his stomach churned. It could jeopardise what he had with the woman, he now believed, he truly loved, even after these few months.

He took an intake of breath. 'Maia, I have really fallen for you, really have big-time, but I have a confession to make.' He noticed her furrowed brow and continued, 'Shona hasn't signed the divorce papers yet.' Then a barrage of detail came out, as Maia stared at him, he couldn't help it, he couldn't stop rambling. He finished with the fact he'd appointed an excellent solicitor who was taking matters in hand to push things through as quickly as possible.

Eight seconds of total silence ticked by ... it felt like eight hours. 'Please say something Maia.' Her face was turning pale and her shoulders sagged.

'Technically, this is an extra-marital affair,' she said bluntly. 'Okay, delays happen with legal matters, but you lied to me in Iceland Ben, and have continued to do so for months. Shona could cite you having an affair and complicate things even further as you're still legally married, and now I feel like a dirty secret. You've had loads of opportunities to tell me the truth.'

Ben quietly said, 'I know ... I know, but even though that's the legal situation, emotionally and in every other way it is over.'

Another six seconds of total silence ticked by ...

'Why have you waited until now to tell me, and not pushed earlier, were you unsure whether you wanted a divorce?'

'I absolutely do want a divorce, but I've been so busy working abroad I haven't kept a handle on things as well as I should, I know. Shona can be really awkward, so I didn't want to provoke her into being even more bloody argumentative.'

'Why is she resisting if it's over?'

'Money! She still lives in the house, and won't agree to a settlement. She ... just ... won't ... budge. It's driving me insane.'

'And you're still paying for the house?'

'Yes, and some of the bills. She also has my car, and I bloody-well want it back. I want my life back. My solicitor has drawn up a final settlement which is very good for her, so I hope she sees reason.'

'You hope?' questioned Maia looking dismayed.

'Look, I'm going to push this through until it's done. I swear I haven't even seen her for over four months and really don't want to either. There is absolutely nothing between us, you can ask anyone, my family, my friends—'

'I wondered about asking your mother actually Ben.' Maia smiled and spoke as though pleasantly interviewing someone. 'Lorraine, in your opinion, does your son still have feelings for his wife, or does she for him? Any chance of them getting back together, do you think? Brilliant Ben, just brilliant!' She abruptly went into the kitchen to pour herself more wine, returned and sat further along the sofa, looking tense.

'I wanted to be up front and tell you straight away in Iceland, but it was easier to say I was divorced, than to explain the complications. You may never have wanted to see me again after the holiday anyway, I couldn't risk that.' He saw the blank look on Maia's face. 'It never seemed to be the right time during phone calls, and I ... I didn't want to spoil anything between us.'

Inside his head he was thinking, shut the fuck up Ben, you're just prattling on now. He was at a loss. Should he move nearer and try to hold her; would she respond, would she walk out, or tell him to get in the car and drive away and he'd never see her again. He felt sick inside and was silent.

It seemed an age before Maia spoke, but there was a coldness.

'I feel really disillusioned by all this Ben. I wish you'd been honest right from the start in Iceland, as I did want to see you again. I have been badly let down because of dishonesty. This isn't a great start.'

Start, he thought, does that mean they will continue, 'I am so very sorry to have let you down Maia. I know there's nothing I can do or say to change things right now, but I promise—' his phone pinged.

'Anything else I need to know?' she said looking suspiciously at his phone.

'Honestly no, it's from my sis Helena, you never know she may have some good news.'

Maia shrugged and took a large gulp of wine.

Ben glanced at his phone and repeated the message, 'no news today, things progressing, will keep in touch, don't worry bro, The Terrier will get it sorted soon as. Hope the time with your lovely lady is going well.'

He held his phone, so Maia could read the message, which she did and took a deep breath.

'Ben, I told you straight away I was in the throes of ending my relationship with Shaun when we were still in Iceland as soon as I possibly could. It was because he was unfaithful and lied about loads of stuff. You know I was in a controlling relationship with Ryan a few years ago too, which also ended up in secrets and lies. I don't want any more relationship complications.' She was sat bolt upright.

Ben took a chance, she looked so upset, and he'd caused this. He put his hand gently on her back to see if she would move away. She didn't, 'I promise you, I'll sort this out. I've never met anyone like you and I will do anything to put this right.'

She nodded, but looked downhearted and gave a huge yawn, 'I'm tired. I'm going to bed.'

'Do you want me to sleep out here and give you some space?'

Maia slightly shook her head, got up and left the room.

Ben climbed into bed after a few minutes. Maia lay with her back to him. He put his arms firmly around her, spooning, he gently kissed the back of her neck and felt his raging passion rise, shuffling his hips back, away from her, now is not the time, he thought and they both fell asleep.

The next day Maia was more subdued than her usual buoyant self, and he tried everything to comfort and reassure her. When they were back from a wander and dinner, lazing on the sofa listening to music, Maia told Ben she wasn't sure if she wanted to hear divorce progress reports, or to wait for him to tell her when it was all over.

'Ask anytime, but I don't blame you for not wanting to know all the details. I don't either, leaving it in the hands of The Terrier now, if she's anything like my sister, lord help the other side!' he said with a fake scared look on his face.

Maia softened into him; she was exhausted from it all. 'You are most definitely not off the hook Ben Lasek and a further period of probation has now begun.'

'For how long?'

'Not sure, I'll keep you updated.'

The situation mellowed and they spent the night in sensual embraces making love. Ben wanted to tell her he was madly in love with her, but the moment wasn't right to make any major pledges or plans for the future until he got the final divorce order in his hand. In the morning he had to leave early. He didn't want to go, but glad they were on good terms again. He still had nagging doubts, even though this was meant to be *their* special time, all he ever heard about was Tom …Tom … who the fucking hell was Tom, some old boyfriend. Ben also had to question why was she wasting her time with some down-and-out old mate of his, it was weird.

After Ben left, Maia lay in bed and thought candidly, his confession paled into insignificance, in comparison to the mind-blowing news about her own history, as a mother. Although she was seriously disappointed Ben couldn't have been truthful from the onset, she believed he was a good, honest man, and they shared the same future wishes, values and humour. She would reveal her truth to Ben someday soon, once her trust in him was absolute. There were risks, as she did not know how Ben would react, he may reject her. Maia would tell everyone about Freya, the beautiful little soul living her life in this world, but that revelation seemed a long way in their future, she had much to deal with in the present.

30

MAIA WAS BACK home at her desk, deciding which of two business leaders would be her choice for the number one slot in her top ten for her Earth Chart article. She needed a good personal story, charisma, and business success; she wanted adversity, maybe rags to riches. They must have a proven record of commitment to the environment in their business practice of course, and one of her choices was, Alexis Leventis with his immigrant family history was perfect.

When Maia interviewed Alexis Leventis, she felt positive vibes about him. He was approaching sixty, Maia estimated. He was a slightly built man, wearing a dark grey suit, blue tie and crisp white shirt. His greying hair was neatly cropped around his hairline. His deep brown eyes were discerning, yet kind, beneath well-defined eyebrows. He had the benefit of clear olive skin from his Greek origins; with visible cheekbones, and the even covering of neat, dark stubble gave him an edgy look. He would have been a very attractive younger man she imagined.

'Good afternoon Ms Hewson. Come in, and do call me Alexi.'

'It's Maia,' she said shaking hands, 'thank you for the interview Alexi.'

They settled with a coffee in his grand city centre office. After preliminary courtesies, Maia began the interview. 'I'm interested in how it all began Alexi. Tell me about the background of the Apollon Group, I understand it's a family business?'

'Indeed it is. My father left the island of Ródos to work in the UK in the 1950s for better employment prospects. He worked in hotels as a cleaner, a porter, a kitchen worker and made his way up to a senior position as Maître D' at a London hotel. He fell in love with,' a broad smile erupted, 'a Northern lass, who was working in the same hotel. They moved back to the North east to start a family; they worked and saved hard, started with one restaurant, then one hotel, and now this … ' He opened his arms wide at the sumptuous office space, the HQ of The Apollon Group of luxury spa hotels and exclusive leisure clubs.

'Me and Gregori now manage the company as both parents are deceased. My brother is much younger and has no head for business. I oversee everything and he is mainly involved with Leisure Club management. He is,' Alexi made a slight dismissive gesture with his hand and under his breath said, 'mou eheis kanei ti zoe patini. Sorry, Maia, it means … he makes my life like a roller skate … he can be unreliable you know, but has good intentions I believe.' He looked pensive.

The Apollon Hotel and Leisure chain maintained

excellent environmental policies, with the latest energy-efficient systems throughout; using low-consumption lighting, recycled everywhere they could, and installed water-saving systems. All bedlinen and towels were made from organic materials and they had reduced heating and air conditioning energy output to efficient standards. Plastics were limited, only used in essential circumstances, with packaging mostly from recyclable sources. Alexi advised the company was looking at the possibility of converting to solar power for some of their establishments and certainly for new builds. It was one of the best examples of an environmentally-friendly business which had emerged from Maia's research.

The interview had gone really well, Maia liked him, he was family orientated, astute, aware of treating staff well, and forward-thinking in terms of business and the environment. He'd make a great front cover for the magazine too, Maia wondered if his wife may be encouraged to be pictured with him. A married couple's photo would have more appeal. Alexi offered her a six-month free pass for two, to any of the spa and leisure clubs, and gave her permission to interview any of his staff to complete her research. Now that, was a result!

Along with Alexi Leventis, there were two other candidates, Maia wanted to showcase in her article. Beatrice Cowen of RecyClothing, was a force to be reckoned with; dynamic and highly committed to producing ethically made clothing. She had impressed Maia with her unfaltering conviction to deal with manufacturers who produced clothing with excellent human rights records. The other candidates,

David and Adrian Harper sourced pure organic products for their specialist food outlet. They worked alongside environmentally sound wholesalers. The company was experiencing budget issues, however their dedication to succeed was impressive. The interviews were going well for Maia's article, much to her relief she'd complete everything well in advance of the end of September deadline.

On Sunday 13 September, Daphne said she was excited about a lazy, luxurious spa day with Maia, it had been so long since the friends had spent quality time together; not since their outing with Rosa at Cafe Dalvik months ago. They used to have a spa day regularly when they worked together for the local newspaper.

Maia booked in for the day at Alexi's signature Apollon Spa Hotel in the rambling Northumberland countryside, for a damn good catch up, lots of treatments and relaxation. Daphne listened calmly to Maia's experiences with philanderer Shaun, and her misgivings about Ben's divorce, and his mother, Lorraine's possible loyalty to his not-even-ex-wife Shona.

'I never understood the true sense of high maintenance partners until now. Ben is too generous, paying the mortgage and most household bills, he also loaned Shona his Audi because her car was repossessed as she didn't maintain the finance payments. Maybe he won't get it back now, and he's running around in a clapped-out Toyota, unless he has use of a company vehicle. She's digging her heels in, but I really wish he'd be more bloody assertive.

They were fully engaged in the conversation, when

Daphne suddenly leaned towards Maia's lounger by the pool and asked in fast, hushed tones, eyes flicking towards the other side of the pool, 'is that Ryan?'

Maia peeped over the top of her magazine and in a suppressed angry whisper, said, 'christ, yea it is! That's all I need when I'm figuring out my new relationship with my current beau, for a previous one to spoil my relaxation. What the hell is, GI fucking Joe with his stupid hair doing here? Hope he doesn't spot me.'

'Shall I ask him over, so you can interview him for your article?'

'Sod off Daphne, you dare!'

Daphne's head tipped back as she laughed aloud, resting on her elbows, in a gorgeous turquoise swimsuit, her shapely, voluptuous dark body beautifully draping the full length of the lounger.

'Shush, don't attract his attention.'

Ryan wore the hotel's leisure club corporate t-shirt and was gathering used bath towels left by customers on the opposite side of the pool.

'Well, how the mighty have fallen. He used to tell me how fantastically well he was doing managing the gym where he worked, and it was going to become a franchise, and he would manage one of the leading ones in the area,' twisting her face adding, 'blah, blah, blah. Seems it hasn't worked out too well has it Ryan?' she looked in his direction.

'He is a looker though,' said Daphne, head tilted staring at him.

'Yeah if you like the Action Man type,' responded Maia, 'the wax-haired tool!

Both lay back on their loungers unable to look at each other stifling their laughter, bodies shaking.

'Ah no, every time he goes by, I'm going to have to hide behind my magazine.'

'Here, stick this over your face,' Daphne plonked a hand towel over Maia's head, 'and keep your face mask on when you come out of the treatments, he'll never know it's you, unless he recognises your boobs or your arse.'

Maia was not amused at Daphne's flippant response at first, then had a fit of giggles, before returning to the conversation about the Lorraine-misgivings, once Ryan had disappeared from view.

'Are you jealous of Shona?' asked Daphne?

'Not really, I know Ben adores me and would be devastated if we split, and thankfully, there's no kids involved from his marriage.'

'Do you want to be with him?'

'I do, it's the early romance stage and I'm loving it. When we meet up it is bliss, just us, walking and talking, eating—'

'And the rest!' said Daphne winking, whereupon Maia dribbled her drink onto her chin mid-laugh.

'True! Enough of my woes anyway, how is Zain doing with his latest exhibition?'

'He's nervous about diversifying away from his established sales in traditional African sculptures, in case his new stuff isn't commercially viable. *He* needs to be more bloody assertive too!'

'Those pics you sent over of his new steampunk African sculptures are a diversion from tradition, but amazing.'

Maia enthused, 'if he's interested, I could ask Sophia if she would consider a marketing strategy. She's well over-the-top I know, but honestly she's a genius with truly unique ideas.'

'Good idea Maia,' said Daphne, 'the exhibition is only a few months away, with virtually no advertising. I'll speak with him, see if he would be interested.

'It would be hilarious to see him interact with Sophia, with his understated genius and her over-the-top flair!'

Daphne laughed and reflected, 'I'm glad we took a chance investing in the new studio. I love the character of Ouseburn and the area is thriving. I've got a good profile up here, but I occasionally miss the hustle and bustle of working in London, especially covering the music scene.'

'Your arts and culture column is the most highly regarded in the area and nationally though Daphne, I'm so proud of what you've achieved in the last few years.' She gave her friend a warm meaningful smile, which was returned in full. No-one's face encompassed unbridled joy as much as Daphne's when she smiled.

Daphne's grin was replaced with a grimace as she said, 'Ryan alert! Ryan alert!' and dove down by the side of the lounger as if she was looking for something, to prevent her laughter ringing out at Maia's fearful expression. Maia put the towel over her face and pretended to be asleep as he walked past. Ryan looked twice at Daphne, she was particularly stunning and memorable. Once he had walked towards the reception desk with his back to them, Maia peeped out of the side of the towel to make sure he'd gone.

'Maybe you should let him know you've seen him here. He could do with a dose of humility,' suggested Daphne.

'I don't ever want to see his face again to be perfectly honest.' As she looked toward the reception area, through the huge plate glass wall, Maia thought she recognised the dishevelled businessman, Ryan was clearly sucking up to near the reception area. 'Hey, when do our treatments start?'

'In ten minutes or so,' replied Daphne.

'Okay, I'm off to the lockers to get fresh towels, courtesy of the lovely Ryan of course,' Maia said, eyes rolling.

Mathew spotted two women walking into the open relaxation area of the spa from the pool, and thought, those two look quite classy, not like the usual old dogs they get in here, wonder if they'd be up for a bit of photography work. Although they're a bit mutton, definitely over twenty five and the camera doesn't lie, I could always air brush their faces, but the bodies look in pretty good nick. Could do a mature middle-aged shoot to appeal to the custom we get in here. A black one and a white one too, nice contrast in monochrome.

Matthew went to the kitchen, lifted one of the prepared glass pitchers from the large refrigerator and took it into the open relaxation area, intending to strike up a conversation. The women were dressed in robes laying on the recliner seats waiting for beauty treatments. He placed the iced lemon-infused, water pitcher on the corner table.

'Good afternoon ladies, are you enjoying your time at our spa?' he introduced himself as Mathew Surtees, area manager of the leisure complex in the Apollon Group Hotels. She looks frigid, Mathew thought about the white girl, but the black one seems relaxed.

Daphne thanked him for the water, as she would never be rude to people, but dropped hints, 'just waiting for our treatments,' and purposefully turned away to look at her magazine.

He took the hint and left suggesting they, 'enjoy their massage experience,' with a leery smile as he slowly walked through the door.

A second after the door closed Daphne said, 'he was a creepy sod, made my flesh crawl, thank goodness he's buggered off.'

Maia was on her way to the changing rooms having spent the last five minutes sinking into her lounger visualising, *Matty S*, written on the reverse of the Linden House photograph. That's where she had recognised him from, when he was talking with Ryan earlier. She'd held her magazine up so his face was obliterated, when he brought over the water.

In a toilet cubicle, Maia's throat constricted and her breath came in gasps. Severe stomach cramping pains and a wave of nausea hit her as soon as she left the lounge area, which resulted in her vomiting into the toilet bowl the instant she entered the cubicle. The cold floor tiles felt harsh on her knees. Once the trembling eased, she rinsed her mouth at the sink and patted her face with cold water before returning.

Daphne looked concerned, 'you ok?'

'I just came over all nauseous,' said Maia, 'sorry to spoil our afternoon Daphne, don't think I'm well enough to have any treatments.'

Daphne said, 'that came on suddenly.'

'I had seafood last night,' Maia lied, 'always gives me a dicky tummy if I have wine with it, should know better they don't mix well with me.' It was a half lie, the combo didn't mix well with Maia, but it was the sight of, Matty S, that revolted her.

'Ah, okay, can I get you a ginger tea or anything?' asked Daphne pouring her a drink from the jug Mathew had left.

Maia turned her face away, feeling sickly even being near the jug he had touched. 'No thanks Daphne, best if I go home. Sorry, we'll do this another time, I've got a six month free pass ... so anytime.' She forced a smile.

Daphne said it was no problem at all, so the women packed up and left.

Maia was quiet during the car journey home. Her head was buzzing, she hadn't the energy to express her suspicions about Matthew to Daphne. It would take more than a quick chat whilst dropping her off to explain the rigours she had been through recently with the revelations from Jordan and Aimee. Daphne stopped near to Maia's apartment building, gave her a reassuring hug, and suggested she comes up to the apartment with her to check she'd be okay.

'I'll be fine honestly, been here before with the seafood-wine combo Daphne, thanks. Really need to rest. So sorry to cut our day short, but I won't be going back there if bloody Ryan's around.' It was a brilliant excuse not to return to that particular spa. Her pale face attempted a weary smile. 'We'll go to another venue next time.'

'Alright, but ring me later and let me know how you're feeling.'

Maia felt Daphne was watching her enter the building, so she turned, blew a kiss and waved as she drove away.

Maia thought she was going to pass out as she got into the lift, her legs almost buckled and she was panting for breath. She was freaking out at the restriction in her throat as she noisily gasped for air. She supported herself with both hands, shocked at the vision of the ghostly face reflected in the interior mirrored lift, which was always unflattering at the best of times, but today was another level of horror. As she gratefully arrived into her apartment she flew to the bathroom and vomited again, retching from the depths of her belly. Her hair was stuck onto her clammy neck and face. Her body was uncontrollably trembling as she lay on her bed. With hardly any strength, she wrapped the duvet over her body, and curled up in a ball. She remained there breathless, dizzy and nauseous.

After laying there a while, she didn't know how long, unable to move, the regular pulsating buzz of a garden strimmer around the apartment blocks roused her brain.

'They must be tidying up, bit late now, summer's over.' Her voice had an echoing resonance. She pushed herself up onto one elbow and felt some calming strength and normal breathing rhythm returned, realising she had a panic attack. Still weakened from the shock to her system, she slowly raised her fragile body from the bed and pulled on her warm, comforting clothes. The soft fabric offered a welcoming hello, caressing her skin. She tiptoed to the kitchen and took deep breaths to quell her flight response, avoiding any swift harsh movement that may regenerate, or induce the panicky feelings. Maia made a rich caramel hot chocolate and went out onto the balcony, with her favourite shawl around her shoulders, to feel the fresh breeze on her face and breathe in its cleansing air.

Maia commenced one of her favourite distractions, people-watching. She noticed a heavily built, overweight balding man, she guessed maybe late-thirties, with his tiny wife walking over the Millennium footbridge across the river. Two young daughters clasped his huge hands; they were skipping and jumping along on either side of him. The four were laughing, and the tinkle of uncontrollable girlish giggles was pleasing. He wore the brightest salmon pink polo shirt, and had a child's small glittery bag over his shoulder. Not a good look sir, pink doesn't do anything for you, Maia thought, but their infectious joy brought a smile to her face. It reminded her that most children were not subject to terrible events at the hands of abusive adults in their lives. She continued to observe the family until the bright salmon pink disappeared.

Maia then reflected on the terror she felt at the salon, and couldn't imagine to what extent young Tom and Jordan must have suffered, being subjected to abuse from that utter bastard, Surtees. She needed to talk with someone about Tom's abuser; someone she could trust, but who? Her parents, Katrin and Phil? She wouldn't want to worry them or drag them into a world of abuse. Her siblings, Andy and Nik? Same thing, she wouldn't want to worry them. Pauline? It would be too distressing for her, and Mike would probably murder him. Daphne? Her pragmatic approach would be calming, and she was there at the salon, she saw him. Rosa? Rosa understood issues of abuse and trauma, and she knew about Tom too, but has her own busy family life, and work to deal with. Maia didn't want to drag her into this situation.

Maia considered calling Craig? An obvious choice, he could offer advice about who to take the information to officially, and potential legal procedures. Of course there was Ben? She had mentioned her childhood sweetheart Tom had died, but there were enough complications between them for now. She could do with his calm comfort though, but needed time and space to tell Ben about past complexities.

The one person she felt would be able to put this in perspective, who understood the issues and who knew the people involved was … Aimee.

Maia didn't know if she had the strength to continue delving into the murky world of child abusers and drug-dealers. It was an alien landscape for her, and she doubted her ability to cope with any further contact with the disgusting nonce, Surtees. She sat motionless staring at the river view and began to sob. Sorrowful, desolate tears dripped down her cheeks. She felt a hollow space deep within as she held onto Tom's pendant.

31

THE FIRST THOUGHT that filled Maia's brain the following morning was, Matthew Surtees needed to be taken down! She was not going to let that abuser ruin anyone else's life.

The smell of toasted cinnamon bagels filled the kitchen and a strong iced coffee was in the making. She resolved, there was every indication from Aimee's attitude and personality, she would be interested in Maia's plan. She sent a message asking when she was free for a call. Aimee's immediate text response was, *Is Jordan ok?*

Maia confirmed he was fine and that she had discovered the whereabouts of Matthew Surtees. If Aimee could identify him as the same guy at Linden House, it may lead to trouble for him; especially if Jordan is willing to act as a witness for drug activity and sexual abuse. Aimee wondered if Jordan was robust enough to go through any of it, but she would support him texting, *"it's hard to find anyone who believes us."*

Maia recognised the significance of the collective, us, terminology and replied, *I do.*

Two days later, Maia and Aimee met at the entrance to the Apollon Hotel, both in leisure wear, carrying sports bags. 'Trouble is, we don't know if he's on duty today, and I certainly wasn't going to ring and find out, in case he asked who I was?'

'No worries, we can come back when he's around if needed, or get a contact number' suggested Aimee.

At the spa reception desk, Aimee asked if Matthew Surtees was available as she was an old friend. He was coming on duty at 2 pm they were told. Turning to Maia whispering, 'may as well take advantage of some freebies.'

The receptionist asked for a credit card. Maia handed over her free spa passes and Aimee responded charmingly with, 'oh, and Matthew will be taking care of payment for any extras. Don't worry, he confirmed any time I was in the area just to book in, do check with him if you wish.' She scanned the price list and with a dazzling smile said, 'we're both having, The Luxe Package and could you put some champagne on ice please sweetie.'

To Maia's incredulity, the receptionist accepted the whole premise. They changed into robes and Aimee perused the food and drinks menu, and the spa itinerary, she turned to Maia and said, 'let's get all the treatments in before that fat bastard turns up.'

'I can't thank you enough for doing this Aimee. I'll pay for the extras if they want to charge for everything if it's not him?'

'It's definitely him, the sleazy way he spoke to your friend the last time you were here is spot on.'

Maia admired this woman's resilience. In a cosy private

corner with champagne cocktails and fresh fruit, Aimee spoke a little about her background. Her mother died of an alcohol related illness, and her mother's partner had sexually abused Aimee from being eight years old. Her mother had taken his surname, so Aimee thought he was her father as she was known by his name in school. It wasn't until social services intervened and she was taken into care, they found her original birth certificate showing her registered name, Bancroft.

Aimee told Maia, 'no idea who my birth father is, don't really care. I became Aimee Cheryl Bancroft from that day on and have never looked back. I love the name Bancroft, it doesn't relate to anyone alive that I know, it's all mine, and I've kept it as part of my married name,' in plummy accent, 'I'm double barrelled now you know.'

'I know,' said Maia, 'suits you, it really does,' she repeated, 'Aimee Cheryl Bancroft-Dara. Brilliant.'

Maia was astounded at Aimee's toned athletic body, as she removed her robe, she clearly looked after herself.

Aimee knew she was admiring her stature. 'You've seen photos of the little chubster I was,' and laughed. 'I went through hell, years of eating disorders, bulimia in the main, I could vomit at will. Then I joined a gym, started to work out, got healthy, stronger and felt great with the help of Sami. That's how we met, he was my personal trainer, honestly he's great and I love his family so much.'

The women indulged in all of the luxurious treatments on offer, enjoying the exclusive champagne lunch, with as many extras as Aimee could conjure up. Maia felt a real connection with her, she would've been happy to talk all day;

and even tell her about her experience of having a child adopted. Aimee would understand and be at ease with Maia's tough decision. They were interrupted by a knock on the inner relaxation salon door, which slowly opened. Matthew Surtees walked in with a disconcerted look on his face when he saw the two women staring back at him. Aimee stood, preening to her full height, put her arms on her hips drawing her robe back, revealing her exquisite bikini-clad body.

'What's up Matty, don't you recognise me?'

Maia will never forget the astonished look on his face, he was clueless! She wanted to laugh aloud.

'It's me ... Aimee ... Aimee Bancroft from Linden House Children's Home,' she wasn't bothered who heard, 'we met in the Grapevine Wine Bar a while ago when you wanted to do a modelling photo shoot?' Nodding at him awaiting recognition.

Matthew glanced at the few other women sitting around on the periphery, whose necks stretched and strained, open-mouthed looking on as their attention was hugely piqued by the conversation.

'Oh yes ... right ... Aimee, yes, um, I seem to recall the name,' aware everyone was glaring at him. He straightened and foolishly offered his hand out to formally shake hers.

Aimee looked at his hand, and turned away. 'Hey Matty, we're nearly done here. We'll get dressed and meet you in the bar in twenty minutes, for a catch up.' She offered her sweet dimpled smile.

'Err ... um, okay. See you then.' His face was pillar-box red as he turned abruptly and shuffled back out of the door.

'That was so impressive,' admired Maia. Surreptitious

glances could be seen on the nosey women's faces, before returning behind magazines.

Aimee smiled and winked. 'Hey, I know you won't want to speak to him, don't blame you. But I'm going to meet him and ask some, you know, interesting questions about where I might meet his mate, Charlie,' she winked again, 'don't worry, I'll sound him out.'

The Charlie-reference penny dropped in a second for Maia. They finished the champagne, got dressed and Maia wished her good luck, and asked her to promise to ring her if anything turned strange.

Aimee rolled her eyes, 'I'll handle that Telly-Tubby, no worries Maia.' She looked stunning in designer jeans and top, with the softest skin-tight oxblood leather jacket, and bejewelled stiletto boots.

Maia shook her head with a smile and actually said, 'wow!'

Aimee smiled, held one arm in the air the other on her hip in extravagant model's pose, pouted, then smiled. 'I'll ring and let you know if I find anything out.'

The two women had an extended warm embrace. With a knowing look and deep understanding of their joint goal, they squeezed each other's hands before parting, as Aimee had to travel back to Leicester that evening.

Aimee rang Maia later from the train, to say although Matthew didn't directly say he could supply her with cocaine, he stated, he did have contacts who definitely would, and would offer her the details, anytime. It was enough confirmation Maia needed, it was definitely the man who sexually abused Tom and Jordan, then went on to exploit his power over them. She needed evidence of either the abuse or drugs, but had no clue how to obtain it.

Maia called Craig to keep him updated about the progress of her day. She gleefully told him about the interaction at the spa.

'Do you want a job here Maia? You seem to have traced a drug-dealing nonce! Problem for you is, Jordan is the only victim and witness that you're aware of; and whilst him and Aimee seem credible, it's maybe not enough for an investigation unless there's more evidence. You should be able to contact whichever team deals with non-recent abuse for your area, as they would be interested in the sexual abuse information. It's whether Jordan is strong enough to go through the process.'

'I won't force him Craig, he needs to do this for himself, as he wants to end all contact, and move forward from his past.'

Craig then suggested, 'if you've got a relationship with this business owner who employs Surtees, is there any mileage in offering information about the drug activity to him? He may be interested in shaking off association with Surtees, unless of course he's part of it.'

'Alexi ... yes,' said Maia, 'I'd thought about him, I get along well with him, can't imagine he's involved. I'd trust my judgement and say he isn't, but it is a risk as you really don't know people. Charismatic men get away with anything.'

'Even murder,' suggested Craig. 'Maia, seriously, be bloody careful. These people won't pull any punches. Promise me you won't go digging into anything, and don't go anywhere or meet anyone without me, or Ben if he's around. I'll be there in a flash if you need me.'

'Or, Luiza could be my body guard, she'd be great too.'

'That's true,' admitted Craig, 'probably do a better job than me. A word of advice, if Jordan has been involved in drug activity, even if it's years ago, he may need to be cautious about any legal implications. If he admits to playing an active part in running drugs, the police will certainly investigate, and the last thing the lad needs is a custodial sentence. It'll prove more compelling if Surtees' employer is the one making allegations.'

They chatted and updated events in their lives, loves, family and finally ended with Maia saying she would sleep on it, and see if she felt she could approach Alexi. Maia did not know whether she would get anywhere, however she did know, she had made a life-long friend in Aimee Cheryl Bancroft-Dara.

32

THE FOLLOWING MORNING Maia was determined to continue on her path, and contacted Alexi for a follow up meeting. He was pleased to invite her for coffee on Friday afternoon to discuss the lead article featuring the Apollon Group. Maia wanted to thank him for being so helpful during her research.

Alexi's personal assistant Michalis, his nephew, welcomed Maia into the large office, a prime spot overlooking the city. A simple mezze was beautifully laid out on the oversize coffee table. Alexi was wonderful company. He was charming, clearly devoted to his wife and family; he told Maia of enjoying trips to Rhodes to see family, and showed pride in how successful his children were doing in the family business.

Maia talked about her Icelandic heritage and the recent visit, which rather intrigued him. He was a curious, interested man and asked many questions. It was an enjoyable meeting, but Maia was anxious about the information she was about to impart. 'Alexi, please forgive me, but I may have some news about one of your employees which is not good to hear.'

He looked puzzled and a little amused as he poured another coffee.

'There is no easy way to explain this. Um ... do you recognise anyone in this photograph?' Maia showed him the polaroid of a group of youngsters, with two adult females and one male outside the children's home.

Alexi put on his glasses and paused, looked closer, squinting, 'is that ... Matthew?'

'It is, he's written his name and a date on the back.'

Alexi turned it over and saw the list of names written on the reverse. He looked up shrugging, still amused.

'One of the boys in the photograph has evidence that Matthew has been associated with drug activity.' Maia pointed to Jordan. 'He seems willing to go to the police with information.' Maia tried to discern any evidence of Alexi's association, but his expression gave nothing away at all.

Alexi looked into her face, 'but this picture doesn't prove anything.'

'No, it doesn't, but I really wanted to warn you in case the police investigate the allegations. The other thing Alexi is,' she paused and took a deep breath. 'Matthew abused those two boys in the photograph when he was a casual care assistant at the children's home in the mid-nineties. The boy, now an adult, is considering taking his case to the non-recent child abuse team. I knew the other boy,' she pointed to Tom, 'we were close ... and ... he told me about the abuse too ... but he died recently. I'm so sorry to burden you with all this Alexi.' Maia exhaled generously, glad to offload the information, but tensed, waiting for his response.

Maia almost didn't hold it together. She refused to let Alexi see this was very personal as she could lose all credibility. It was such a gamble, he was a powerful man in the business community; he could have her thrown out of his office, and disparage her evidence; worst of all, withdraw his support for her work.

Maia continued, 'I saw Matthew at the spa recently and wondered if it was the same guy in the photos.' She pointed to Aimee in the picture, 'this girl formally identified him. She spoke with him and he did recognise her from those days. She had a private conversation with him later and he confirmed he could access drugs if she wanted them. He isn't a good person at all. Look, I really don't know if his victim is going to talk about the drug involvement to the police as there are implications for him, but he definitely intends to about the historical abuse. He so badly wants to free himself from Matthew's association with his past, and save anyone else he may still be abusing now. He understands the risks, and may need protection from potential recrimination.'

Alexi's skin turned sallow as he glared at the polaroid photograph. He remained completely still. His mouth, a fixed horizontal thin line of defiance, or was it anger? Maia had never seen such suppressed emotion. Alexi's face burned, his eyes flashed, and he was breathing deeply. The strain inside him to hold it together was powerful. Maia felt the tension zipping around the room like lasers, she half expected to see burn holes in the walls. It was deathly quiet, but for the faint hum of city traffic below. Maia didn't know what else to say, or which way this would go. If Alexi was involved in the drug activity, this could be excruciating and perhaps dangerous for her.

Alexi rested his forehead in his hand and said, in a low, almost menacing, voice that actually sent shivers through her, 'I had already started an internal investigation of my own about Surtees. I've had my suspicions about his financial dealings within the business for some time, and now this.' He flung the photo on the table, 'this proves I'm right about the type of person he is. Thank you for bringing this to my attention. I now have business to attend to, so if you wouldn't mind.' His tone completely changed as he arose; he fastened a jacket button, and gently pulled it straight, shoulders back.

Maia stood too. She looked deeply into Alexi's eyes. He was in his heart, a good man. 'I had no idea,' he said quietly, 'I wouldn't have employed him all this time if I'd known.'

'How could you possibly know Alexi?'

They had a warm handshake. As he said, 'goodbye Maia,' he put his hand over hers and patted it firmly but gently.

He knew, Maia sensed it, he knew it was personal. She felt a welling inside and managed to say, 'good luck Alexi, you're too good a person to be dragged down because of people like him.'

As she left the reception office, she heard Alexi's raised voice demand of Michalis, 'get Surtees over here now!'

33

MAIA SAT WITH Jordan as they completed the online, *Report a Crime,* section on the Northumbria Police webpage that evening. The electronic system advised any information given would be transferred to the control room for action. The allegations proved sufficient concern to the police, so Jordan was given an appointment at the neighbourhood team covering Central Newcastle and an officer would be available to take an initial report.

The day arrived when Jordan needed to present himself at the police station, and, to Maia's relief he hadn't backed out and absconded. The two were having a late breakfast at Century House in Newcastle rail station.

Maia recognised a slim, athletic woman, with fire-red spiked hair, standing at the bar chatting to the staff. It was Iceni Queen Boudicca. Should she say something; introduce herself perhaps, but it may seem over-friendly and unwanted, there was nothing more than a mid-run nod when they passed. Boudicca may ignore her, or worse want to befriend her. An odd situation. Maia had the utmost respect for this woman who had clearly suffered some trauma in her life, despite the fact, at 11 am, this ancient royal was downing a tumbler with a small measure of amber coloured liquid; whisky, or brandy perhaps. A bit early, mused Maia, but whatever gets you through the day she concluded. The running blade was covered by black combat trousers, maybe there was a prosthetic limb in place today, and Boudicca's tattoos were hidden beneath a nondescript sports top, and leather biker jacket. People survive. Jordan was a survivor too, as was Aimee, who arrived from Leicester at that very moment.

Maia had invited Aimee to stay with her for a few days to support Jordan, once he had made the decision to tell the police about the abuse. Aimee bought a coffee, she couldn't face breakfast. Maia had never witnessed such apprehension in Aimee. They gathered in a quiet area, sitting on a comfy corner sofa surrounding a large low table.

'How are you feeling about all this Jordan?' Maia asked nervously. She was anxious that he would walk away and dismiss going to the police with information about Surtees.

Jordan stopped eating for a second, looked vague, shrugged, then said, 'got nowt to lose. I'm never going to get shot of the scumbag if I don't change stuff. Definitely don't want to be associated with the twat ever again.'

Maia sighed with relief inwardly. She was so eager to hold Surtees to account, and she was aware she had to restrain herself from pressuring Jordan to do something he didn't want to. Maia had been clear with Jordan suggesting he takes some independent free legal advice too. She would rather give it all up than see Jordan come to any harm. He had maintained his new volunteer position on an inner city urban green project, and his living circumstances seemed stable. He was attending a drug and alcohol dependency support program through his GP surgery. Maia felt happy his future could turn out okay. He had his teeth fixed too, which was a bonus.

Maia had grown to really like Jordan and it was positive to see him now, transforming from the unresponsive soul she found on the streets some months ago. Nonetheless, she must question whether this was all about her, and her misguided ambition to punish someone, anyone, for Tom's death.

Aimee joined in. 'Course he can do it! You're one of the tough ones now who's not gonna take any more crap off anyone. They won't let me come in the interview with you, but I'll be waiting at the door, and we'll deal with whatever is needed afterwards.'

With a mouthful of breakfast, Jordan nodded in affirmation, with a muffled and cheeky, 'cheers ladies.'

The three arrived at the city centre police station, which was a ten minute walk from the bar. Jordan was called into a small side office to discuss information as a witness to an historical crime of sexual assault.

Detective Constable Christine Powell is thirty-eight. Her dark bobbed hair, worn in a neat side parting fell below her jawline; she wore a light grey trouser suit and black shirt. Chris joined the service as a student officer and never thought about an alternative career. She had spent many years working within sexual offences and domestic abuse teams, but to further her career prospects, she was due to be transferred to the Crime Team on her recent promotion to sergeant. Chris did not have an aggressive interviewing style, however was dogged and stoic, with an unceasing persistence which wore down many offenders. Chris was purposefully relentless, and never perturbed in the face of some of the worst sex-offending she could have imagined at the beginning of her service. It only fuelled her desire to put perpetrators behind bars.

Chris looked at the name on the sheet she had in her hand to complete an initial report, and entered the interview room. She could see, Jordan Davis was agitated and put him at ease, offering a cup of tea and keeping the conversation and atmosphere as low key as possible. She did not want him disappearing into the night and miss the opportunity to potentially nail another offender, she enjoyed the long game. Chris explained the steps of what would happen, checking for feedback that Jordan understood the process. Prior to the interview Chris had checked Jordan's details for history of any past criminal records. This did not reveal any current major misdemeanours, but for a few petty theft instances, reported unsuccessful TWOC attempts at stealing cars, and criminal damage to a park gate, he and some kids wrecked as a teenager. Jordan Davis, it seemed, was no deviant or master criminal.

Jordan was able to describe Matthew Surtees' drug dealing operations. He offered compelling information about the network of associates, the locations, and venues they regularly used to conduct their business. He tried to recall the full names of Baz and Sol and gave physical descriptions, also two addresses, that he could remember, where he was taken and given packages to transfer.

It came to the most difficult part of the interview, when Jordan had to reveal he was also sexually assaulted as a boy, by Matthew Surtees, when he was placed at Linden House in Durham. He believed his abuser may also have taken compromising photographs of him. Jordan advised that his friend, Tom Cassidy also suffered the same abuse, but he had died. It was tearing Jordan apart having to talk about this, but he knew he had to face up to everything now, or never.

Chris advised she would make an appointment for him at the Sanctuary Suite to record his witness statement in respect of the abuse. She told him the location, gave him an explanatory leaflet and advised exactly what would happen on the day. The appointment was booked the following week.

Aimee and Maia had a brief conversation with Chris, as they were invited into the room at Jordan's request. Chris made notes regarding Aimee's communication with Surtees, which she repeated verbatim, claiming he could access drugs for her. Maia told Chris about Jordan's friend, Tom Cassidy who said he was also sexually abused by Surtees at Linden House. Maia handed Chris the pictures of Surtees with the children. Aimee and Jordan identified Matthew Surtees in the photograph.

On leaving Maia noticed, the regulation police uniform issue, of black combat trousers, very similar to those Boudicca was wearing in the pub, maybe she was an ex-cop. Made sense for her to be drinking in the nearest pub to perhaps, her old station.

On Friday 25 September, Jordan and Aimee arrived at the interview suite located in an ancillary building of a local authority centre, east of the city. Aimee had extended her stay so she could accompany Jordan through the ordeal. The suite was a small anonymous brick building, which reminded Jordan of the tiny infant school he used to attend. He had vague recollections of enjoying school when he was really small, before his father turned to alcohol and ruined his life. Jordan felt vulnerable, he felt like that small child and thanked his lucky stars Aimee was by his side.

They were guided into the main room by a pleasant young officer. The room had a typically corporate-type mid-blue coloured carpet. It was a low key environment, with two small grey fabric sofas and an armchair. There was a coffee table in the centre and a side table between the chairs, with a lamp upon it. Bright orange printed cushions and some non-descript prints in wooden frames gave the place a less-than-clinical feel. Jordan sat with Aimee on the sofa.

Chris began the introductions, 'I am Detective Constable Christine Powell and I am here today with' ... she smiled at Jordan ... 'would you please say your full name.'

He replied, 'Jordan Davis.' His voice croaked.

'Thank you Jordan.' Another reassuring smile, 'can you also confirm here in the waiting room is your friend Aimee Bancroft-Dara, who is here to support you.'

He looked at Aimee, who was holding his hand. 'Yes, that's right, this is Aimee.' He felt Aimee squeeze his hand.

Chris continued. 'In the next room is D.C. Edward Dodds who you met when you arrived, he is here to ensure the recording equipment is running correctly. He will listen to what we talk about today and will ensure you won't need to repeat anything afterwards. At the end of the interview I will leave the room to talk to Eddy to check if there are any further questions I may need to ask you. The interview will be formal, as the purpose is to obtain your account as evidence for the police investigation. It will be played in court, so you don't have to attend in person.'

Chris led Jordan into the interview room. He turned and Aimee gave him a smile and thumbs up. The interview room was similarly furnished, they sat in two comfortable chairs, with a coffee table between. Chris offered Jordan a glass of water from the jug on the table, which he took, but wished he hadn't as he almost spilled it his hand was shaking so much. He took deep breaths.

Chris explained about the camera that would record the interview up in one corner of the room. She ensured Jordan was ready to begin, and reassured he could take a break if needed. She explained she may need to make a few notes. He nodded. She then talked through the steps of only telling what was truthful, stating exactly what he saw, or heard in as much detail as possible. The information must only be from his perspective, not what others had told him. Chris explained he can speak up if there was anything at all he was unsure of, but not to guess at anything.

'You are here today following your account of sexual assault by Matthew Surtees at Linden House, a Children's Residential Care Home in Durham, during the summer of 1995. Can you please tell me about the incident?'

Jordan recounted as much as he could remember about the assaults. The first time it happened he felt as though he was in shock, and that he had imagined it, but then it happened every time Surtees was on duty. Jordan was able to talk for almost fifteen minutes, hesitating and correcting some of his testimony, concentrating on the reality of what had occurred. He was often reticent to say the words for body parts. He desperately tried to remain focussed throughout, hardly looking up at Chris. He had fallen into the deep, dark well of his dreadful past experience.

When it was clear he had completed his testimony, without interruption, Chris began the ancillary questions from her notes.

'How many times did this happen?'

'I don't remember, but every time he was on night shift duty.' Jordan shrugged. 'We dreaded it.'

'You mentioned Matthew Surtees spoke during the assault. Can you repeat what he said?'

Jordan hesitated … 'don't make a fucking sound or I'll kill you.'

'You said you were aware of a smell, can you describe that?'

'Yes, a really strong tobacco smell, more than cigarettes. Like from a pipe or a cigar … and … he stunk of sweat, you know, body odour, and his breath was kind of … sour smelling. Jordan wrinkled his nose and felt nauseous. He shakily picked up the empty glass, realised it was empty, so Chris poured in water from the jug on the table.

'What, if anything happened after the assaults?'

'I was sick in the bin in my room, and my mate Tom

would help me clean it up. He told me Surtees had been in his room as well.'

'Did you tell anyone?'

'N … no, I couldn't.' then under his breath, 'who would believe us anyway.'

'You spoke of a flashing light, tell me more about this.'

'I think it happened sometimes, not every time, I just remember the room lit up and I heard a click, a whirring sound like an old-fashioned camera. One time, it was pitch black at night, Surtees brought Tom into my room, made us both take off our pyjamas and forced us to touch ourselves here, Jordan pointed to his genital area.' He said quietly, 'there was loads of flashes that time.'

When it was apparent there was nothing else to report, Chris thanked Jordan for the information and complimented how well he had done, then led him back into the waiting area.

Jordan emerged to Aimee's waiting embrace and when they were outside he said, 'I did it Aimee, I told them everything!' He managed to repeat what he had rehearsed with Aimee. It was a weight of his shoulders, but his soul still ached deep inside for his lost childhood.

'Good lad!' said Aimee. The taxi she ordered arrived, and they went to Maia's apartment, calling at Greggs for Aimee to buy copious amounts of baked goodies. Jordan told Maia all about the interview.

'Well done Jordan, I'm proud of you.' Maia hugged him, 'Tom would be so proud of you too.'

There was a tangible silence that could be felt between the three. Maia could feel all of Tom's presence, his breath, his smell, his laugh, his voice ... everything that he was. The improbable three friends shared some food, and chatted before Aimee had to return home, and Jordan left for his accommodation, saying he was working on the green project the next morning.

Later that evening after Maia had been for a run, she became aware Alexi Leventis had made contact with the police about Surtees financial activity. He rang her, but she hadn't picked up his call whilst running. He left a brief voicemail, *"I've set the ball rolling with the police, and suspended Surtees from employment, also commenced the process of terminating his contract."*

Maia truly hoped there was enough evidence to cause Surtees at least some grief in his so far, charmed life. She had done everything she could and would now have to wait and see.

34

'WHO THE HELL does that jumped up goat-banging Greek fucker think he's talking to?' Surtees grumbled to himself as he walked out of Alexi's office, after being summoned. Then repeating Alexi's words with a scowl, *"your management of the Apollon Leisure Group is under investigation."*

Surtees knew there were some inconsistencies with the finances, but believed the stupid accountants wouldn't trace anything to him. At least that's what he tried to convince himself of as he stormed away from the building. He sat in his car revving up, and seething. 'It'll never show up in an audit, and he's got the nerve to fucking suspend me while he investigates. That bastard won't find anything!' He sped away, tyres shrieking, banging on the car horn at an unsuspecting couple crossing the road ahead, who had to scuttle out of the way to avoid an impact. Surtees was incandescent! As he drove he considered the option of his family legal team getting involved pronto, in case there was any hassle. Alexi and Gregori can stick their job, he didn't need them anymore, but it had been an easy number for the salary he was paid.

He thought about Gregori Leventis; they'd got along well initially as it was he, who had enlisted Surtees in the role of supervising the drugs team at the trap house for a percentage. He recalled Gregori's anxieties about Alexi finding out. Gregori distanced himself from ongoing communication, and focussed on the wizardry of secreting financial gains from illicit deals, into an offshore account.

Surtees turned up the music in the car and said aloud. 'Looks like I'll need more deals if the goat-banger is stopping my salary, but the idiot hasn't mentioned the car,' referring to the company leased BMW he was driving. Surtees didn't reflect much on his life, but he did feel resentment and lots of it.

Resentment about this latest travesty with Alexi. Resentment when Gayle, the stupid cow, walked out leaving him to fend for himself. Resentment the night club he owned went bust and took a huge chunk of his parents' financial contribution with it. The whole enterprise failed because of his poor management, and he lost a fortune on the final sale of the building too. Still, all of it was someone else's fault in his opinion. Surtees never accounted for the lost thousands he'd spent on trying to influence business associates by throwing money around, wining and dining to win favour; because he didn't know how else to impress, he had to buy people.

He'd racked up a significant amount of credit card debt in the past on those extravagant solo holidays too, also what he paid on male and female prostitutes if he couldn't get free sex. He'd also managed to write off three cars for dangerous driving since his teens, and one of those occasions, resulted in his licence being revoked for three years for a drink driving offence.

Resentment and bitterness about everything others had done unfairly to make Surtees' life difficult, raged inside him. He eventually calmed at the thought that his current operation had expanded, and he remained under the police radar making significant income. 'Dirty money they call it, nothing dirty about it,' he smirked. For now he needed to increase the imports and the circulation. A few days had passed, when he contacted Gregori to establish how that side of the business was going. He received one message from him on a number that wasn't in his contact list, which indicated there would be no further communication at present.

Over the next week, Surtees thought it strange he could not make contact with Gregori but dismissed it as sour grapes since his suspension from Apollon. Sitting at home in the huge echoing, now sold, Georgian terrace. He threw the phone onto the coffee table, along with the other detritus he left lying around for the new cleaner to sort out. The place was a mess since Gayle left. He drank two bottles of beer and finished a large takeaway pizza, watching his laptop. His phone alerted, the one he used for business at least. It was a message from an unknown number, but referred to a meeting with Baz at, 'the house,' Surtees fully understood the location.

Maybe the latest shipment had arrived. If that, Greek git Gregori, as he now referred to him, was letting things slide, Matthew certainly wasn't going to. It was 7.45pm on the first day of October, and he decided it was time to step-up and take control of the operations. He would never return to working for the Leventis brothers.

Matthew closed the laptop ending the stream of naked bodies in various stages of sexual acts on the screen. He zipped up his trousers, and stood quickly knocking a half empty beer bottle over, the foamy liquid spread across the coffee table, then dripped onto the floor. He put the jacket on, that he'd flung on the floor earlier, and checked the pockets for car keys. He kicked the empty pizza box across the floor on his way out of the room, left the house, got into the company car and drove off.

The trap house was twenty minutes' drive north, beyond the outskirts of the city. The remote non-descript terraced house was located on the edge of a crumbling, depleted small town, heading towards open countryside. Several rundown residential streets ran parallel to a small row of boarded up offices, shabby discount stores, and two takeaways. The house Surtees headed to, was the end dwelling in the last row, with nothing but fields to the rear for miles. No-one bothered the occupants. The door was always locked and blinds drawn.

Surtees unlocked the door with his own key, and entered the tobacco drenched, smoke-filled room. It was quiet, but for the low volume of voices coming from a TV. A young skinny man was laying on a small stained, grubby sofa; his gangly legs dangled over the arm. In the gloom, the flickering screen reflected across his unshaven face. Surtees recognised the kid as a regular at the premises. He didn't look up, and grunted, 'gone out,'

'Where?' Surtees demanded.

'Dunno,' the lad shrugged not taking his eyes off the screen, 'they told me to stay here 'til they came back.'

Surtees walked into what would be the dining room of the decrepit house. There was a large bag of white powder on the table in the centre of the room, surrounded by a variety of different size plastic bags. Surtees picked up the large package, placed his hand underneath it and grinned at the hefty weight. There was drug paraphernalia, scales and utensils set up ready for cutting. He took out his phone and rang Baz's number, he was supposed to be in charge of this shift. No answer, it didn't even go to voicemail. He tried Sol, another dead phone line. He wondered where all the shitbags were? They'd need to get their arses in gear. He thought about that scrote from the care home, and of a few other degenerates who may come in handy when circulation increased. The useless sods will do anything for a few quid. He walked right through the kitchen area and out of the rear door.

Surtees lit up a slim cigar as he looked across the empty fields, he always smoked them, gave him a sophisticated edge, so he believed. He thought he heard a vehicle or two in the distance. There wasn't much traffic on these roads, it's not as though the town was a delightful tourist destination, and few residents were employed. He assumed it must be Baz returning to the house, to arrange distribution of the drugs. He thought he'd try Gregori again, although he never got his hands dirty, Surtees knew the line would be dead, and it was. He had a rare, anxious moment, but dismissed it, flicking the discarded cigar into the urine-smelling rancid sewer of a back yard.

Raised voices coming from the front of the house alerted him. As Surtees entered the back door, the young lad who'd been lounging on the sofa, shot past him and pelted towards the open countryside. Surtees was entering the middle room, about to shout to Baz, he expected to see coming through the door. It was not Baz. A large imposing dark figure, with a visor reflecting his own terrified face was heading straight for him at speed. In a shocking millisecond he realised it was a police officer in full riot gear. He turned, attempting to run but two more officers appeared through the back door, and before he'd taken another step, they grabbed him.

A plain-clothed middle-aged male officer appeared, and asked him what he was doing there, whilst the uniform officers searched the building. Surtees stuttered that he came to see his mate Baz, and had no idea what all the stuff was, or who it belonged to. The officer cautioned him and told him he was being arrested for supplying Class A drugs. They searched him and took his phone and car keys. Surtees was really panicking now and could feel his bowels relaxing. As he was led to the car, he saw the young man handcuffed and struggling, as the police manhandled him into the back of a van.

Nothing was said in the vehicle and he only responded as required when being booked into custody at the station. Surtees was advised by the custody sergeant, he had the right to free legal advice, also to have someone notified he was there. Surtees demanded to speak with his father immediately. The custody sergeant, a patient older officer, said they would make arrangements for his father to be

THE IMPROBABLE THREE   265

informed of the situation. Surtees again, demanded to call him, however this was not permitted.

He was taken to a cell, suffering the humiliation of his jacket, belt, watch and shoes being removed and placed in a paper bag. He was given paltry refreshments, and left to sleep in the small pokey room, with a thin mattress on a tiny bunk. Surtees held his belief he would be out of there the next day, and he would ensure his solicitors were made aware of the bastards who had subjected him to this indignity. He lay on the bunk, hands behind his head with a smirk on his face, they didn't realise who they were dealing with, and their jobs were now in jeopardy.

It was 10.30 pm and Surtees' house was currently being searched and his car was seized. They found phones at his home and one in the car. His laptop was also seized. Recent information the police received from a credible registered informant had been corroborated, and was compelling enough for them to make the arrest at the trap house.

The custody officer made the call to Matthew Surtees' father, advising him of the position, and that his son had requested the family solicitor to represent him, when he was interviewed in the morning. His father was not prepared to pass on the solicitors' details, advising the officer that Matthew's mother had recently died. The family were bereaved and involved in legal matters concerning their properties and investments, so alternative legal representation would be required.

At the custody desk the next morning, Surtees was advised of this information. He, however, insisted he should have the opportunity to ring his father. A decision was made for this contact to proceed, as there was little threat of information being leaked, so there'd be no jeopardy affecting police enquiries, and this was facilitated. All ongoing searches relating to the enquiry were nearing completion too. Surtees was told to use the telephone located on the end of the desk.

'Hello Dad, I know the police have already rang you about this mess. It's nothing to do with me, they've made a gross error and I want to put in a claim for maltreatment by all the officers involved. Can you get one of the solicitors from the firm to make contact here and arrange to come and represent me. It's urgent as they won't wait forever.'

There was a pause … 'Matthew, I can no longer help you.' was the solitary response.

'What the hell do you mean by that?' He raised his tone somewhat, suppressing the urge to shout, in response to the custody sergeant's raised brows.

'Your mother is gone and she would always protect you in the past, but she isn't here now.' His dad sounded defeated. 'I simply cannot take on your problems any longer.'

'Come on Dad,' he implored, trying to retain a semblance of calm. 'This is so unfair. I haven't done anything wrong, it's all a big mistake.'

'Then you have nothing to worry about son.'

'But I really need one of our legal team to help out again, they've stepped in before.'

'No, this time you're on your own. I just can't deal with all this right now son, I've got enough on my plate.'

For the first time in his life, Surtees heard weakness in his father's tone of voice and when the line went dead, he knew it was over. No one was bailing him out this time. For the briefest moment, grief impacted upon him, since he heard the news of his mother's death from his sobbing sister over a month ago. He swore at the top of his voice and told his father to burn in hell, then he smashed the handset onto the counter, which broke into pieces.

The two detention officers grabbed either side of him. The ageing custody sergeant, brows still raised, informed him stoically, 'Mr Surtees, a duty solicitor will be appointed. You can expect to have criminal damage to police property added to your offences too.' He looked slightly amused, at the mangled phone on the counter.

Surtees was marched back to the cell to wait until the duty solicitor arrived. He continued to deny all knowledge of the source of the drugs on the premises, and the people involved. Surtees stuck to his account; he was simply visiting a friend, who was not there when he arrived. He had no knowledge whatsoever of any nefarious activity taking place in the property, otherwise he wouldn't have gone. He insisted he had never visited the premises before. He was released under investigation. In those few days since he left Alexi's office, his life had changed dramatically.

Surtees returned home briefly to grab some belongings. The aftermath of the police search was evident; he winced at the thought of what they may have found, but the amount of cocaine would be deemed recreational use only, he'd get a slap on the wrist for this, he was sure. He quickly packed some clothing, rang to rent a car, as the BMW had been towed away it seemed, and headed off to see his father. During the journey, he planned how he would soften his father up; he'd be kind and helpful and listen to him droning on about his mother, even though it had been weeks since the funeral. The stay would at least be free room and board, with a view to eliciting more financial support.

Surtees stayed with his father for two weeks and was given money from his mother's estate which boosted his finances. He was devastated when his brother Xander had a chat with him about his stake in, *Zanders* the new family bar-restaurant, which was prospering by all accounts. Xander felt it best to transfer the business loan they arranged into his, and his father's names only, therefore removing Matthew from the business concern, and any future profits. The family felt it may prove destructive to their business should there be any charges made against Matthew. It was a precaution, they said, and promised to reinstate him once he was legally cleared of any wrongdoing. No amount of pleading would change the decision, he realised his family wanted him out of the picture.

Surtees moved back to Newcastle with every intention of opening his own bar, and continuing with his drugs business, which he intended to expand once police enquiries cleared him. He was disgruntled that his father had sold the Georgian house, it had been an investment his mother had managed, but his dad no longer had any interest in renting it out. Surtees would have to find another home, but was hopeful of receiving a share of the proceeds from the sale. He was disinterested in looking for employment and could easily stretch his reasonable inheritance to fund his lifestyle for a while. He thought about taking a holiday soon, he smiled, he had always enjoyed being a lone traveller.

He intended ceasing contact with his former drugs associates, to reinstate the lucrative activity alone, believing he could create his own empire with no-one else calling the shots. He could easily find a way of laundering his own profitable proceeds. It couldn't be that difficult if Gregori managed it, and he was sure Gregori would divulge his contacts. He pondered his future, looking at available flights to any Greek island, or further afield, where it would still be warm and sunny in October. He'd take a holiday until things died down, once all of the spurious charges held against him were dropped.

35

THE CROWN PROSECUTION Service looked at all of the evidence and deemed Mathew Surtees should be re-interviewed. The narcotics seized had a street value of over £1 million so far, which reached the benchmark to deem him a flight risk. During the five weeks since his arrest on 1 October, the police downloaded data from Surtees' telephones and laptop. The Officer-in-Charge, now Detective Sergeant Christine Powell, was progressing the criminal investigation into Surtees' drug involvement. She was assigned the case on completion of a witness statement from Alexis Leventis. Having interviewed Jordan Davis when she was based within the Sexual Offences Unit, she was aware of his drug activity and historical sexual abuse from Jordan's testimony.

Surtees had booked a week in Tenerife where he hoped there'd be some British holidaymakers avoiding the onset of winter, when he was advised he was required for re-interview, relating to recent inquiries. He wholeheartedly believed there were no charges and the interview was a formality to clear everything up. He desperately needed this police involvement to end, so he could get on with his life.

'I'll be on my way to sunnier climes soon, away from this shit-hole. These pigs are as thick as Alexi if they think they can get one over on me.' These words were spoken under his breath, as he parked up and got out of his newly acquired luxury vehicle bought with the inheritance from his mother. He'd arrived at the city police station at the designated appointment time. Surtees was led to an interview room, and was offered the explanation that he was required to attend for further interview, as all searches were now complete.

DS Chris Powell, in her now recognisable uniform of grey suit, but this time with a pale blue shirt, not black, took the lead in the interview and began by asking a question. 'Mr Surtees, you were arrested at a residential property, we now know was being used for the preparation and distribution of drugs. Have you ever been to that property before?'

Surtees replied. 'I've already said, I've never been before and was just meeting a friend. I know nothing about the place.'

'Does your friend own the property, and do you have regular access to it?'

'I've no idea who owns it and, no, I don't have regular access to it.'

'Do you know the young person, Robert Fawcett, also known as Robbie Fawcett, who was in the house when you were arrested?'

'Never seen him before in my life.'

It wasn't long into the interview when the officers recognised Surtees would only respond to the male, secondary interviewing officer sitting next to Chris, albeit she was asking the questions. He also showed contempt for the assigned solicitor beside him.

Chris continued. 'At the time of the arrest there was a large bag of heroin on the table. Can you tell me anything about that.'

'I didn't see it and even if I had, I wouldn't know what it was.'

'Do you have a car?'

'I had a company car at the time.'

'Is it a black BMW 8-series coupé with personalised registration MTW 5URT'

'Yes, that's my own private number plate I had fitted.'

'Who has access to the vehicle?'

'Only me, just for my business use with Apollon Leisure.'

'Would anyone else, other than you, have driven the vehicle over the last few months?'

'No, as I said, just me.' Matthew's responses were becoming increasingly terse.

'Two mobile phones were recovered, one at your home address placed on a bedside table, and the other was in your vehicle. Do they both belong to you?'

'The one by my bed is for personal calls only, any other phones are used for business.'

'Does anyone else have access to the phones, for example, would they have the unlock device pin numbers?'

'No, not at all.'

Chris continued with similar mundane questions, and Surtees became confident there was no evidence against him whatsoever.

'Why am I here, if this is a formality, it's taking ages.

Why are you continuing to ask me the same questions over and over?'

'We simply need to establish your whereabouts or any involvement Mr Surtees, and this is the correct procedure. Thank you for the information, this seems a good point to have a break before the final interview. Would you like a coffee or tea?'

'No. I'll get a proper coffee, a Starbucks, soon as I'm out of this shi … place,' he quickly corrected his language, as a custody officer led him out of the door heading for the cells. Chris followed him out of the interview room.

Surtees wondered why the hell they had him in a cell, when they clearly had nothing on him. Twenty minutes elapsed and he was escorted back to the interview room, increasing his frustration. He constantly tapped his fingers on the table and his right knee bounced frantically under it, restraining him from exploding and yelling at the incompetent cow who sat in front of him.

Chris calmly explained the situation. 'Mr Surtees we appreciate you've answered all of our questions, however there are a few things not tying up.'

Surtees seethed inwardly as his lower jaw jutted forward gritting his teeth.

'You stated that you've never seen or met Robbie Fawcett before the night you were arrested.'

Surtees nodded in acknowledgement.

'Can you please reply for the recording.'

With an immense sigh, 'I have never seen him before, ever.'

'Mr Fawcett has been interviewed and confirms he had seen you at the house on previous occasions.'

'He's lying.' Surtees lifted his forearms off the table, slumped back in his chair, folded his arms and looked away from the officers.

'Not only that, a neighbour confirmed they had seen your vehicle there on four occasions in the last three weeks. Can you explain that?'

Surtees, still looking at the side wall said, 'rubbish, could've been anyone's car.'

'When you were arrested Mr Surtees, you were in possession of a front door key to the property, yet you claim not to have access to the house. Can you now explain how you got that key?'

Surtees said nothing. A silence of five seconds passed like a lifetime, when he was encouraged to reply by the duty solicitor, who he ignored. For the benefit of the recording, the second officer stated he had not replied.

Chris continued. 'You have stated you alone had access to the BMW registration number MTW 5URT.'

Matthew offered a curt nod. The benign solicitor alongside him indicated that was sufficient as a response.

'For the benefit of the recording, Mr Surtees has acknowledged he had sole use of said vehicle.' Chris paused. 'The Apollon Company GPS records show, in the last three months, this vehicle has been located at the property on nine occasions. Can you explain this?'

Surtees remained simmering in silence. He was unaware that Alexi had welcomed the police to investigate his financial transactions with the company, which included viewing all records for the company vehicle. They were able to track his journeys which included trips to the trap house.

Mathew Surtees was stunned, his mind was racing with the realisation those Greek bastards knew he was being investigated, so that's why Alexi let him keep the car. He may even have instigated it all. Surtees was fired-up, still not realising the seriousness of the list of charges, he could only focus on how he'd get revenge and implicate Gregori, that foreign scum!

Christine Powell continued. 'You have also confirmed the mobile phones that were seized were for your own personal or business use. The cell tower information from your mobile phone company is also consistent with you being in the area on these occasions.'

Christine's colleague, and second interviewer braced, sensing Surtees' suppressed frustration may boil over any second as she continued.

'Information from your phones has been downloaded, and the data on numerous messages indicate you were concerned in the supply of drugs. Can you explain this communication?'

Surtees had internally switched off his senses, as he looked vaguely between the officers faces at the wall behind them, making no eye contact. He continued to disregard his legal representatives advice. The second interviewing officer stated, 'for the purposes of the recording, Mr Surtees has not acknowledged the question.'

Christine continued maintaining her stoic conduct and monotonous tone. 'Furthermore in the house, you state you haven't previously visited, there was a bag of heroin which you claim not to have seen. However, your fingerprints were recovered from the bag. What is your explanation for that?'

Surtees felt powerless, yet tried to counter the questioning. 'You know who you need to ask these questions to? The Leventis brothers.' He crossed his arms and believed Christine may want to halt the process and divert her enquiries elsewhere. But to his horror, she cautioned him again. His confusion was evident.

'Following examination of your laptop, a significant amount of data was retrieved.'

Matthew Surtees face drained to ash grey.

'In addition to your arrest concerning the supply of Class A drugs, I am further arresting you on suspicion of being in possession of indecent images of children.'

As she left the room with the solicitor for a briefing about the serious Category A images, Surtees began writhing and kicking, pushing at the table shouting, 'you fucking bitch. I'll kill you!'

Detective Sergeant Christine Powell hit the emergency buzzer strip at hip-height around the room, and two custody officers quickly entered the room to subdue him, and take him back to his cell. Matthew Surtees was charged and the custody sergeant denied bail. He would appear before magistrates the following day, and remanded in custody pending trial.

36

FRANK O'BRIEN, A journalist at the Daily Record in Newcastle, had kept a close eye on Matthew Surtees' activity for some time, and recently relished reports he'd been charged for drug offences. Following a conversation with his ex-partner, Michaela, last week, they concluded their drinks were spiked before being intimidated and coerced into their involuntary actions at Surtees' home on that fateful night in 2014. Michaela commented she believed Gayle, had left Surtees. Frank wondered if Gayle may be a great asset regarding the life and times of this abuser. He could never forget the guilt he felt and the humiliation Surtees had subjected them to. He knew there was more to his story than these recent charges.

Frank grinned, tapping his pen on his neat goatee-covered chin, as his Mac screen reflected the image of his bright blue eyes. Scrolling through a number of archived articles and photos, he stopped at a picture of Surtees from some years ago with scantily clad and bejewelled podium dancers from his failed night club, Euphoria. He was looking sleazy and obviously inebriated, stoned, or both, leering at their breasts. Frank's editor was keen to support the exposé, most readers responded to a good local sex scandal, it would get plenty of clicks and make great copy; *Bankrupt former nightclub owner Matthew Edmund Surtees arrested on suspicion of drug dealing and possession of indecent images of children.*

Michaela agreed to make contact with Gayle to assist Frank's investigation, as she was also keen to expose Surtees. Michaela had deleted the meek apologetic messages from Gayle after the debauched night, she couldn't bear to speak with her, but remembered about the email address. Not long after she sent an email asking to make contact, Gayle rang and couldn't stop apologising for allowing the events of that night to happen. Michaela calmed Gayle and reassured her none of it was her fault. She explained Frank was following up anyone who had fallen victim to Surtees intimidation and abuse. They agreed to meet, and at Gayle's request, Frank didn't attend their meeting.

Michaela saw Gayle arrive at the mutually agreed, quiet wine bar and ordered a small glass of red wine for each, she recalled Gayle enjoyed red wine. Michaela was struck at how young, fit and healthy she looked, from the over made-up, pout-lipped woman, with the abundant frond-flicking lashes she had previously met. Gayle told Michaela, 'he was the instigator of it all. I had no idea he had planned any of it. He had a way of making you feel stupid and unadventurous, plus all the drink didn't help.'

Looking deeply into Gayle's distraught face, Michaela said, 'Matthew told me everyone knew the rules of this type of game. You had to try something you wouldn't usually do with your partner. He produced loads of sex toys that I never imagined existed. He tried to insist on anal sex with me and suggested it with Frank too.' Michaela explained she and Frank separated soon after the traumatic night as they felt all trust had gone, and she never knew what happened to Allan and Evie. They severed all contact.

Tears sprung into Gayle's eyes, 'I'm really so very sorry, you were the only friend I had at the time and I let all that happen to you.'

'You had little to do with it Gayle,' Michaela reassured. 'He is a skilled abuser.'

Gayle settled and sipped her wine. She spoke of how Matthew would threaten to withdraw finances unless she dressed in sexually provocative clothing, some of which she disliked immensely and found physically restricting. She drew the line at bondage as she felt scared of being incapacitated in his presence. Recently she had reflected some of her memories were vague and dumbed-down, and she wondered if he had put some form of sedative in her drinks or food.

'I definitely wondered about that too, it felt almost dreamlike. It wouldn't surprise me if he'd got his hands on some Rohypnol or something to spike our drinks.' Michaela felt her own anger and shameful disgust rising. 'The horrible bastard!'

'He was always taking videos and photos of me too,' said Gayle. 'He'd appear with his phone held in front of him recording me while I was in the shower, or getting ready, and even on the loo for god's sake.' Gayle inwardly shuddered and continued, 'I was in the TV room and switched the telly on, when a paused naked image of me appeared on the screen. I discovered Matthew was covertly recording footage when we had sex, but I knew nothing of it.' Gayle had challenged Matthew about the footage. He laughed and said his, *"Matt's Movies"* were an extra benefit when he entertained guests. That's why he always separated the men to go into the TV room to play games. Not long after that night, I walked out of the door leaving everything behind and I never looked back. I've learnt a lot Michaela. He was a master of grooming and coercive control before I understood what it was, but I see it so clearly now.'

Michaela was immensely supportive as she listened to Gayle pour her heart out, and believed she had never talked to anyone about her experience. Gayle said she had met, 'a really nice lad,' and reconnected with her family and friends. Michaela was pleased to hear this, and that Gayle had returned to work. She was taking up studies with ambitions to join the police. Michaela encouraged her, believing she could start a great new career protecting women because of her experience.

Following that conversation Michaela relayed the information from Gayle to Frank as they settled in their favourite coffee shop in the city. It was a pre-arranged meeting to discuss how Frank's investigation into Matthew Surtees' personal life and family history was progressing. Frank had prolifically contacted people who were associated with Surtees' night club, until its demise. He had gleaned snippets of information, and lots of rumours of dealing drugs and Surtees' unsavoury, leery nature with workers and customers at the club, both male and female. Above all, most people from the business side commented that Matthew

Surtees was a compulsive liar, couldn't be trusted and his business was brim-full of corrupt dealings.

A woman who had managed one of the bars within the club likened him to, a Walter Mitty type character, with delusions of grandeur where he would pretend to be on the phone to some wealthy business associate in Dubai, when it was evident there was no-one on the other end of the phone. He was a joke to her.

One or two who had brief business partnerships with Surtees alluded to him seeking funding from his parents when he was in dire straits, until the funds ran out. The banks wanted their loans repaid, and the business folded at a significant loss. Many staff didn't receive their final pay cheques and Surtees went underground, fleeing to his parents' home until the dust settled. There were some dangerous people after him for repayment of debts too, which most of his former associates suggested his family probably paid them off.

Michaela felt it appropriate to be present when Frank interviewed the women who had worked at the club during Surtees tenure. Frank was grateful for her support. It was becoming clear Surtees had made advances towards many girls working there and wouldn't take 'no' for an answer. In general most of the, now older women, interviewed would recount his creepy, aggressive style, but they did not want to be associated with any report that would reveal their identities as they were now happily settled in life, but gave details anonymously.

Frank and Michaela were waiting in the coffee shop for a former worker from the club, Gina, they never knew whether former associates or victims would appear for pre-arranged meetings. Michaela received a text, looked toward the cafe door and spotted a woman looking around. She was probably in her early forties, dressed in jeans, with a heavy jacket on this cold November day. After they settled into conversation, Gina was willing to divulge information, that had worried her for years.

Gina became visibly upset when she spoke of a young woman called, Ashleigh, who had just started working at the club in 2003. Ashleigh told her, Matthew raped her in his office when she refused his advances. She became pregnant, and had a termination. Gina helped Ashleigh through the procedure and encouraged her to go to the police, but Ashleigh refused to report the crime.

Gina said, 'I received a postcard from Ashleigh months later telling me she was now living near Newquay. She'd met a nice bunch of friends, was working in a bar, and was learning how to surf. Bless her, she only sent it to thank me for my kindness. There was no return address and I have no way of contacting her. Anyway I very much doubt she would report anything ... people don't.'

After further discussion, Gina left, and wished them the best of luck to help expose Matthew Surtees for what he is. Michaela and Frank glanced at each other, aware of the humiliation and shame which washed over them when they were together, listening to others' testimony.

Following extensive background research Frank had tracked down a man called, Jerry, who was at university with Surtees, and now lived in Edinburgh. Frank travelled to meet him as Jerry was happy to speak with him. Jerry explained, Matthew was invited as a replacement with group of students on a final university hurrah in Ibiza, as someone had dropped out.

Jerry recounted his experience, with animation, in a gentle Scottish accent, 'I suggested a superhero theme, and coudnae believe it when Matthew arrived in the hotel foyer in a full rubber gimp suit on our first night. I remember at the time saying, what the hell's all this, ye pervert? Most o' the lads burst out in roars of laughter. Jesus, huvnae seen the like before. Only his eyes showed through the mask, the mouth was zipped up an' when he unzipped it for a drink, there was a feckin ball between his teeth, sorry for swearing Frank. What a wierdo. He wore a spiked dog collar and leather lead too. It wus embarassin' he got young lassies te trail him around on all fours, an' they kept askin' us how he went to the toilet 'n' the like. Us lads just disowned him. He was a joke, a nutter. There was something … you know, off, with him. The way he looked at women, starin' an' all.'

Frank asked, 'were you aware of any, let's say advances, he made towards anyone?'

Jerry continued, 'a few o' the lassies were nervous around him. We learned one lass was in a right state saying she'd been assaulted in the early hours on her way back to the hotel. Grabbed from behind, but it wasnae clear what had gone on, and she coudnae be sure who did it, likely traumatised and drunk no doubt. There were rumours about drinks being spiked too. Awfy business.'

'Did anyone suspect him?'

'I guess you cannae just accuse people willy-nilly with no evidence,' said Jerry. 'I've two daughters now and it terrifies me thinking of it.' Jerry was shaking his head. 'This was all years ago, and I'm glad there's more information nowadays that says us lads should pipe up if awfy things are going on.'

Frank and Jerry continued to converse and Jerry offered additional, vague memories about Matthew, being quite unremarkable at university. Jerry's demeanour was much more subdued than when he initially met with smiles and handshakes. 'Jesus, I just hope my girls will be safe when they're older, goin' off out into town on their own.' He wished Frank success with his investigations and suggested if he thought of anything else he'd be in touch.

On his return train journey from Edinburgh, Frank wrote up copious notes from the interview with Jerry. Deep in thought, Frank enjoyed the view of the north east's rugged coastline, and the vast expanse of the sea stretching to the horizon. He got to thinking about beach resorts in Europe and couldn't get the thought out of his mind that Matthew Surtees sexual abuse must have been going on for two decades at least since 1995. He also thought, probably not restricted to the UK, or places he'd worked. He should broaden his search for victims to include anywhere Surtees had been abroad on holiday. Time and location are not barriers for serial abusers. Frank offered Michaela his thoughts about extending his search abroad when she met him at Newcastle station. He relayed Jerry's account to Michaela, who voiced her sincerest sympathy for anyone unfortunate enough to cross Surtees path, 'that poor girl, and saying nothing, but it's totally understandable why people don't report assaults. Can you imagine us having to sit with a police officer and recount the events of that night.' Tears sprang into Michaela's eyes. 'You could end up with PTSD or something, all because of that bastard.'

Frank leaned forward and took her hand, 'I know ... I know, you'd just feel so stupid and humiliated. It would be so ... so, degrading.'

There was a fierce look on Michaela's face. 'I hope he's going to rot in prison for years, the dirty bastard. All those lives he's ruined.'

Frank had a doubtful look on his face. The information he was gathering was consistent. He had commenced investigations into various care homes, where Surtees had worked casually as a student. He'd begun tracking down workers, and now adults who had been in care during the summer months Surtees may have worked there. There were some quite positive leads where people wished to discuss more information with Frank and Michaela, but most refused. Their meetings were becoming more regular, and more relaxed now that time had passed since that dreadful night. The fact many more people were coming forward reporting similar experiences of Surtees gave them some relief, it wasn't just them who had been duped, also the drive to report a story and expose his terrible acts was satisfying.

As if by way of drawing a line under their experience, Frank chanced his arm, saying, 'I've tried to contact Allan and Evie from that night?'

Michaela nodded solemnly.

'Allan did answer once, but when he realised who I was, he cut the call and must've blocked my number as I can't now get through. I'm not going to push it, it's too sensitive. Folk will come forward if they want to.'

'You're a good bloke Frank,' Michaela looked into his soulful blue eyes. 'Too nice to be an embittered old hack.'

Michaela and Frank enjoyed their familiar banter. He chanced his arm again. 'Well ... would you be interested in this non-embittered old hack taking you out to dinner sometime? Even for old time's sake.'

'Oh alright, go on then,' said Michaela, 'hate to think of you all alone, with only your MacBook for company, eating microwave ready meals for dinner.'

Their eyes met again and warm smiles radiated between the couple, sitting in their favourite coffee shop, with vapour rising from fresh cups of coffee.

37

MAIA INVITED ROSA for lunch, to catch up about the latest news regarding the whole Surtees debacle, also what was happening with Ben. Rosa had been a patient ear for Maia, one of her best qualities, despite her quirky randomness, she was a good listener. Maia noticed a deep red mark under Rosa's ear, when she arrived.

'Bloody straighteners! I'll never get the hang,' Rosa explained.

'You are the clumsiest person in the world Rosa. Step away from the kitchen and don't touch my new wine glasses.' Maia laughed.

'Please yersel,' Rosa commented as she wafted by, 'I'll park my arse out on the balcony and you can bring the offerings soon as you like, Slave.'

'Cheeky sod!' came the retort from the kitchen. 'The blankets are on the chairs; we should have about an hour before it gets too cold to sit out, Newcastle in November can be rather chilly. Oh look, Nik has dropped off some tapas for lunch, just needs heating up, isn't that lovely of her?'

'Thank the lord, I don't have to suffer your Bolognese speciality yet again.' Rosa stopped before heading onto the balcony and was admiring Daphne's beautiful hot air balloon watercolour on the wall, 'some folk are so talented aren't they?'

'Yes, true,' replied Maia, carrying a tray full of Cafe Dalvik goodies and a bottle of red wine, with two intact wine glasses. 'What about Daphne and Zain expecting a baby, how lovely!

'Such a shame she can't make it tonight, but the sickness and fatigue early on is horrendous. It'll be a little cracker with those two stunners,' Rosa paused. 'Me and Steve are trying for another.'

'Oh?' said Maia looking at the wine as she set the tray onto the table.

'It's okay, nothing yet,' reassured Rosa, now enveloped in a thick fake fur blanket on the balcony. 'Before we embark on this delicious feast, courtesy of your darling sister, have you seen this?' she held up her phone. The online local news showed Frank O'Brien's preliminary report on the disgraced Surtees. 'Look at that picture, the slimy bastard.'

'Horrible, said Maia, so glad Alexi reported him, 'I've got a feeling his brother, Gregori was connected to the drugs thing with Surtees. He'll have torn a strip off Gregori for sure, deservedly so; he'll clean up the mess and say Surtees was acting alone. Alexi won't want shame upon the family, so they'll pile it all on that fat twat. I felt Alexi was glad of an excuse to get rid of him as he didn't trust him one bit with the company finances. No more swanning around in a top end BMW for Fatty Matty Surtees.'

'Just wait until the outcome of the historical child abuse investigation too ... if it happens,' said Rosa. 'That Frank O'Brien article makes definite hints about lots of dodgy goings on. Obviously he can't outright state Surtees is a nonce, but he's definitely left it open for people to come forward. Decent for a journo eh? They often want to exploit these sort of situations for their own profile, and expose victims to the wolves, don't they ... eh Maia?' A toothy grin.

Maia offered a mock withering look in response. 'I could suggest Jordan speaks with him, maybe, as it may encourage others to come forward. Wouldn't surprise me if there were more children in the homes where Surtees worked. Now he's been put away, Jordan may feel more confident about the truth coming out in public, but I don't want to disrupt his life right now.'

'Trouble is, it can take years for people to get the justice they deserve, and only if it can be proven. But then, maybe Jordan won't feel so isolated if he knows many others have suffered the same,' said Rosa.

'The utter bastard,' said Maia, 'another sentence on top for sexual abuse will keep him out of everyone's way for longer you'd hope. I do hope Jordan keeps his nose clean and finishes the rehab program. I was so worried he may lose his volunteering work and be set back to homelessness with the stress of all this. Glad Aimee is keeping an eye on him too, I'm worn out with it all. You'd love her Rosa, and Jordan is a brave lad. Tom would be so proud of him, I wish he was here to see Jordan's recovery ... I just wish he was here.'

Rosa rested a hand on Maia's and looked sympathetically toward her. Then her toothy grin emerged and the expression changed. 'Hey, do you think Fatty Matty will be put away with the other nonces; Rolf Harris, Gary Glitter and the like. They were convicted recently weren't they? Christ 2015 has been rife with them. At least there'll be some recreational facilities; art lessons with ol' Rolfy, a nice painting to adorn his cell.' Rosa spread her arm wide. 'Maybe a bit of a Glitter Band greatest hits sing-a-long of an evening, and I'm sure, Fred the weatherman will keep them updated with a daily forecast too. What a bunch of absolutely creepy dangerous bastards, and that's without that other depraved fecker, Sa-vile!' Rosa always emphasised the, *vile,* pronunciation.

Maia enjoyed the imagery her beloved friend conjured up of nonce recreational activity in prison. She looked at the picture on the news report on Rosa's phone, and spoke directly into Matthew's image, 'you abusive foul, fat, filthy fuck-face! I hope you never see the light of day for the rest of your miserable life.'

Unlike Maia to express that level of profanity and hatred, so Rosa tilted her head and said softly, 'ah Maia, bless you. Do you feel better for that now honey?'

'I do actually. Ab-so-fucking-lute-ly!

Maia and Rosa sat quietly on the balcony with a glass of crisp white wine in hand and the tapas ready for picking, catching up about their lives and loved ones.

'This place is lush, and a night off for me too ... perfect. You're so lucky to have this lifestyle, and with Ben joining you soon too,' Rosa said followed by a gentle smile, then balanced it with, 'and you're thirty soon short-arse, good job someone's finally plucked you off the shelf.'

Maia smiled. 'But, you're not so badly off Rosa. Honestly, your lovely devoted Steve and scrumptious Anthony. Hope there's another on the way soon.'

'Yeah hope so … but first, fill up my glass, Slave!'

Which the Slave did.

'You know Rosa, if it hadn't been for Tom keeping that phone and the notebook, it wouldn't have led me to Jordan or Aimee, and Surtees would still be as free as a bird.'

They looked at each other, clinked their glasses and said instinctively and in unison, 'to Tom.'

38

MAIA VISITED PAULINE and Mike, and updated them about her findings about Tom's death. 'It does seem to have been a freak accident, there's nothing to suggest he was depressed, or on drugs and drinking to indicate suicide.' She explained about the ongoing investigation regarding Surtees, and Pauline nodded towards Mike, commenting it was as well he was imprisoned, as it would be Mike being done for murder, to which Mike agreed.

'I am relieved it wasn't drugs or anything,' said Pauline, 'he had a rough year or so when he was on them, which we knew about, but we stuck with him and he came out of the other side a better person.'

The three sat in silence for a few moments in the cosy front room of the Cassidy home. 'Christmas tree is lovely, you always get a real one,' said Maia, and very early too, it's not December yet.'

Christmas for the Cassidys was always full of fun, love and laughter, family rituals and overspending! Mike and Pauline looked at each other, and Pauline began to cry. He put his arm around her and said, 'it's our first Christmas without Tom, he always came for Christmas Day, with Fiona, she was lovely. He would have been thirty two next year. Still can't believe he's gone.' He held Pauline, 'hey, hey come on love,' he said with such tenderness.

'I know, but I'd be putting his gifts under the tree now, and I just can't bear the fact we won't see his smiling face again.'

'I know love,' Mike had tears in his eyes but valiantly tried to smile as he said, 'we'll miss opening the daft joke presents he used to get us ... remember ...' He didn't finish the sentence. The couple remained in stillness and silence and Maia almost felt voyeuristic at their grief. Then she had an idea she hoped would cause distraction.

'You know, I'm in touch with Jordan, Tom's friend and caught up with Aimee who stayed with you, we could arrange to meet up in the new year maybe.'

A slight smile appeared on Pauline's face at the mention of Aimee.

'Look what I have here.' Maia showed them a recent image on her phone of Jordan and Aimee, which was taken the last time the three of them got together.

Pauline gazed adoringly for some time at the two fully fledged adults, 'he looks healthy and she's absolutely beautiful!' she exclaimed.

Mike smiled shaking his head, 'you'd never forget Aimee.'

Pauline and Mike enjoyed hearing about their lives, and were enthusiastic about meeting them both. Pauline tentatively mentioned meeting Tom's sister Abigail to Mike again, but he hadn't changed his mind, 'I couldn't care less about his birth family after the way he was treated and abandoned by them. Not sure I could put my feelings to one side, I may say something out of line.'

Pauline tried to assuage the situation, 'but Mike, Abigail had nothing to do with Tom going into care, she was only a baby,' her expression hardened, 'it was the parents who scapegoated him at every opportunity, until they eventually got rid of my brilliant boy from blighting their lives.'

Mike added, 'no doubt they told everyone he had gone off the rails or he was bad inside, or summat.' His anger was evident, the usually calm, gentle-giant of a man, left the room to go to his workshop, his sanctuary.

Maia felt his disquiet too, could she keep her own emotions in check if she met Abigail? She'd have to. It wasn't her fault, and the point was to support Pauline, and she was indeed, rather curious too. The meeting with Abigail was arranged at a quiet traditional front street cafe near Pauline's home.

Maia and Pauline were settled in the cafe with a hot drink, Maia turned at the sound of the tinkling bell as the cafe door opened and got quite a shock. It was as if Tom was walking through the door in his teenage years. Abigail was his double! Pauline noticed Maia's reaction, caught her eye and nodded, 'told you, they could be twins.'

Pauline waved over to Abigail who was at the counter getting a coffee, she mouthed, did they want anything?

Maia quickly asked, 'does she know who I am or why I'm here? Did you mention I was a girlfriend of Tom's?'

'Oh yes, I wouldn't bring anyone along unless she knew about it. Abigail asked about Tom's dad, which I thought was lovely, because she meant Mike, but I said he was busy and couldn't come.'

Abigail was wearing a fur-lined navy parka coat and walked over to the table. Apart from her striking attractive likeness to Tom, with sparkling bright green eyes, she seemed quite drab. Her long mid-brown hair wasn't in any particular style and Maia noticed it didn't appear to be that well-groomed. Could do with a touch of conditioner, she thought. Abigail wore no makeup and her clothes aged her. Maia again thought, what I could do with some great clothes on that figure, making up those eyes and a bit of blush on those cheekbones.

Abigail approached the table with a timid, 'hello.' She took off her coat, revealing a tan A-line cord skirt which reached her knees, a cream cable-knit jumper with a terracotta scarf, and plain black non-descript winter boots. She wore little jewellery apart from small gold sleeper earrings and a dainty gold bracelet on her right hand, and a slim gold bracelet watch on her left.

Pauline introduced Maia, and Abigail smiled sweetly at her. Maia noted she even had the slight quirk of uneven teeth on one side of her smile. This actually made her really happy to see, yes they could definitely have been twins.

'Please, I'm Abbi, no need for my Sunday name,' she said with a little smile.

Pauline had brought a few photographs of Tom soon after he arrived at her home, smiling, looking already settled. Abbi became quite emotional and quiet as she soaked in every photograph looking at Tom's features, studying him closely. She said it seemed he had a wonderful relationship with his mam, glancing with appreciation at Pauline, and his dad.

Maia said how much Tom was loved by Pauline and Mike, it was important Abbi understood these people were the most important in Tom's life. There was absolutely no resistance from her to the comment whatsoever.

Abbi went on to say how she never really understood why Tom didn't live with them, or why they never saw him. She asked about him when she was younger, but her parents were vague. Maia asked what explanation they gave for Tom's absence in the family. Both Pauline and Maia were waiting for the response which, true to their expectations was; his behaviour was so terrible, his mother couldn't cope because the father worked away a lot, so he was placed in care.

Pauline indicated to Abbi in no uncertain terms, she probably did not understand everything about what happened with Tom, and Abbi agreed. Pauline was able to offer lots of descriptive and personal information about Tom, about his personality, about his wishes and his dreams, about what a wonderful person he turned out to be, and he had an incredibly happy life with them.

Maia echoed those sentiments, 'we all still miss him terribly, always will.'

Pauline suggested, 'maybe on another occasion I could tell you more detail about Tom's past if it feels right.'

Abbi acknowledged her comment.

Maia said looking at a photo of her and Tom one Christmas, 'it's still raw.'

Abbi said, 'I've realised what a significant loss it's been

for me, never knowing my big brother. I wish things had been different. Never having the opportunity to have a relationship with him and now being cruelly taken away.'

'Why didn't you try and contact him?' asked Maia.

'Truthfully I felt guilty and wasn't sure he'd ever want anything to do with me, and my ...' Abbi hesitated, 'God-fearing parents with their discipline, would never allow me to. It was how I was brought up, to obey the rules of the house. I had little freedom as a young girl and even in my teens. They wanted to know exactly where I was, where I had been, where I was going, and who I was with, all of the time. I thought it was normal parental protection until I attended college to do a business course, then I realised other girls had much more freedom and trust with their parents, so I started to make friends.'

She laughed and recounted tales about her rebellious teenage years, which were mild to say the least. Maia never got tired of seeing her smile and laugh which reminded her so much that Tom had existed; he had lived in this world and she'd loved him.

It also struck her, here was Freya's aunty by birth, maybe she would grow up looking like Abbi, a sobering thought, which she may never know. She made a vow the paternal grandparents would never know about Freya.

Abbi went to Hull University, in part to get away from her parents' clutches, as she needed to live her own life. Maia estimated Abbi was in her mid-twenties as she remembered Tom saying he thought he was about five or six when she was little. It wasn't long before Maia could see, and sense the parental relationship Pauline would likely be involved in with Abbi. She would be taken under the Cassidy wing no doubt.

Abbi spoke about the wider family, 'my mother has a brother who moved to Australia, so there are cousins I only know from Facebook. I now live in Yarm in a flat share, it's great, I never returned to my parents' home after uni, which they are still not happy about.

Pauline asked if they were still living in Billingham.

'Still in the same house, and would you believe they decorate the house every other year with the same wallpaper and paint. When they replace furniture, they scour the shops for the same items.' Abbi continued with a shake of her head, 'honestly its weird. They have the same bedding, curtains and towels they've had for years, only replacing like-for-like items when they've worn thin. They have the same ornaments, lamps, fruit bowl, crockery, pans and cutlery, and never replace them. All in exactly the same place as when I was young.'

Maia added humorously, 'really? That is a bit strange. I change my colour schemes every six months, and I'm always re-jigging stuff around.'

A delighted look appeared on Abbi's face. 'Me too! I think I've gone in the opposite direction to them, because of the way they are. I'm sure they've wanted the best for me, but honestly their routines are so strictly adhered to; even in the garden. They buy the same plants every year, same colour and put them in exactly the same place. Nothing ever changes. I even use Abbi now as they insisted on correcting my friends, or anyone else, that they must call me Abigail my name in full, it was so embarrassing.' Abbi looked ashamed now.

Maia guessed there had been times when her parents had sucked every ounce of individuality or flair out of her. Abbi began to really relax now, showing more of Tom's personality, it was definitely in there.

She asked tentatively, 'was Tom the little terror I've been led to believe?'

Pauline said, 'there were times Tom didn't know how to deal with the world because of his childhood experiences, and he needed support through those times. Most of the time he was thoughtful and caring, very loving, but sometimes he was naturally mischievous.'

'Oh good,' said Abbi wistfully, 'glad to hear he had some spirit. I feel so much closer to him, I'm glad you agreed to meet with me.'

'We have footage of him singing in a band. Maybe someday you'd like to see those videos?' said Maia.

'Yes, good idea,' added Pauline, 'we also have loads of film of him; on holidays, playing football, when he got a motorbike, a guitar, you name it.'

Abbi was thrilled at the prospect. 'Doubt my big brother would ever have been allowed those things if he'd stayed at home,' Abbi said ruefully, 'they'd be really annoyed knowing I'm here, but I don't care.'

Great to see a glimmer of Tom-like rebellion. Maia caught Pauline's pleasing glance, likely thinking the same. Abbi had claimed him as her big brother. Pauline gave Abbi the photos and they hugged. They both saw Abbi crying as she left for her train. Maia held Pauline's hands and said it was the best thing Tom had over twenty wonderful years with her and Mike. He lived a life full of love and laughter.

Pauline agreed, 'I doubt very much his real parents would have put up with him playing guitar and singing at all hours; messing about with his school mates on games and making such a racket in the bedroom, plus the motorbike phase, creating all sorts of havoc.'

'Come on, let's get you home. Maybe you can now persuade Mike to meet Abbi.'

Pauline agreed he may be more receptive as Abbi didn't seem so close to her parents, 'it may be good for Mike to connect with her to help him deal with his grief.'

As they got up to leave, Maia linked arms with Pauline, turned directly to her and said, 'Pauline, you did make a big mistake earlier.'

Pauline looked surprised.

'You do realise ... you and Mike are Tom's *real* parents. Tom told me exactly that years ago. He loved you both very much and let's face it, Tom almost lived two lifetimes in one the way he threw himself into everything. And he was happy, he was loved, and he didn't take his own life, I'm sure of that now, it must've been an awful stupid accident.

Pauline seemed contented by Maia's words. 'How's things with this new chap, Ben, you're seeing, I've spoken to Katrin on the phone and she told me about him.

'He's great Pauline, I'm sure you'll meet him at some point. My thirtieth is coming up, so we'll all have a get together then.

39

Lincoln, December 2015

'DOOR'S OPEN, LET yourself in!' said Maia.

Ben walked through the door and almost tripped over her weekend bag. After a brief hug and welcoming kiss, Maia checked everything was locked and she was ready to go. Life had been overwhelming Maia recently, and she needed time out. She was looking forward to a few days away in Lincoln. The plan was to have a stopover in York to visit Craig and Luiza. Ben carried Maia's bag, and they took the lift down to the parking bays on the lower ground level. A dark blue Audi Q5 was parked in an empty bay next to Maia's car.

'Is that—?'

'Yep, got it back and ready for lots of adventures wherever we go in it. No more Mr Nice Guy, ably assisted by The Terrier.'

Maia squeezed his hand.

Ben continued, 'I'm hoping we can get the champagne out this week sometime as I expect to hear it's all going through. Shona's been digging her heels in about the house, but the deadline is tomorrow for her to finalise the finances. She has to go now or buy me out, as it's listed for sale. The estate agents are primed and ready; the house will go quickly I'm told. All the direct debits have ended, but she is getting one hell of a great settlement. It's so worth it though.'

Maia was gobsmacked, not often it happened, 'I'm proud of you, but think I should take credit for giving you the metaphorical kick up the butt you needed!'

'Speaking of butts,' Ben put his arm around her shoulder and let his hand slide down over her hips and rest on her buttocks as the car boot popped open. 'Hope I've passed my probation period Miss Hewson,' he said with a mischievous grin.

The time spent with Craig and Luiza was fun. Craig and Ben hit it off really well with a similar sense of humour. Luiza got a little tipsy, mixing up some of her sayings. After an entertaining evening of great food, and many drinks, they decided to go retro and play the original Trivial Pursuit board game late into the night. A difficult enough task to manage for Luiza when sober. A sport and leisure category question came up. Ben asked her, 'how high are the bales on a wicket?'

Luiza was extremely puzzled repeating the question, 'what did you say ... how high are the balls on a whippet?'

Craig and Ben laughed and replied together, 'about the same – two foot!' both measuring the distance from the floor with a hand.

Later on, Maia was complaining about turning thirty, saying she was sure she was getting crow's feet, to which

Luiza stared downwards, asking if it was a medical complaint. Maia adored her, explaining what crow's feet were. She was so happy for Craig, Luiza really livened him up as he could have a tendency to become morose. It settled her to see her wonderful friend so content.

Craig and Maia's eyes met and she knew Craig was wondering if she'd disclosed to Ben she had a daughter. Maia looked away and with fondness watched Ben laughing, she could not bring herself to think of the rejection that may be ahead, should he not be able to accept the fact she already had a baby, and any child they may have together would always be *her* second, not *their* first. She was young at the time and could not be absolutely sure Ben would handle the information about her baby sensitively, as she secretly crossed her fingers. She'd wanted honesty and Ben had divulged the information about Shona, he could easily have kept it a secret, she couldn't blame him if he hadn't said anything at all. Freya weighed heavily on her mind, she must tell Ben. They said their goodbyes the next day and Maia whispered to Craig, 'I'm going to tell him.'

Lincoln was lovely. It snowed on and off and the shops were adorned with Christmas decorations, which was only a few weeks away. The couple wrapped themselves up warmly and took plenty of exercise yomping up and down, Steep Hill, wandering around the cathedral, eating great food and thoroughly relaxing, snuggling together in each other's arms on the sofa after their wintery walks. Maia felt settled, hopeful and excited about the future. Of course, Freya was on her mind as always, and now there was opportunity to talk about her, she would choose her moment carefully. It happened as they were relaxing in the large apartment which was converted from an old Victorian mansion near Bailgate.

As they sat in each other's arms, with soft music playing, a glass of wine for her and whisky for Ben, she began, 'do you remember I told you about Tom and the situation with Jord–'

'Yes, yes, yes, Tom and Jordan, it's all I ever hear about Maia! Look if you can't move on from something, or should I say, someone, is there any hope for us. Seriously, how long is it since you broke up with Tom, he was only your teenage boyfriend. It's really sad the guy died so young, and maybe even took his own life … I mean, it's tragic, but what the hell is all this stuff with Jordan? Who is he to you, I just don't get it Maia.'

Ben had sat upright, which shifted Maia from her prone position, she put her head in her hands and began to weep. This was it, the moment when she confessed everything. It was make or break. She'd kept this huge secret from Ben, yet had berated him for not being honest. He could walk right out of her life, right now, and she'd never see him again.

Maia looked up at Ben's confused angry face as he said. 'What the hell is going on?'

She replied. 'There's something I've been meaning to tell you, not even my family know.' She noticed Ben was distancing himself slightly away from her. She took his hand, and placed it on her heart with hers over the top and looked straight into his eyes. 'Ben, I … I had a baby when I was eighteen at uni. Freya … and … and she … Freya … was adopted.'

She was sobbing now, 'Craig knows … he helped me when …' Maia couldn't speak or stop the floodgates opening. She had never spoken of this to anyone else. Ben stood with his glass in his hand and walked towards the window. The atmosphere was tense. Maia had tried so hard not to become over-emotional. She wanted Ben to say something, anything, she felt nauseous, this was it, he could be gone in an instant.

Ben sat beside her, put his glass down on the coffee table and stroked her face, fingers cooled from the ice in his drink. 'Why didn't … why couldn't you tell me?' Ben drew his arms around her tightly. After a few moments when her tears had subsided, Ben said, 'I'm going to make a guess, and say Tom was the father.'

Her eyes widened as she stared at him.

'It's okay,' he half smiled, 'There had to be something more than you being childhood sweethearts. Being honest, I have felt like … like I've been competing with a ghost whenever Tom is mentioned.'

Maia was stunned and could only nod to confirm, 'Ben, if I've ever made you feel less than precious to me, I'm so sorry.' She melted into him as she cried, this time with relief, she knew now this guy is a keeper. So often she had suffered angst over Freya's adoption and the thought of telling everyone, it was a secret she had nurtured for ten years, hidden away in the depths of her soul.

The couple spent the rest of the evening huddled on the sofa under a woollen blanket as Maia told Ben all the facts and feelings about her pregnancy, giving birth to her daughter, and giving Freya up. They talked into the early hours as Maia recounted Tom's history of abuse and what she, Aimee and Jordan had discovered about the situation.

When all the information was out in the open, she finished with, 'Tom's funeral was on the twentieth of March, two thousand and fifteen, the year I said goodbye to him, during a solar eclipse ... and it was Freya's tenth birthday that day. It couldn't have been more significant for me, I wish I'd told him about the baby, he was a father and never knew.'

Ben held her tight as she broke down again. When she calmed, Ben asked sensitive questions and commented, 'maybe if you'd told Tom, you wouldn't be here with me now, so ...'

'Maybe he wouldn't be dead either, I could've stopped it all from happening.' Maia was quiet now.

'But maybe not,' said Ben, 'Maia you cannot keep holding on to the fact Tom's death is something you could have prevented. I often wondered why you were so intent on saving Jordan for want of a better phrase, you're over compensating, trying to put something right, but you can't Maia. It's sad but it's happened, and all I care about now is that you are okay. And, I need to get Craig a decent bottle of whisky for looking after you all those years ago.'

Maia smiled through her tears, 'I'm going to suggest Craig tells Luiza too as it must be a burden for him to keep it to himself all these years and I know he worries about me. I honestly don't know if I can tell my family, I feel like I've betrayed their trust.'

Ben agreed the timing had to be right and he would support Maia, with whatever decision she made.

After and age of comforting silence, Maia said, 'I have a scan image and a photo of Freya, I brought them in case I got the courage to tell you, would you like to see them?'

Ben nodded, 'of course.'

She showed Ben the images, and a few tears rolled down Ben's cheeks, he sniffed and wiped them away looking at the image of his beloved, Maia as a scared young girl with her baby. In a whisper he said, 'it must have been so difficult for you, not much more than a child yourself. You do know I love you, don't you?' He held her face in his hands again.

'I love you too Ben, very much.'

The next morning, she text Craig suggesting that he let Luiza know about Freya. She had told Ben and all was well. Craig must be busy as all she got back later on was a text, *Will do. Top bloke! x*

'There's something more to tell you,' she said the next day. Ben stopped buttering the spiced toasted teacakes abruptly, as Maia continued, 'I'm afraid you will be *the* centre of attention, at my birthday party.'

'Well, that's okay, I've met all your family.'

'Yes, but not all together in one room, and under the influence of alcohol.'

'I can cope,' he laughed, 'I'll counter your family with my dad.'

Maia smiled, and confessed she still had slight reservations about Lorraine being very close to Shona.

Ben replied, 'they got along okay at first, but not particularly close.' He stopped, coffee cup in hand, but mum hasn't been herself lately. In fact, I've got something to tell you too. She was having a rough time when you visited, we were all waiting for her test results for breast cancer. Mum wanted to keep it quiet until it was confirmed, and if she got the all clear. She had the op to remove the lump, and it all seems positive, she rang me yesterday to tell me, so fingers crossed. I didn't want to bring it up while we were at Craig's. She'll need routine checks, but it's been pretty awful.'

Ben's relief was clearly evident in his face and body as Maia hugged him. He softened into the sofa alongside her as they munched on hot buttered teacakes and strong tea. Once finished, Maia held him, stroking his hair and kissing his face, offering reassuring words. That explained Lorraine's distraction when Maia visited. She had got it so wrong. Lorraine must've been anxiously distracted waiting for her test results. Well, Maia thought, it can be put right the next time she visits.

'I'm so relieved, she's got the all clear. My celebrations next week are going to be great!' Maia said with a rush of pleasing excitement.

40

THE DAY BEFORE her thirtieth birthday on Thursday 17 December, Maia went to Café Dalvik with her mam, to see Nik and Sophia and discuss the catering for the party. They insisted it was all on the house.

'Oh no' replied Katrin, 'we will come to some arrangement.'

Sophia, raised her hand to stop further protestation.

'Ah now Katrin, we've agreed with Maia, the deal is we're getting a professional photographer to pop in for an hour once the food is served to take some fabulous photos for our new publicity material. Because we're all so bloody gorgeous it'll save us a fortune not having to hire expensive models.'

Nik nodded her agreement, put her arms around her mam and sister as they squeezed together in a joyful embrace.

Sophia confessed to Maia and Katrin it wasn't often she felt self-conscious about her size, 'usually I couldn't give a monkeys chuff!' holding up a hand, 'but I wanted to wear something special for the birthday celebrations, so I went to the lingerie department last week to buy some shape-wear. Never tried such a thing, but thought, well, let's give it a go. The assistant was helpful and brought along some all-in-one-sucky-in malarkys. Aaanywaaay, I got undressed and squoze my legs into the suit, had to stop for a breather, then pulled it all the way up.' Sophia demonstrated with gestures of how tough it was. She held her hands up in the air and with a wide-eyed questioning expression asked, 'but how would I take a pee, or even breathe for that matter? I caught sight of myself in the changing room mirror.' She threw her head back at the memory. Her deep throaty guffaw rang out, 'I looked like I was auditioning for Mrs Doubtfire, I honestly looked like Robin Williams in all the padding! I had to get the assistant to peel it off me, she was mortified, the little love. I was exhausted by the end and the poor lass was sweating her cobs off!'

Nik, Maia and Katrin couldn't stop laughing as they imagined the scenario Sophia conjured up.

'So that is that! No sucky-in undies for this lady ... ever! But wait until you see my outfit. It – is – divine! Anyhoo, I've booked us all in at the salon for our hair, nails and anything else you want faffing with?' Pointing at Maia, 'you, me, Katrin, Jen, Daphne and Rosa. It'll be a scream.'

'No Nik?' questioned Maia.

They heard. 'Not bloody likely.' from behind the bar.

Sophia added, 'Nik will pop in with the champers for a drink, you know what she's like, no faff, this would be torture for her.' Sophia turned towards her partner, 'wouldn't it honey, your perfect exactly the way you are.'

'I couldn't agree more,' said Katrin.

Nik brought another round of cocktails; traditional Mojito for herself, a fresh raspberry Mojito for Maia, a Manhattan for Katrin and a flamboyant Mai Tai complete with a tropical bird cocktail pick and rainbow fruit kebab for Sophia.

'Ooh just the way I like it, understated!' exclaimed Sophia with a resounding clap. They raised their glasses and said in unison. 'Skál!'

They were waiting for the little ones to turn up for an afternoon birthday tea at the Cafe, so the little ones; Kate, Nathan, Andy and Jen's children, and Anthony, Rosa's son, could come and help her blow out her candles. They all played pass-the-parcel and musical chairs and miraculously every child won a prize every time, all the parents and children had a lovely time.

Maia had a lovely celebratory meal out with her parents and Ben on her birthday, then all the grown-ups joined her for celebrations on Saturday evening. Nik and Sophia excelled themselves, Helena, Ben's sister absolutely adored the pair. Maia's parents, Katrin and Phil sat with Ben's parents, Lorraine and Ivan, and seemed to get along famously. Pauline and Mike arrived and joined in their group too. Maia had an opportunity to speak quietly with Lorraine, asking how she was since her surgery, apologising she hadn't known about it. Lorraine said she wanted to keep it quiet until she had all the results and apologised for being so miserable when they first met, and they embraced in a meaningful hug.

Sophia was on top form, she could have made a career in stand-up with her natural razor sharp wit. At one point

Maia saw her gesticulating and having an intense conversation with a bewildered looking Zain, no doubt offering him creative marketing ideas. Daphne caught her eyes with a broad grin, as they shared a moment of pleasure at the scene they had predicted would happen during their spa day. Maia was content her friends, and family were all in good relationships, as she was too, she squeezed Ben's arm as she stood by his side for photos.

Sophia looked resplendent in a velvet, midnight-blue evening dress, cut low at the back. She discovered the beautiful designer gown whilst having a rummage, by invitation, through Pauline's old clothing. She had the vintage dress re-vitalised and refitted at a local dressmakers. A modest colour by Sophia's standards, however the chiffon sleeves and embellishment of tiny gems on the cuffs and around the neckline and bodice were amazing. Sparkling Sophia style, and classy. She literally lit up when she walked by as the lights caught every tiny twinkling reflection. One of the highlights of the evening, was Ivan, after several glasses of wine, deciding to lead everyone in his favourite traditional Czech polka, with Sophia as his dance partner.

41

'BLOODY HELL, THIRTY years old!' Maia exclaimed to her reflection in the bathroom mirror the following morning after the celebrations … or was it afternoon.

Maia supported her heavy, fuzzy head by resting her hands on the bathroom basin to scrutinise her face in the mirror. The small bright LED lights embedded around the circular frame did nothing to either soft-focus, nor brighten the harsh image of tired eyes, grey skin and fatigue evident in her face. 'Work hard and party hard,' she said to her reflection with a smile, 'definitely no run for you today, you old sod.'

Maia was exhausted. She was still feeling the remnant after-effects of the whole Surtees saga, and the strain of supporting Jordan's disclosures, and having to divulge the awful details to Alexi. There was also Ben's delayed divorce, and her revelations to him about Freya. 2015 had been an intense year, and she had high hopes for 2016. She was pleased things were back on track with Earth Chart, and her article being well-received. A contender for the front cover was Harriet Cooper's last comment.

Maia gazed at Tom's rune pendant in the mirror. She understood Ben's feelings about, living with a ghost, now he knew about Freya and that she was Tom's child. Maybe she wouldn't wear it so often. She must move on. The dark bronze pendant was about the size of an elongated penny. The symbol running downwards was etched in silver. It consisted of a, V, on top of a diamond shape, which sat on top of an inverted, V. It reminded her vaguely of DNA helix. She chose this pendant for Tom because it translated from the Viking rune alphabet as; love, music, harmony, and with the deepest irony, male fertility. She re-read the rune translation from when she bought it in Iceland recently, *Inguz teaches us that we are driven by the hope of changing something, and from this we draw strength to carry on in life*. She kissed the pendant, she always did for good luck and smiled. She took it off and placed it on the glass shelf below the mirror. Maia could finally let go, and joyfully accept she really did now love Ben Lasek.

Maia ran lukewarm water into the basin, pressed a blob of sharp, citrus-scented Vitamin C facial scrub into her hands, then worked it into her skin. She did an involuntary chortle, thinking of the time Rosa used it exclaiming, *"by ya bugger, that doesn't half scrag your jowls!"* She loved her dear friend so much.

To Maia's delight, a few uneventful days went by before Christmas was upon them. Ben had returned from the Highlands, and they chatted excitedly about their plans to move in together permanently now Ben's financial situation was stable. This would be defining for her, for them both, she hoped to fully endorse the promises they had made to each other in Lincoln about always being completely honest, no matter what.

Ben and Maia had spoken of a five year plan, then laughed at themselves, as real life rarely sticks to a timetable. There was even cautious talk of an Icelandic wedding, and future children, all of which was on the back burner for now. Ben had asked, and she had accepted his marriage proposal. Maia was never bothered about traditional values of getting engaged and weddings, but with Ben everything felt natural, still, no rush. It felt balanced and they were equal partners in this. It would be worth the cost of a wedding to see what Sophia would wear.

New Year 2016 was a whirlwind of sorting out the living space in her apartment to accommodate Ben. By way of Maia's goodbye to single life, she invited Rosa and Daphne over for supper, as Ben was in Pendle seeing his parents and clearing up the last few things before making the permanent move.

Maia had confided everything to Rosa about Freya recently when they had a coffee after an exhausting paddle boarding session, watching a beautiful sunrise. It was poignant, and they held each other and cried. Rosa agreed it would be good, if Maia felt able, to write a letter for Freya's parents to keep for when she's ready to hear more about her and Tom. Maia said she would need Rosa and Ben to support her when she was ready to tell her family.

'I hope mam and dad won't feel betrayed for not telling them at the time.'

Rosa reassured her, that would most definitely not be the case, but understood her anxieties.

Ben moved into Maia's apartment and they were adjusting to life together. Both very busy with their own careers, though early signs were good. The more time Maia spent with Ben, the more reassured she became he was a reliable, loyal man, romantic and very sensual too. They spoke about Freya when Maia felt the need to express herself about the daughter she may never know. It was a deep loss and Ben was of great support to her, always giving time for quiet reflection.

42

The Psychiatric Unit, March 2016
DOCTOR TARA SANCHEZ-BRIGHT was the newly appointed Forensic Psychologist on the vulnerable persons wing of the prison. The petite thirty-six year old entered the room. Her black abundant hair was drawn back with a colourful Ikat print headband, creating a tumble of natural corkscrew curls down her back. Her dark olive skin, almond-shaped hazel eyes and neutral expression remained steadfast. Matthew Surtees had been imprisoned on remand for four months and was subject to ongoing psychological assessment. Tara had read the previous risk assessment notes and anticipated the same narrative would be played out again during this session

Matthew Surtees was desperate to tell his story. He knew no-one had believed him so far. He remained full of vicious resentment about everything and everyone. It constantly seared and bubbled inside him like a boiling cauldron, yet his exterior presentation was of arrogant indifference, particularly when faced with a female in a professional capacity. He had little to think about apart from planning revenge when he got out of prison. Tara listened to a recording of the last session.

I killed the ranger. It was me. He deserved it. He attacked me once, defending that scum who helped to put me in here. I know who that Scrote is, and all the others who were part of the conspiracy against me, along with Baz, and the bastard Greeks. I'll ruin them all when I get out.

According to Surtees' testimony, he discovered where, the dead ranger, as he named him lived and tracked his daily routines. He never spoke his name and described how he found a perfect blind corner to cause an accident on a winding track, the dead ranger regularly used. Surtees claimed he was there and described the events. As the dead ranger's work van approached and came within view, he had faked stepping out in front of it. Tara listened to this part of the recording a few times.

I wanted to scare the shit out of him. The idiot must've been looking at his phone or something. I'll never forget his face (he laughs aloud) *when he suddenly looked up and realises a person was walking in the road. He swerved to miss me, he lost control as it had been raining and smashed into the wall. I checked, and he looked dead.*

Tara double-checked the previous research notes and discovered a Countryside Ranger who lived at Edera Cottage, and who was employed at Northumbria National Park named Thomas Cassidy, was killed when he crashed into a wall in March 2015. She found the archived newspaper report online, which tied in with Surtees dates. It was concluded an accidental death, and would remain a question of suicide. However, there was no note or indication

Cassidy was going to take his life, so it remained an open verdict. Most likely an accident on a slippery road surface.

Dr. Sanchez-Bright, made brief headings to start her assessment of forty-year-old Matthew Edmund Surtees;

> *Determine if, M.E.S. in the socio or psychopathic range of personality disorders.*
> *Sex offending since teens? (Further details awaited).*
> *Continually demonstrates need to be inextricably linked to Thomas Cassidy's death.*
> *Is the statement a fictitious, grandiose narrative? (Obtain details of full investigation in public domain).*
> *Is the account true and he was instrumental in causing the death?*
> *Any evidence? Could be charged with manslaughter*
> *No remorse or empathy, Narcissism disorder.*
> *Plan for long-term psychiatric assessment and rehab plan.*

Tara was ever the professional, however in a moment of pure humanity, after she listened to the recording, and read the notes again, she began packing up for the day, and under her breath whispered, 'that's one I hope never sees the light of day.'

43

Newcastle, 20 March 2016
MAIA WAS THINKING about Freya. She thought about her often, especially today, 20 March which was her eleventh birthday, and a year since Tom's funeral. Maia always took the day off work or as near as she could and would avoid any other contact to devote time to her thoughts. Maia harboured a deep resonating hope Freya was happy and her life was wonderful. She looked at the photo they took minutes after Freya was born which they gave to her on the maternity ward. There was a glimmer of a smile as she was looking down at the new-born baby wrapped in a white blanket; hers and Tom's perfect daughter.

An adoption worker told Maia they would keep a copy of the photo for Freya's life book. They also encouraged her to write her a letter then, or anytime in the future and they would forward it to her parents. At the time Maia wasn't emotionally strong enough to write anything. The adoption worker took some basic details about her and Tom; where they were from, their full names, dates of birth, a physical description and a little about their lives and their families.

It would offer Freya some background, and her adoptive parents would be the guardians of the information to share with her when the time was right.

Maia was playing hers and Tom's favourite album quietly in the background. She felt so close to Tom she could almost feel his presence. He would fully understand the blessing of Freya being brought up within a loving secure family, as he was. Maia did not want any erroneous information of Tom's death to reach Freya, if she or her family discovered old news reports or anything. There was so much more she could know about him. Maia felt a responsibility to speak for Tom. This was the most important letter she had ever written in her life, she read it aloud one last time;

Dear Freya

I hope you and your family are well. I think about you a lot and would like to explain how you came to be adopted.

A little information about me and your birth father Tom to begin with. My name is Maija, that's the Icelandic spelling, but I usually use Maia. I am thirty years old now, and I work as a journalist. My parents are Katrin and Phillip. My older brother is Andri and my younger sister is Monika. We call them Andy and Nik. Katrin is from Iceland and our names come from there.

Me and your birth father Tom were teenage sweethearts and this was our first relationship. We loved each other and had many happy times together. Tom was a singer in a local band and we both loved music. He was brought up by a wonderful foster family. His parents are Pauline and

Mike and they are the best people in the world. Tom was really happy living with them.

We dated for 18 months and though we parted, we remained good friends and I did see him from time to time. We weren't together when you were born but had met up and spent time together before I moved away, and that is how you came to be here. I was eighteen at university in York when I found out I was pregnant, and I was really scared I couldn't be a good mother. It broke my heart into pieces to give you up, and it doesn't mean I didn't love you Freya, but I knew I couldn't give you everything you would need in life. I wasn't in labour long, and your birth went without any problems. You were the most beautiful, healthy perfect baby, and the name Freya was exactly right for you, it means, Noble Lady.

I have to tell you the sad news that Tom died in a car accident when he was 31, in March 2015, it was the saddest day, but he has left us all with happy memories. When he was a teenager Tom would sometimes do outrageous things, often to make people laugh or just because he dared to. He tried to be positive in life and he stood up for people if they were being bullied. He was a kind and compassionate person.

I've enclosed a photograph of me and Tom together when we went camping one weekend with friends as teenagers. He loved the countryside and worked as a Ranger for many years. There is also a photo of Tom when he was older in his Countryside Ranger uniform, and you can see how handsome he was. He had a very cheeky smile. I've also enclosed some photographs of me as a little girl with my family, and as I am now.

I have also enclosed a necklace Tom gave to me for my 16th birthday. It is a precious gift, and I know he would want you to have it. It is sent with lots of love from me and Tom.

Maia xx

Maia picked up a small pink velvet box and traced the silver heart embellished on the lid with her finger. She opened it and kissed the jade heart displayed on the pink cushion. It looked lovely on the delicate chain she bought. Carefully closing the lid, she wrapped the box in pink tissue, then placed it together with the letter and photographs inside the small padded package. She checked the address of the Adoption Agency again and sealed it, placed it in her bag being careful not to crush it.

Her phone pinged with a text from Ben to say he was waiting in the car outside. Maia stood, slid her bag onto her shoulder and walked to the door. She rested one hand on the handle. She paused, and drew her other hand towards her neck. She lifted the rune pendant to her lips and kissed it. It would be one of the last times she wore it. Maia drew in a deep breath, then gently blowing out a long exhale, said, 'well Tom … it's time to introduce everyone to our daughter Freya.'

Maia sent the package containing the letter, photos and necklace for Freya to the Adoption Service post-box system. They explained it is a confidential physical conduit for the exchange of correspondence between adoptive and birth families. An adoption worker reassured Maia they will make contact with Freya's parents and forward the package, but would delay this until an acceptable date after her birthday. Maia understood the significance of this date for Freya's family.

To her amazement the Adoption Service advised they had some information, and forwarded a letter to her, from Freya's adoptive parents which had been held on file for years. It was returned to the service marked, 'not known' from Maia's student address after she had moved tenancies. Maia had completely forgotten about updating her address and never dreamed Freya's parents would write to her. It is a precious, reassuring letter. At the time it was written Freya was a healthy, happy toddler who loved listening to nursery rhymes and was developing well. The brief description told Maia that Freya had beautiful bright green eyes, Maia had burst into tears, *"just like Tom."*

The evening Maia told her family about Freya was incredibly emotional. She scanned her mother's face to ascertain if there was resentment that Katrin did not know a granddaughter was born. There was not. The family experienced renewed grief for Tom, when Maia told them he was Freya's biological father.

Rosa and Ben were superb in their support, with encouraging smiles and nods, sitting either side of her. Ben gently held a protective arm around Maia, until the point at which Katrin cradled her as she wept. Maia was still her baby daughter after all.

Maia chatted with Katrin questioning whether to tell Pauline about Freya, and Katrin rightly questioned who has a right to know about her biological father? 'No one, apart from Freya,' Maia answered without hesitation. Katrin was unsure whether to tell Pauline as yet, so the outcome was to keep the information within close family for now, however she would support her, if and when, the time was right to tell Pauline and Mike.

Maia asked at the Adoption Service if adoptive parents ever sent photographs, which was affirmed, though not guaranteed, sometimes for confidentiality reasons. Maia had rang the service twice to see if a response had arrived from Freya's adoptive family to her letter, then realised she was unrealistically raising her expectations. Maia accepted this as a painful part of the process and respected the system in place. She had relinquished all of her parental rights and may never hear anything further, even when Freya is older and can make up her own mind. Simply because Maia was now ready, she could not make any assumptions, Freya or her parents would be.

It may never happen, and all Maia can do is wait ... and hope.

Tom Cassidy, in his words 13.09.2002

I'm glad you're my girlfriend Maia. I'll always love you.

Maia wrote underneath ... and I'll always love you too Tom.

Epilogue

It is March 2018, Maia and Ben have been together for almost three years and all is well. They announced their engagement at a family night out in Café Dalvik in 2016, not long after Ben moved in. They are well-settled into their new family home to the west of Newcastle City, and plans are in place for a winter wedding in Iceland in 2020. Ben set off to Alaska on his next six month contract. Maia misses him desperately and intends flying out to see him as soon as she can. Ben was upset before he left, following a phone call with his sister Helena, as their mother Lorraine is under investigation with her oncologist following breast cancer surgery in 2015. More tests are required, and though nothing is conclusive as of yet, it's a terrible strain on everyone until the results are received. Ivan, especially is devastated. Everyone remains hopeful for a positive outcome.

An announcement that brought joy to the Hewson family is, Nik and Sophia are getting married in the summer. They already have a Civil Partnership, however, *"Sophia wants the whole shebang,"* Nik revealed, accompanied with a lengthy eye roll. Maia commented it would be a spectacular event and she can't wait to see the bridal gown. Andy, Jen, Kate and Nathan go from strength-to-strength, Kate loves school and Nathan is doing well at the pre-school group he attends with his gran, Katrin. Phil has eventually retired, joined a gym, has lost weight and is virtually evangelistic about keeping fit and healthy, and has finally worked out how to use a smart watch.

Further good news is Daphne and Zain have a healthy baby boy, Dalmar, who is now a robust toddler. There's no baby news for Rosa and Steve, and Rosa chatted with Maia about the possibility of starting the adoption process. The three friends regularly gather at Café Dalvik to catch up, and Maia joins Rosa at many sea-swimming events, especially the sunset gatherings, complete with bonfire and yoga. On a recent girl's spa day out at Apollon Leisure with Daphne, Rosa and Aimee, Maia spoke briefly and congenially with Ryan. He remains working in the leisure complex and in Maia's words, *has now been promoted to head towel collector.*

Pauline and Mike meet regularly with Abigail, Tom's sister, and to Maia's prediction they have become her surrogate parents. Katrin and Maia decided to tell Pauline about Freya. Pauline was full of questions as to why Maia never told Tom. She and Mike suggested they would have cared for the baby, which was a noble gesture, but without considering the implications. It was a difficult time emotionally for them all. However, Pauline and Mike understand the issues around confidentiality regarding Abigail and her parents not being told about Freya for now. The Cassidys were, however, overjoyed to meet with Jordan and true to form have taken him under their wing, offering him guidance and support whenever he needs it. He's doing well, he is clean and is now head barman at Reds Bar, he hopes to make manager soon. Everyone is thrilled to hear Aimee's announcement that she is pregnant, after two years of fertility treatment. Pauline and Mike are besotted with her engaging personality and keep in regular touch.

Alexis Leventis, was pleased with the Apollon Group article Maia wrote in Earth Chart, which boosted interest and investment in the company. They remain friends and meet for lunch occasionally. Alexi advised his brother, Gregori had turned a corner and had thrown himself into the management of the Leisure Clubs. He also received information that Matthew Surtees was badly beaten in prison. The injuries sustained required admission to hospital for treatment of a broken jaw and rib, also a dislocated shoulder. He had severe cuts and bruising everywhere, and in Alexi's words, *"around the genitals."* Maia did not question how the Leventis brothers knew this information.

Detective Sergeant Christine Powell, is impressed with Police Constable Gayle Mortimer, who has recently joined their team on a temporary attachment. Chris returned to the sexual offences team, following a period in criminal investigations. Gayle made significant efforts in her studies and shows keen observation for the signs of abuse. Chris mentored Gayle and saw a positive career ahead in the police force. Neither women, as yet, know of the mutual connection that would inform an enduring future professional, and personal relationship. Chris Powell often meets with her former colleague, Betty Trewhitt, who was critically injured during a police chase and had to retire early as a result of life-changing injuries. Chris meets her red-haired friend for drinks and spoke about the promising new officer who appeared to have an instinct about abusive behaviour.

Frank and, the now, Mrs. Michaela O'Brien continued their exposé of Matthew Surtees reign of terror and sexual predatory behaviour. Team O'Brien, continue to update information that has been gleaned from investigations across the UK and abroad. They have appeared on television chat shows regarding the story, and are currently in discussions with a global streaming service who are keen to use the story for a true crime series.

Maia is involved in further environmental research for Earth Chart, regarding a plastic waste company who appear to somehow be making unrealistic huge profits. There's something, she hasn't quite grasped about the arrangements, which seems odd. She is fully aware there are unscrupulous people involved in the environmental sphere who will happily make money in underhand ways. *Not everyone is a good guy*, she said to Ben. She has little evidence to take to Harriet Cooper as yet, and certainly wouldn't want to look a fool making allegations erroneously. She recently spoke with Craig about her misgivings, when he and Luiza returned from a trip to Poland, and as always, he is intrigued by the situation. Maia is determined to seek out the truth. Craig and Luiza have not seen Maia's ex, Shaun since he was moved from their department.

Ben bought Maia a delicate white frame for the photo of Freya when she was first born, which is safely stored in a keepsake box, with letters from her adoptive parents, which they send every year. Tom's rune pendant is placed in the box too, with his photo, and other mementos from Maia's time with him, including the cinema ticket from their first date. Whilst Tom Cassidy will never be forgotten, Maia Hewson is enjoying living every moment of her life in the present.

Acknowledgements

The Improbable Three is the first manuscript I started and as a former social worker, it holds a special place in my heart. I left the Adoption Service in Newcastle in 2016 and I am so grateful for the time I spent with that team. We worked hard, we cried, we laughed, and we ate (a lot) together. What a team, you all know who you are!

A huge thank you to my sister Valerie, and to my friends June and Diane who continue to read my initial drafts and help every story come to fruition. My books wouldn't be here without your support, and I am always indebted to you.

Further grateful thanks to Carol, who, apart from being an amazing former colleague, and lovely person, is a consummate editor of the written word. Carol offered to read the whole manuscript prior to publication and provided the most wonderful feedback. Thank you Carol, I'm so appreciative for your insightful comments.

I give my thanks and highest regards to Hayley Webster, an editor and author of supreme talent. Hayley encouraged my thinking about this manuscript when I was unsure how to progress. Her insight and ability to enable me to reframe the narrative was invaluable. Hayley also graciously agreed to acknowledge my work with the quote, *I found the book really moving and powerful*. I am ever grateful for your testimony Hayley, thank you.

I have dedicated this book to three remarkable women I had the privilege of working with, who sadly are no longer with us. Eileen, Cate and Helen. They all died way before their time and didn't get to see retirement after years of dedicating their working lives and passion to helping children in difficult and often tragic circumstances. I wouldn't consider them an Improbable Three, but certainly, an *Incredible Three*. I could write pages about each woman, however will now try to encapsulate how I remember them.

Eileen was assigned to show me the ropes when I moved to the team at Newcastle, and her pragmatic, down-to-earth insightful mentoring and humour never left me. Eileen was always present to calmly see the team through the most fraught circumstances, bringing thoughts and emotions back to a sustainable level. A capable person to be with in a personal or professional crisis, a rock to all who knew her. Thank you Eileen.

Everyone knew when Cate entered the office, always accompanied with drama. Too many instances to repeat, however Cate turning up to work with blood trickling down her forehead, having walked under a car park barrier as it descended, was typical. She had a new joke for us every morning from the chaps she went for an early morning swim with. You brightened our days, thank you Cate.

Helen had a stoic wisdom I've rarely experienced, with

an unfaltering ability to see the world from each individual child's perspective. Along with wisdom, her wit was a joy. I'll never forget Helen's surreptitious comment in a meeting with a rather defensive buttoned up co-worker sat in a corner, *"Mel, I'm finding it difficult to concentrate with Whistler's Mother over there."* Still makes me smile, thank you Helen.

I had the privilege of working with some amazing foster carers and adoptive parents during my career. I take my hat off to those who could instinctively understand what a distressed child needs. As a professional, walking away knowing you have placed a child with a trusted family who would respect and nurture them, made my role all the more fulfilling. Thank you to all the Pauline and Mike's offering their hearts and homes to children in care.

This book could not have been written without the support and expertise of my husband, and former police officer, John. His professional knowledge and experience has influenced so much of this book. Thank you John for your patience and support, love you. And to my sons Dan and Joel, you two were such a pleasure to come home to from those tough days at work, and I'm sorry for the times I was late picking you up from after school club. You have no idea how much inspiration you give me every day, love you both to bits.

As always and of most importance, my unrelenting heartfelt gratitude goes to you lovely readers. To anyone who reads this book and may have experiences of their own in whatever capacity, you are precious. Every individual life story has its own challenges, strength and value. In the words of Aimee Bancroft-Dara to Jordan Davis, *"we are survivors, whatever happened to us as children was **not** our fault."*

About the Author

Mel was born and bred in Newcastle, the second of four children and hails from a large extended family. She is married with two adult sons. She spent most of her career in Children's Social Care. When she is not writing, you will find Mel socialising with friends and family on Newcastle's Quayside, taking walks along the stunning north-east coast and has been known to take a dip in the North Sea. The Improbable Three is Mel's third publication. You can say hello to Mel and find details of her books on her website melfrances.co.uk

THE LETTER FROM ITALY – *A Broken Friendship in a Broken World*

Verna believes her husband is stranded in lockdown during the global pandemic in northern Italy? Suspicions arise between Verna and her best friend Hannah, their thirty-year friendship is fractured by a bitter argument as Covid reaches UK shores. Can they forgive and forget when a letter from Italy arrives revealing a devastating secret? Will their beautiful bond be broken forever? This gripping tale explores the power of forgiveness and redemption in the face of betrayal.

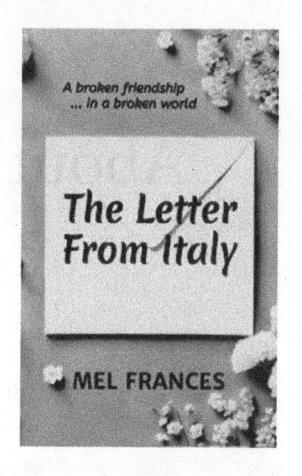

DESTINATION MAISIE –
The Trip of Her Lifetime

In 1960 Maisie was born illegitimately in London and placed in care. Reuniting with her birth mother and half-sisters in Manchester at seventeen, raises questions of belonging. Decades later, Maisie embarks on a life-changing trip to Crete with her granddaughter, Fran. Both women's lives are changed forever, as dark family secrets unravel, leading to devastating consequences. In a world where we all need a safe place, will Maisie ever find her true destination?